for Chinaeme + Lauren happy birthday

ALL the YELLOW POSIES

Elaine DeBohun

Threaded Entanglement
BOOK ONE

All the Yellow Posies
Book one in the Threaded Entanglement series

Cover illustration by Sarah Anne Bachman
Cover design by Morgan Hockensmith
Headshots by Sarah Mattozzi Wright

Content warning: This story includes suicide and suicidal ideation.

Second Edition: April 2024
ISBN: 9798218408848 (extended edition hardcover)
ISBN: 9798320768236 (paperback)

Printed in the United States of America

For Stephen and everyone who loved him

truthful narrative of healing after loss; that while there is inevitable pain that comes from loving deeply, it is always worth it to love anyway. Everything may not happen for a universally accepted reason, but we are not powerless. It may just be that disorder and fate interweave us in their celestial dance, and we must loosen our grip on the illusion of control and learn to dance along with them.

You may be able to pinpoint me in this story, and who knows —you might just have your own cameo woven in as well. Only one thing is certain in this web of mingled yarn: we all become storytellers in the end.

Happy reading,
'Marceline'

All the Yellow Posies

THE FOOL

naivety – innocence – beginnings

August 1919 — January 1921

Chapter One

The notorious Virginia humidity steamed off the sunbaked pavement in waves as I began my walk down Caroline Street, slipping into the nostalgia of old summer memories. Memories of my school friends and me, lying across the rocks dotting the river's edge, soaking up the sun with a basket of cold sodas and ham sandwiches at our side. That's how we would have spent a sweltering day like this.

I fanned myself with the classified paper as I passed by the familiar store windows, filled with locals already eager for shade.

With my 21st birthday a few days behind me, I was withering away. Trapped within the walls of my family's drab estate house with only rolling hills and suitors for company, I ached for the lost independence of my school days. I was one high-society function away from losing my mind, and that morning in particular, my parents would be too busy fussing over the Equestrian Society, with their mint juleps and pipes, to question my whereabouts. They didn't pay much attention to me anyway—unless I was doing something wrong, of course. I hardly fit the narrative of the daughter they'd wished for: proper and obedient, intelligent but not *too* intelligent. I was their only child, but I might as well have been a changeling left by the fairies, and I couldn't imagine I'd be missed. Besides, I'd be back before they even realized I was gone.

Unfolding the classified, I focused on the listing of the apartment I'd circled. I tried to imagine the intimate space and the freedom that might come from calling such a place my home. No stuffy, elitist luncheons; no corset fittings or remarks on my etiquette. And best of all, no marriage proposals. I was expected to conform to the ways of an upper-class lady, but I was more interested in the companionship of the books in the family library, more interested in folklore and mythology, than birthday parties and sports teams.

I had no interest in finding a husband, only in finding myself. The war was over, the influenza was fading, and I could feel in my bones that the world was on the edge of a renaissance.

I wouldn't let myself miss it.

On the corner, Goolrick's Pharmacy, the popular lunch spot I'd frequented as a student, was swarming with the lunchtime crowd. A few patrons sat across the classic marble bar, cooling themselves with bubbly Coca-Colas and ice cream sundaes piled high with hot fudge and cherries. From the other side of the window, a man standing at the counter caught my eye, bringing me back from my root beer float daydreams. He was magnetic—tall and imposing, with dark hair and a lean physique. Without warning, his gaze slipped past the young blonde he was chatting up on the stool, and found me on the street. I pulled my wide-brimmed hat down to hide the flush as I scurried past Mr. Goolrick sweeping the walkway.

Poor Mr. Goolrick. His wife—my former teacher—had been the first to perish when the flu tore through Fredericksburg, closing my school and everything with it. Life had only just begun to resume a sense of normalcy, but the reminders were impossible to avoid. Much like sharing lipstick and nights at the theater, basic human contact had also been part of the death toll.

It felt strange not to wear a mask as I walked down the street, though I was grateful. The heat was miserable. I'd dressed to impress my potential landlord, hoping to appear responsible, serious, *older*, and I was satisfied when I'd left the house in my pewter quarter-sleeve blouse and striped French linen skirt. But the last couple blocks of my walk felt interminable, and I began to seriously question my choice as the perspiration dripped down my temple.

I'd never noticed the tall, ivory building before, perhaps because it looked more like a home than a storefront. Many of the old colonials along the major streets had had their first stories converted to shops over the past few decades and 1111 Caroline Street was no exception; the simple iron sign that read *Thompsons' Tailoring* was the only indication of a bustling business within. I knew of the family by reputation only, but it was a spotless one. From what I'd heard, they were likable people—second generation Irish Americans with a strong work ethic. Even in the post-war recession, their business seemed to thrive, and it was local knowledge that Mr. Thompson was dedicated to his craft.

I couldn't have known when I knocked on the door, hot and out of breath, that an invisible thread had drawn me there, to the man who would change my life.

"Afternoon, Miss." A blond gentleman in a charcoal vest and striped tie greeted me on the other side. He looked to be about my age. "The shop is just right through the door on the left."

"Oh—I'm actually not here for the shop," I began, thrusting the damp classified in his direction. "I saw that you all have an apartment for rent." I opened the paper and pointed to the drawing of the building.

"Uh," he stumbled, "I don't really—"

"I'm hoping that it isn't already spoken for?"

"I wasn't aware that he had put out a classified ad. See, this is my father's shop."

"Oh," I said, awkwardly trying to look past him. "Is he here?"

"He's a little tied up," he said, glancing inside. "But come in and out of the sun, at least."

He stepped aside and I walked into the small foyer. On the left, I could see the teeming weekday hustle of the shop.

"I'm Jamie Thompson by the way," he said.

"Louisa Morgan. Most everyone calls me Lou."

"Nice to meet you, Lou," he replied. "Let me talk to my Pop and sort this out."

Jamie walked away, leaving me alone in the foyer. The hallway was spacious, with sun pouring through the windows to warm the cherry wood floors. I looked around slowly, taking in the intricate staircase and a door at the end of the hallway, likely leading to the back of the shop. Seeing a mirror to my left, I stepped closer to inspect my appearance. Wiping the sweat from my nose, I wondered if it were possible I'd gotten even more freckles since I'd left the house that morning. My face was still flushed from the heat. At least, that's what I told myself. That it was the heat.

I tucked my chestnut hair under my hat and adjusted my posture as Jamie rounded the corner.

"I'm sorry," he began, walking back into view, "he's going to be held up for a while, but I can give you a tour of the upstairs."

I motioned to the staircase. "After you."

We exchanged wholesome grins like two children meeting in Sunday school.

"Your father's shop seems like a busy place," I said, following him up.

"It is. My brother and sister work here too."

"A whole family affair then?"

Jamie laughed, as if he'd heard that a million times. "All but I."

There was a small landing with a single door at the top of the staircase. He took out a key to open it, kicking the bottom with his foot as he led me inside. "Damned door. It can give you a little trouble sometimes," he warned.

I admired the molding on the high ceilings, accentuated by crisp daylight as we walked into the fully furnished antique white foyer. My fingers traced the walls as I walked to the bay window and looked down onto the lively street below.

"I hope it's not too noisy," said Jamie.

"It's everything I could ever want." I turned back to him, giddy. "I can't believe *you* don't live up here!"

"No one has lived up here in years. I thought about turning it into an office, but it seems you've beaten me to it."

"Are you in school?" I asked, seating myself on the settee.

"I go to the Medical College of Virginia. I'm studying to be a doctor," he said nonchalantly, as if it weren't the best medical school in the state.

"Thank goodness for that," I said. "God knows we could've used more of them with the influenza."

"I got to see it up close and personal while volunteering. Richmond was completely overrun."

"Oh my." I leaned forward with unabashed curiosity. "You didn't get sick, did you?"

"No." He laughed. "I didn't get sick."

"You're fortunate." I stared off, summoning the memories of my school's inundated infirmary. Of the "no-hugs rule" and of poor old Mrs. Goolrick. "How did you manage to stay well while you were treating people?"

"Proper sanitation, masks. Maybe just pure luck on my side," he said. "I'm thankful for the hands-on experience."

"If you wanted hands-on learning, why not join the army as a medic?"

He shrugged. "I figured I'd be most useful at home."

"I was just curious," I said, suddenly aware of my prying. "I'm a reporter by nature."

Jamie leaned toward me. "In that case, I've got a story for you."

"Oh?" I asked, intrigued. "Do go on."

"My older brother just got back from the front, as a matter of fact. He dropped out of Princeton and went over as a sergeant in the 27th division but was promoted to captain on the field."

"Your brother that works downstairs?" I asked, looking to the door.

Jamie nodded.

"How did he manage that?"

"He doesn't talk about it. But apparently, he made quite the name for himself over there."

"What's his name?" I asked.

"Captain Holden Thompson."

"Holden," I repeated, letting the name sit on my tongue. "How unique."

"It's a surname on my mother's side."

"Tell me, why didn't you take up the family business like him?"

"Holden used to help around the shop when he was younger—he always kind of took to it—so my father was quick to give him a job when he got back. As for me, I'm a terrible tailor. I'll be headed back to Richmond soon to catch the fall semester."

I watched Jamie as he continued to talk. He was the kind of upstanding young gentleman that any traditional father would be happy to have joining his daughter at the Christmas table. A doctor-to-be, he would blend well into a family like mine. He was handsome, no doubt, but it seemed clear from the start that we were only meant to be friends.

"Enough about me," he said. "I want to hear from you. What's your story?"

"My family is from Culpeper. I just graduated from the Fredericksburg Teachers College, so I'm familiar with the area."

"There are plenty of teaching jobs here for graduates of the Teachers College."

My eyes found the floor. "You see…I'm not really interested in being a teacher. I was hoping to try my hand at writing."

"What kind of writing?"

"That's to be determined. Maybe write for a local paper. Or even better—a paper that would allow me to travel. I don't know. It's all up in the air, really."

Voicing my vague plans made me feel very childlike next to Jamie, who was able to lay his life out perfectly before me as if it were a map.

"Funny. My brother said the same thing," he said. "He studied English before the war."

"Is that so?" I asked. "I can't wait to meet him. He sounds so interesting."

Jamie smiled, as if he couldn't say what he really wanted to. "Interesting. That's one way of putting it."

"Of course, I'm planning on finding a job to support myself until I figure everything out. I have the down payment today," I continued, trying to assume the image of a financially dependable tenant. I'd asked my father for bits of money here and there—*to buy some new hats* and the like. Nervously, I glanced at my pocketbook that held the wad of cash, hoping it would be enough to last me in the meantime.

"I think my Pop may be looking for a receptionist downstairs. I could ask about it for you if you'd like."

My face lit up, unable to believe my luck. Asking my parents for money wasn't an option, and there was no promise I wouldn't be cut off completely after pulling a stunt like this. However, if I had a job—if I could prove that I could make my own way—maybe they *could at least* respect me.

"I can inquire about it myself," I assured. "I'm sure the interest would look better coming from me."

Jamie rose to his feet. "Well, let me introduce you."

I followed him down the stairs and into the shop, which smelled of fresh linen and leather. A blend of fancy perfumes from the women who walked through the door every day still lingered in the air. The floors were made of the same cherry planks as the foyer and the upstairs, and they were lined with a scattering of thick, oriental rugs. A small wood stove presented itself in the middle of the room, patiently awaiting winter. My eyes followed the bolts of fabric and layered ties that lined the walls, at last landing on a young woman working in front of an oval mirror.

"My sister, Marceline," said Jamie, following my gaze.

Marceline tucked her strawberry blonde hair behind her ear, looking intently between her client's reflection and the pinned velvet she held in her fingers. She looked perfectly put together in a blush blouse and long skirt, not a button out of place. *If only I could look that professional.*

"My father, James Thompson," he continued, turning my attention to the desk on our left.

Mr. Thompson was tall and thin, nicely fitted in a three-piece suit, with his long-graying hair in a center part, slicked back behind his ears. The expression on his gentle face was notably cheerful, a contagious smile if ever I'd seen one.

"Well, hello there!" he exclaimed warmly. "It's a real pleasure to meet you..." He glanced at Jamie for a name.

"Lou Morgan," I said.

"Lou! A lovely name. What did you think of the upstairs? I hope you found it to your liking."

"It's perfect."

"Isn't she a beauty? We may not have a glass storefront, but she's got good bones, this place."

"Was it a home previously?" I asked.

He grinned, big and wide. "It was *my* home, in fact. I opened the shop downstairs in 1889—the son of Irish immigrants with hardly a penny to my name!"

"It seems to have worked out in your favor," I gushed. "You have quite the reputation around town."

"Treat everything as an opportunity and things will always work out in your favor." He reclaimed his seat again behind the desk. "Are you from the area, dear?"

"My family is from Culpeper, but I went to school here at the Teachers College."

"Ah, yes!" he exclaimed. "I've known some of the staff members for many years now."

Our conversation was interrupted by the slam of a door toward the back of the room. Another man walked in, extinguishing his cigarette in a nearby ashtray. My eyes widened, recognizing him immediately from the counter at Goolrick's.

Marceline turned over her shoulder with an expectant look. "You're late…again."

He offered only a cheeky smile in return.

Then it hit me.

That must be Holden.

He didn't seem like a Princeton boy nor an army man. He was tall, but not quite as tall as Jamie or Mr. Thompson. Dressed down in comparison to his siblings, he wore a white shirt and brown blazer, with caramel pants cuffed just above his flashy Spectator shoes. His dark hair and strong brow were a stark contrast to Jamie's lighter features, and I wouldn't have guessed that they were related at all.

As if he felt my gaze on him, he glanced up at me and our eyes met for a second time. He strolled over to Jamie and me with a troublesome smirk, and I stepped back, intimidated by his obvious confidence.

"My brother, Holden," said Jamie, introducing him. "This is Lou. She's going to be renting the apartment upstairs."

"I think I saw you when I was at Goolrick's today," said Holden, who was even more striking up close. His jaw and cheekbones were cut like marble, symmetrically drawn together by a chin dimple of just the right size.

"I don't recall," I lied.

His sapphire eyes widened. "Don't you?

My cheeks burned.

"You look a little warm."

"It's hot out," I snapped back.

"Holden, leave her alone," ordered Marceline, who was watching us from her station at the mirror. "I'm still waiting on that hem, whenever you want to come back to work."

He turned to his sister and then back to me. "It must be a hundred degrees today," he said, shedding his blazer.

Two could play at this game. "It's nice to meet you," I taunted back. "I'm sorry—what was your name again?"

He laughed, revealing one deep dimple on his left cheek.

"Holden!" called Marceline. "*Hem.*"

"All right, all right," he mumbled, swiveling away from me. "Duty calls."

Catching my breath from the exchange, I turned my attention back to Jamie.

"Never a dull moment!" Mr. Thompson joked.

I laughed along, careful not to look in Holden's direction as Mr. Thompson motioned for me to come closer. I leaned my elbows on the desk with eager eyes.

"Rent is due the first of the month, and you'll need to lock up the front door when you leave and the shop is closed. Can you manage that?"

"Yes sir," I answered with a huge smile.

"Welcome to the neighborhood, Lou," he said with a confident nod. "I hope you'll make yourself right at home."

Chapter Two

The tailoring shop was in full swing when I stumbled through the door with my luggage on the last Saturday in August. I'd left my parents officially that morning with a smile on my face, eager to start my new life and holding faith that the rest would come. I didn't need their financial support, and I would prove it.

"I thought you would be back at school!" I exclaimed, surprised to see Jamie waiting for me in the foyer.

"Not until next weekend," he replied.

"Well, I'm certainly happy to see you!"

"Let me help you with those," he offered, reaching for my suitcases.

"Thank you. You're a godsend—if you take these two, I can get my typewriter," I said, shuffling my luggage.

Glancing into the shop on my climb up the stairs, my eyes found Marceline, who lifted her hand in a friendly wave. I shifted my prized typewriter to one arm so I could do the same.

The second Holden appeared at her side, I bolted out of view, running straight into Jamie. My Corona typewriter slipped from my hold, crashing against each solid wood edge of the stairs before finally hitting the floor.

The sound of a slow clap echoed in my periphery as I walked down to survey the damage.

"That's really not good for those," Holden said from the doorway.

I was too distraught to fight him. "I can't believe it," I murmured, reaching for the shattered remains.

"I'll take care of it."

I snapped to my feet. "What do you mean—will you throw it away?"

"Surely you don't expect it to work?"

I glared at him. "You'd like that, wouldn't you?"

"Don't be mad at me." His grin was nothing short of wicked. "I'm not the one that dropped it."

"You're such an ass, Holden," Jamie murmured.

"Do what you will with it," I said coolly, vowing not to let him see my heartbreak.

Jamie unlocked the door at the top of the landing, and frustrated, I kicked the bottom as hard as I could muster. "Your brother is intolerable," I said, well aware that I was caught somewhere between attraction and revulsion.

"He really can be," said Jamie. "Trust me, I know. I'm the youngest."

"I can't believe I dropped my typewriter," I groaned.

Jamie stacked my suitcases by the window. "Things happen. You can't blame yourself too much."

"It's just" —I halted, aware of how silly I was about to sound — "I always hoped I would write some kind of work of art on it. Something special."

"Well, maybe a different typewriter is meant for your work of art," he replied with a sympathetic smile.

I couldn't help but wonder if it was a bad omen. Unable to purchase a new one with my limited savings, I mourned the loss of my typewriter, and all my hopes with it.

I'd made it a point to ask Mr. Thompson about the receptionist job when I moved in, but two days went by without a response. By the end of the week what little money I'd scavenged was draining, and my financial circumstances were dire.

Crossing my fingers and dressed for the role, I forced myself down the stairs to inquire a second time.

"She finally shows her face."

Holden stood in the foyer hallway, eating a peach, as though he'd been waiting for me to emerge from my cave like a predator.

"What do you want?" I asked, sliding past him.

He stood up and walked over to me, stopping only to lean against the door frame.

I did the same on the other side, crossing my arms. It was a shame he was so unpleasant. A waste of a beautiful face. "Can I help you?" I asked, reluctantly admiring his lopsided smirk.

He raised an eyebrow, looking me over with a smug expression. "I think the question here is *can I help you.* Are you here to ask about the job again?"

"I see you've talked to Jamie."

"He's told us all about you—and you know? I was delighted to hear we had so much in common." He grinned.

"I wouldn't really know," I said with a shrug. "I can't say he's said much about you. Or maybe…I just overlooked it."

"Ouch. It hurts that you find me so unmemorable."

I smiled at him slyly. "Good."

"I deserved that," he admitted. "You have my attention."

"That's the last thing I want," I replied.

He laughed and looked away before biting into the peach, which, to my dismay, accentuated the sharpness of his jawline. "If we're done with this little spectacle," he continued, wiping the juice from his mouth, "I can help you get that job."

"Let me guess—out of the kindness of your heart?"

"No." Holden took another bite. "It's a chore to make my own appointments."

We stared at each other for a moment, each waiting for the other to say something more.

"I don't think I properly introduced myself the other day." He held his left hand to his chest, and to my surprise, I noticed a gold wedding band on his ring finger. "Nice to meet you, Lou. I'm Holden."

"Are we finished here?"

"Do you want my help or not?"

Something about him felt innately untrustworthy, but my need for the job overruled my suspicions. I gritted my teeth, willing myself into the shop with him trailing behind.

"Good morning, Mr. Thompson," I said, finding him in his usual seat behind the desk.

"Morning dear, what can I do for you?"

"I wanted to ask again about the receptionist position."

"So sorry, the time has just gotten away from me. Let's see…do you have any experience with tailoring?"

Holden joined his father behind the desk. He widened his eyes and nodded slowly, coaxing me to mirror him.

"Some," I lied, hesitantly following his lead.

Holden shrugged. "Well, if that's true, she's already more qualified than what we're looking for."

"How are your organizing skills?" asked Mr. Thompson, turning to me.

"They're excellent—I would say it's my strong suit."

"How about we take her to lunch," Holden interjected. "To see if she's a good fit."

"That's an idea. Everyone who works here is family, so it's important to find the right person," said Mr. Thompson.

I nodded in understanding.

"Perfect. I'll grab Marcie and we'll head to Goolrick's," said Holden.

Mr. Thompson suggested we walk since it was such a beautiful day and Goolrick's was only a few blocks down. It was miserably humid and cloudy outside, but I would come to learn that Mr. Thompson thought every day was beautiful. For that, I envied him.

"I'm so happy to have another lady around," said Marceline as we walked ahead of the men.

Until that day, she and I had merely coexisted in the same building, occasionally exchanging a passing hello. She was the polar opposite of her brother, the perfect balm to his intensity. Under the darkening sky, I tried my best to ignore Holden's gaze on my back as the pharmacy came into view.

The familiar smell of hot fudge and vanilla ice cream tickled my senses as we walked inside.

Seated by the glass storefront, the full view of Caroline Street stretched out like a living mural before us. Marceline and I sat together, across from Holden and Mr. Thompson.

"Ham salad for me," Mr. Thompson announced.

Sipping on my ice-cold cherry Coke, I scanned the familiar menu quietly.

"You always get that, Papa," said Marceline.

Holden shrugged, looking rather absent. "No need to ruin a good thing."

Marceline turned to me. "What are you going to have, Lou?"

"The chicken and cucumber salad, I think."

"Marvelous choice," she replied as the waiter appeared alongside us. "I think I'll have the same."

Jotting our sandwich orders down in a flash, the waiter returned to the bar. I noticed Holden watching the pedestrians outside, but before he could meet my gaze, I turned back to his sister. "Do you enjoy tailoring?" I asked her.

"Marceline is the best tailor we have," said Mr. Thompson, in that boastful way that fathers have. I envied that, too.

"I love it," she said. "I'm proud to be a woman in a solid profession, but I'm even more grateful that it's something I love."

I leaned toward her, intrigued.

"I need to pick up my prescription," said Holden, knocking the table a bit as he stood. "Since we're here."

"I'm sorry about my brother," whispered Marceline as he walked back toward the pharmacy. "I promise he's not so harsh when you get to know him."

"I don't find him harsh," I lied. I looked over my shoulder to find that he was doing the same from the pharmacy counter, one eyebrow cocked as he subtly studied me watching him.

Holden walked back to the table with a brown bag of whiskey, which he pocketed as he took his seat. Marceline smiled at me, reaching for her root beer as our waiter returned with our sandwiches. Holden was quiet as we all conversed, apparently absorbed in the scenes happening beyond the window.

"I believe in equal pay for women," said Mr. Thompson in between his bites. "A woman can do just as good a job, if not better, than a man. So why shouldn't she be paid equally?"

"It's a rarity to find a job with equal wages," added Marceline.

"And soon enough, you ladies will have the vote. You mark my words! It's history in the making."

I found the Thompsons' stance refreshing, especially in contrast to my conservative parents.

Marceline turned to me. "Jamie told me that you studied at the Teachers College and you want to be a writer?"

"That's the idea," I replied, catching Holden's attention as if he'd just been woken up from a long nap.

"It's going to be hard to write without your Corona," he teased, showcasing the smirk that I would soon come to know as his signature.

"Please excuse him," said Marceline. "He's forgotten his manners."

I smiled, feeling vindicated, before turning back to Holden. "You remember the brand?"

"Believe it or not, I have a pretty sharp memory," he replied. "Corona is a nice brand. I prefer Royal, myself, though."

Marceline glanced at her father, looking amused.

"What do you write?" he asked me.

"Not much," I said. "But I'd like to write for papers."

"I'll bet you're a wonderful writer," said Marceline.

"Yes, I'm sure of it!" agreed Mr. Thompson.

I split a nod between them, unused to the flattery.

"Journalism," said Holden. "Why journalism?"

"People intrigue me," I admitted, thrown off by his interest.

Holden looked at me intently. "Me too."

"And what do *you* write about?" I asked him, taking a guess at his own interest in the profession.

"He never lets anyone see," Marceline poked.

"We should finish up," said Holden, dodging my question by turning our attention to the raindrops hitting the large window.

By the time we got back to the shop, a light rain had ushered in the smell of fresh grass and summers past.

"All right, Lou," said Mr. Thompson, pulling out his key. "I can offer you the apartment as part of your paycheck, along with seven dollars a week."

I tucked a piece of damp hair behind my ear. "Do you mean it?"

"We open at nine."

I raised my brows, exchanging a quick grin with Marceline as he moved to unlock the door.

"Now that that's been decided." Holden inched toward the alley, as if he had somewhere to be. "I think I'm going to head out early. I don't have anything else on the books."

"Again?" Marceline's tone was one of annoyance.

Mr. Thompson motioned for him to go ahead, unwilling to linger on the issue.

"See you tomorrow," Holden called, disappearing around the corner. "You too, shop girl."

Thanking Mr. Thompson and Marceline, I made my way upstairs, completely unprepared for what greeted me at the top of the landing. In front of my apartment door was my Corona typewriter, miraculously intact. *But how?* It had only last week been damaged beyond repair—or so I'd thought. I ran my fingers over the familiar keys.

He'd fixed it.

Holden, with his sparkling eyes and devious grin. The thought brought a smile to my face and a fleeting softness to my chest.

Chapter Three

Time passed quickly in the day-to-day workings of the shop. With Mr. Thompson teaching me everything I needed to know, I'd mastered booking appointments and garment pickups in no time. Even though I was employed for the first time in my life, my new routine hardly felt like work. I sat at a nice desk and wrote with smooth pens. Beautiful gowns came to life before my eyes, and the news and politics discussed by the gentlemen always gave me something to ponder.

Even Holden wasn't that bad. Sometimes, he was pleasant. And every now and then, he was nice.

As for the mysterious resurrection of my typewriter, I tried not to read too much into it. After all, though he was charming in a way—if you could look past everything that made him so insufferable—he was obviously spoken for. He'd only done it as an act of kindness. The *why* was what troubled me, and for that reason, I brought it up to him only once.

Holden was posted up against the wall of the neighboring building, cigarette in one hand and a mug of coffee in the other, looking like he hadn't slept at all the previous night.

"Good morning," he said.

Ignoring his confused look, I shut the door behind me and

walked down the stairs to meet him. "Morning. Can I have a cigarette?"

He shrugged and handed me one, lighting it promptly.

"You look tired," I remarked.

He exhaled a breath of smoke. "I live a tiring lifestyle."

"Surely. I'd imagine repairing typewriters is pretty time consuming."

"I don't know what you're talking about," he replied, looking me dead in the eye.

"Liar."

He grinned. "Fine, you caught me," he admitted. "I just couldn't bear to throw it out."

I reached into my purse and handed him a few bills but he shook his head. "Why not? You saved me from having to buy a new one."

"I don't want your money."

"Then how do I thank you?"

"I'm sure you can think of something." He turned to me and laughed at my shocked expression. "I'm kidding! If you want to thank me, just thank me."

"All right. Thank you."

"You're welcome."

"Where did you learn to do that, anyway?" I asked.

"I learned while I was in the army," he replied, flicking his cigarette butt to the ground. He turned back to me with a smile before opening the door. "You learn how to fix a lot of things in the army."

After that day, Holden's redeemable qualities began revealing themselves to me little by little. He held the door for the old ladies and told them when their hair looked nice. His snarky jests, I realized, were all in good fun, and kept us entertained. And he wasn't terrible to look at, either.

As an only child, I was both entertained and intrigued by the sibling bond of my coworkers. Every morning when Holden was late, Marceline complained to me about how he never took anything seriously. Holden, on the other hand, teased his sister relentlessly. He also openly loathed many of her clients and acquaintances, claiming they were judgmental, phony, and worst of all, tremendously boring. Marceline had one client in particular that her brother despised more than the rest, and after watching the woman spew unkind remarks in the shop more than once, Holden had not-so-lovingly nicknamed her *Lemon Seed Eyes*.

I was organizing the register one afternoon when he walked over, seemingly eager to watch the drama unfold from the best seat in the house.

"What is it this time?" I asked.

"Use your imagination," he said, motioning to *Lemon Seed Eyes,* who appeared to be complaining.

"Demanding the impossible, I see," I replied, following his gaze.

"My poor sister," he scoffed. "I'd rather be shot at by Germans."

"Holden," I shushed.

He huddled closer to me behind the desk. "We could have finished the war sooner if we'd only had her on our side."

"She's going to hear you," I whispered.

"Her complaining could have been an effective weapon."

I covered my mouth, swallowing my laugh.

"Just look at her, Lou." We both peeked over the desk at the soured face in Marceline's chair. "She's going to go home after this and suck on another lemon," he whispered in my ear.

I couldn't help but cackle between my pleas for him to stop, and soon, he was laughing along to his own commentary. Marceline glanced over with a slight grin, and then, immediately wiping it from her face, turned back to the mirror to focus.

Luckily there were plenty of clients to offset *Lemon Seed Eyes.* Mrs. Robinson was as sweet as the homemade pastries that she brought us every month—this crowned her as a favorite among the family. I loved writing to Jamie about the shop's regulars, always jotting notes so I wouldn't forget to tell him whose husband was having an affair, and whose son had gambled away the family fortune. It was like a fun character study, each letter its own little weekly paper.

Mr. Thompson was the busiest tailor in the shop by far, followed by Marceline. Holden was good at tailoring—he was good at everything, really, but he didn't seem to have much of an interest in expanding his clientele. Where Marceline was meticulous in her work and pushed herself in the pursuit of perfection, Holden merely skimmed by. She never outwardly voiced it, but I wondered if that was part of her irritation with him; that he would always be taken more seriously than she, even when he didn't have to try.

Holden seemed to float through life, charming friends and strangers alike with a sense of confident detachment. When he wasn't bending the will of everyone around him, he appeared to be elsewhere; in a distant land in his own mind where no one could follow. And it was this quiet, deeply private side, free of the showy facade, that captivated me. I often caught him scribbling out of the corner of my eye, as if he were running out of time, always careful to hide his words when I walked by. I spent more time than I'd like to admit trying to catch a glimpse of his work doodles.

Despite sporting a wedding band, he never mentioned his wife. It was almost as if she didn't exist. And while I thought this was strange initially, it wasn't long before I learned why. It took only a few exchanges between Holden and Marceline for me to gather that his family didn't approve of her. It was November before I finally got a chance to form my own opinion of Bette, and I'll never forget the first time I saw her: the perfect blend of fire and ice.

Thanksgiving was a week away, and the shop was so busy it was half-past two before I'd eaten anything. I assured Mr. Thompson that I was fine, but ever the solicitous father figure, he ushered me to the back door to at least take a smoke break. I sighed in relief as the crisp fall air hit my lungs, grateful to be out of the stuffy shop, full of body heat from the holiday traffic. Feet aching, I collapsed onto the second stair and lit a cigarette. I'd only inhaled a few gentle drags before my attention was drawn to a muffled conversation in the nearby alley.

I was immediately able to pick out one of the voices as Holden's, but the other one stumped me. *Her* voice, whoever it belonged to, was so soft that it almost sounded like Holden was talking erratically to himself. I fell under the sudden impression that I'd stumbled upon something private, but before I could extinguish my cigarette, Holden rounded the corner with a small suitcase in his hand.

Dressed in black from head to toe, the woman's expression was uninterested under her short, platinum bob. Holden's back was turned as he continued to talk to her, oblivious to my presence. She finally nodded in my direction and he turned around. Sitting on the stair with my cigarette, I lifted my hand to wave, but her glance was icy and I shrunk back.

"Ah." Holden awkwardly rubbed the back of his neck, looking between her and me. "Bette, this Lou. She works here now."

She examined me beneath the long eyelashes that hung over her slate eyes. "You're the one who lives upstairs."

"I am. It's nice to finally meet you," I said.

She managed a tight-lipped smirk in return. "Likewise." Bette started to pull her cigarettes out of the beaded purse that hung from her shoulder, but was interrupted by Marceline opening the back door, and swiftly returned them.

"Holden, we could really use you inside," Marceline scolded.

Bette met her glare, then walked away, neither woman acknowledging the other. And just like that, she was gone.

"Don't look at me like that," said Holden, turning back to his sister.

I cowered in between the two of them as I sat on the middle stair.

"Look at you like what?" she taunted.

"She was dropping off my typewriter. I told you that earlier."

"When did you possibly think you would have the time to write with us being so busy?"

"I wanted to have it with me in case."

Marceline looked at him with a stale expression before shutting the door loudly behind her. Holden ran his hand through his hair with a sigh, and I went in for another drag of my cigarette only to see it had completely burnt down.

"Well," I began, "Bette seems lovely."

Holden laughed. "She's just quiet because she feels unwelcome here," he said, nodding toward the back door. "She's fantastic. Actually, I think you'd hit it off."

"Is that your Royal?" I asked, motioning to the little black suitcase.

"It is."

"Can I see it?"

He raised an eyebrow playfully. "As long as you don't take it near any stairs."

Chapter Four

When I returned from visiting my parents at the end of November, I found the shop's interior adorned in cedar boughs, courtesy of Mr. Thompson's wife. A potpourri of cinnamon, cloves, and oranges sat atop the wood stove while it burned, and, to my delight, the scent wafted up to the second floor, infusing my space with the festive aroma.

Jamie, who was home for the holidays, joined me in the decorating of my first Christmas tree. I didn't have much in the way of traditional ornaments, so we strung a few popcorn garlands along its branches and added tinsel and pinecones to finish the look. It looked a bit pitiful set against the grand bay window with all its intricate molding, but I was happy. Both to have a tree of my own, and to catch up with Jamie.

That week, the weather had dropped to toe-numbing temperatures. It was a blustery day and the wind whipped at our faces, but the storefront of Chennault's coffee shop had a bright orange awning, so it was hard to miss, even with watery eyes.

The inside was as radiant as the outside, and the color of the dandelion walls warmed my bones as we stepped onto the mosaic-tiled floor. Embracing the immediate relief from the December gusts outside, we looked around the cozy shop for an open seat as smells of fresh coffee floated through the air. It was a small establishment, only about a third of the size of our own, but there was always a line, and for good reason. Chennault's had the best coffee in town.

Insisting that it was my treat, I brought two cups filled to the brim over to the table Jamie had picked out by the window. "One for you," I said, pushing a mug in his direction. "And one for me."

"Thank you."

"Thank *you* for the company today," I said. "Now, tell me everything."

"What's there to tell? I study, I sleep, I look at sick people."

"Jamie." I rolled my eyes. "I mean have you met *anyone?*"

He angled his chin, as if to tell me that one sister was plenty and he didn't need another.

I stared at him expectantly. "Well?"

"There is a girl I like," he admitted. "Since you ask."

"Oh?"

"She goes to the nursing school."

"That sounds like a match made in heaven."

"Yeah, well, I don't even know her name. I've only ever seen her in passing."

"Perhaps you should ask her," I suggested, raising the mug to my lips.

"I'm really busy with my classes."

"Excuses," I scoffed. "I hope you make time to study her next semester."

He laughed, taking the opportunity to change the subject before I could prod more. "That sounds like something Holden would say."

"Does it?" I gulped. "I guess I *am* around him a lot. Sometimes I pick up on people's mannerisms without realizing."

"I've been meaning to ask how it's been working with him."

"Holden?" I paused. "He's been friendly if that's what you're wondering."

Jamie chuckled to himself. "He's been on good behavior, then?"

"We're friends," I clarified.

"Friends?"

"I don't know if he told you, but he fixed my typewriter."

"He what?" asked Jamie. "Also, no—he doesn't tell anyone anything. He fixed your typewriter?"

"He said he learned to fix them in the army."

"Well, that was nice," he said quietly, appearing puzzled. "And out of character…though, I guess it's not *that* out of character."

"What do you mean by that?"

Jamie laughed to himself and then looked at me like I should know. "You're a pretty girl. And Holden, some might say…"

"Oh," I interrupted, feeling myself blush. "He said he just couldn't bear to throw it out."

Jamie smiled, looking unconvinced. "Right."

"Well, I appreciated the sentiment anyway. It saved me from having to buy another. Oh, and I met Bette the other day." I took another sip of coffee, hoping I appeared less flustered than I felt.

"How was that? Marcie told me that she came by."

"It was a little tense. I wasn't sure what to think."

Jamie said nothing at first. It was hard to tell whether he liked or disliked someone because he was incredibly adept at hiding his facial expressions. Even his glare had a sweetness to it. "I hardly know her," he said finally. "We never even heard of her until after they were married. He'd only been back from Europe for a few months. At most."

"He didn't tell anyone he was getting married?"

"He told Dane but none of us got the memo until afterward."

"Dane?" I asked, taking another sip. "Who's that?"

Jamie's eyes lit up. "Our older brother—surely Holden has at least mentioned him?"

I slid my cup onto the table slowly. "I had no idea you had another brother."

"Half-brother. From when my father was married before."

My brow wrinkled as I questioned if I'd somehow overlooked a mention of an eldest brother.

"He's lived in Europe for a long time. I don't think he's been home to visit since before the war."

"Was he a soldier too?"

"He's a painter," he said. "Holden stayed on with him for a while in Paris after the armistice. They've always been very close."

"Do they write?"

"All the time."

"He's always writing something at work."

"I would bet money that they're letters," said Jamie. "Ask him next time, if you dare."

In the days following, I studied Holden from behind the desk until my opportunity finally came. With Marceline and Mr. Thompson occupied in the back, I confidently strolled over to where Holden sat in the hall, clicking away.

"What's this?" I asked, flicking the paper in his Royal.

No response.

"Are you writing to your brother?"

"Yes," he replied, at last meeting my eye. "I am writing to my brother."

"Jamie told me that he lives in Europe," I said, admiring the typewriter's glossy shine.

"Jamie has no idea where he lives," said Holden condescendingly. "He hasn't seen him in years."

"If *you're* so close, why haven't you ever mentioned him?"

He laughed, leaning back in his chair. "You are so nosy. Has anyone ever told you that?"

"As a matter of fact, yes."

"Imagine that," he said with a smirk. "Makes for a good journalist though, I suppose."

I moved in to take a closer look at the paper in the Royal when Holden held up his hand in protest. Unsure if he was kidding or not, I drew back, making eye contact at an uncomfortably close distance. His glistening blue eyes, which looked more aquamarine as he faced the window light, studied my face and his expression softened. "Don't even think about it," he warned.

Before I could counter, Marceline walked over, handing me a little red envelope with my name written on the front.

"What's this?" I asked.

"Christmas Eve invitation," answered Holden offhandedly.

"Such enthusiasm," said Marceline, throwing his invitation onto his lap before turning back to me. "Our parents put on a Christmas Eve dinner every year. I hope you're able to make it?"

To Dane from Holden
December 6th, 1919

I received your letter mid-November, but I think it's out of order. Did you send two at once? It's been busy at the shop. You know how it is, all of the rich people and their need to impress other rich people with their overpriced garments. Even with all of the business this season, I still haven't made the money I was hoping for, and I'm finding it increasingly difficult to save anything due to my own boredom. This place is so painstakingly dull. It's the same thing day in and day out. Even the nightmares have subsided a bit. I almost miss them.

In other news, Pop hired a new receptionist who is also renting the upstairs apartment. Her name is Lou, and she claims to be a writer, though I haven't read anything she's written. She is witty, though. Witty enough to keep up with me, even. You know better than anyone that's a sign of talent. Aside from being unbearably nosy, she is a fine asset to the shop. Don't worry, I'm not tempted. But the sun freckles along her nose and cheeks may be enough to change my mind. I'm only kidding. I'll admit that I did fix her broken typewriter, but that was done for my fondness of the craft and has nothing to do with the lovely green shade of her eyes.

Bette sends her thanks for the postcards you sent. She and Marcie had a run-in the other day at work and she is convinced as usual that everyone hates her, so I appreciate your sentiment. We went out with some friends she met in a club a few weeks ago, a couple of gentlemen. I think one was part of the Mob. Do you think they are looking to hire? Again, kidding. I wouldn't involve myself with any of that. Unless the pay was exceptional. I did have to stop Bette from nearly drowning herself in the river by accident, due to her drunkenness that night. I wasn't much better off but we managed to make it home unscathed. However, I did lose my nicer pair of Spectator shoes. See what happens when you aren't around to keep an eye on me?

It's bizarre to be home for Christmas this year...stranger than we even imagined. But I do look forward to that Christmas brisket. As always, I hope all is well on your end and I hope to hear back from you soon. Merry Christmas.

Holden

Chapter Five

According to Holden and Marceline, their holiday dinners usually meant friends and family were elbow-to-elbow at the crowded table, but the guest list seemed to grow smaller with each passing season. Last year, indoor gatherings were prohibited in hopes to curb the spread of influenza. The Thompsons decided that an intimate dinner would be best this time around too, since it would be Holden's first Christmas with them after returning from the front. I would be the only invitee that wasn't immediate family. But in the words of Mr. Thompson, *I might as well be family, anyway.*

Jamie and Marceline pulled up in a black Model T sedan to pick me up for dinner around twenty after six. They waved in unison as I walked out the front door with my fur-lined coat in my arms. I was wearing an Aegean velvet gown, complete with button-down long sleeves, a sash at the waist and flower embroidery on the bottom.

"Oh, Lou!" exclaimed Marceline. "Your dress!"

I opened the door and squeezed into the backseat with my coat as Marceline turned around to talk to me.

"I love it," she gushed.

"Look." I maneuvered to give her a closer look at the triangular pockets. "I couldn't bear to cover it up with my coat."

"*Marvelous* choice."

"And what about you?" I pointed to the soft finger waves falling over her vanilla fur neckline. "I love what you've done with your hair."

We chatted about fashions, tabloids and other frivolous topics as we headed toward Spotsylvania county. Jamie, as usual, was the best sport. I appreciated the distraction from my clammy palms and tight chest, which had only grown clammier and tighter with the ride. I tried not to think of Holden, dressed up for the occasion, and where he would sit in relation to me at the table.

The Thompsons' house was much bigger than I'd anticipated—a brick colonial with a long, beautifully landscaped walkway. A lit Christmas tree dazzled in the parlor window, putting my own shrub to shame.

"You look handsome, Jamie," I said, motioning to his three-piece charcoal suit.

"I've got Marcie to thank. She tailored it."

Marceline pinched her little brother's cheek. "It helps to have such a pretty subject."

Jamie knocked once on the stained-glass door. I stood next to Marceline, able to make out the faint sound of a Victrola playing just beyond the entrance. Mr. Thompson opened the door in his best pinstripe suit and smiled, motioning us to come inside and out of the cold. Aromas of beef and rosemary filled me with delight upon entering the house.

Mr. Thompson reached out to take our coats. "My favorite pair," he said cheerfully. "You both look lovely."

"There goes all of my attention," muttered Holden, leaning in the doorway to the dining room in his normal white shirt, suspenders and blazer.

Marceline placed her hands on her hips and looked at him. "Would it have killed you to try a little bit?"

"You either get fancy attire or punctuality. You can't have both, Marcie," he replied.

I peeked into the dining room to look for Bette, but she was nowhere to be found. Before I could ask about her, Mr. Thompson walked over with a tray of drinks.

"Take one, take one!"

"Thanks, I've got my own," said Holden, pulling out his flask.

I grabbed a glass of Vine Glo from the tray. Wine lovers only had to purchase one of their legal grape bricks, add water, and follow the warning on the label like a set of directions: *do not keep the mixture in a cupboard for twenty days, because then it will turn into wine.*

"God awful juice," Holden scoffed.

"You only feel that way because you've been in Europe."

"Exactly." He took a swig from his flask, nodding to Marceline. "My taste buds are developed."

"Lou, come with me. I'd like you to meet the lady of the house," said Mr. Thompson, pulling me aside.

I followed him down the hall and toward the kitchen, admiring the wood-carved furniture along the way. Stepping into the kitchen, we were greeted by a tiny woman with short, dark hair—the same color as Holden's—standing by the stove. One of the members of the cooking staff brought a sauce dish over to her, which she tasted and nodded with approval before turning to us with a welcoming smile.

"Mrs. Thompson, it's so nice to finally meet you," I said.

"Please, call me Madora." She untied her apron and removed it, revealing a gingerbread silk dress pleated at the waist. "I've heard a lot of wonderful things about you, young lady."

Mr. Thompson pulled his wife to the side, draping his arm over her shoulder. I felt a warmth between them that seemed to penetrate into the walls of the house, and I couldn't help but wish they were my own parents.

"You have a beautiful home," I said.

"It feels nice to have it full again," she remarked cheerfully. I didn't have to ask to know that she was referring to Holden being home.

"Go ahead, Lou," suggested Mr. Thompson. "Find everyone in the parlor. We'll let you all know when dinner is ready."

I shuffled back down the hallway, past the collection of artwork and photographs that adorned the walls. About half-way, a painting of Notre Dame caught my eye, and I lingered to study it, intrigued by the endearing feeling it gave me. In the parlor, I found Marceline, Holden and Jamie standing around the mantel with their drinks as the tree twinkled in the corner. They seemed to be hot in conversation and I felt awkward entering the room, so I stalled in the doorway for a moment and listened, hoping to inch my way in unnoticed.

"You would vote for old Woodrow again, really?" asked Holden. "Poor sap isn't looking so great lately. Perhaps he'll die before the election."

"That's incredibly morbid," remarked Marceline.

Holden shrugged.

Jamie stood looking tense with one arm resting on the mantle. "What do you think, Marcie?" he asked. "About the president's fall campaign?"

"What does it matter what I think? I don't get a vote."

"Not yet, you don't."

"Not *ever* if Wilson stays in office, for Christ's sake," Holden scoffed. "You know he doesn't believe in equality."

"How so?" asked Jamie.

"Our magnificent country is prejudiced against its own citizens. Have you seen the way we treat our Black veterans?"

"I've never really thought about it."

"Maybe you should sometime." Holden took another sip from his flask. "It's medicinal," he said, turning to Marceline, whose stare was somewhere between judgment and worry. "Lou!"

Jamie and Marceline turned to look at me as I hovered in the parlor's entryway.

"What do *you* think about Mr. Woodrow Wilson?" Holden asked. "Don't pick tonight to suddenly become shy."

"I think one glass of Vine Glo isn't nearly enough," I joked, entering the room.

Jamie extended his hand. "I'll get you some more."

I could tell by his expression that he was tired of the conversation with his brother and wanted an excuse to make his escape. "Thank you, Jamie."

The crackling of the fireplace filled the quiet room as I searched for something to say.

"Bette couldn't make it tonight," said Holden, addressing the elephant in the room. "She wasn't feeling well."

"Sorry to hear that," I replied.

Marceline sipped her drink as if to stop herself from making an unkind comment.

"The painting of the cathedral in the hallway," I began, changing the subject, "is Dane the artist?"

"Good detective work," Holden replied. "It's nice, isn't it?"

"I'm quite taken with it."

"Notre Dame. It's in Paris."

"I know where Notre Dame is," I said with a smile. "Have you been?"

Jamie reappeared around the corner with my Vine Glo. "Ma says dinner's ready."

"I've been to Notre Dame," Holden went on, ignoring him. "But it wasn't my favorite church in Paris."

"Which was your favorite?"

Holden leaned over, whispering something in my ear as we made our way to the table. "I'll show you one day."

If it weren't for Jamie walking over to hand me my glass, I would have stopped breathing all together.

I took my seat next to Jamie, across from Holden and Marceline, with Mr. Thompson at the head. Sipping on my new glass of Vine Glo, I watched as plates of celery, salted almonds, stuffing with brown gravy, corn, candied sweet potatoes and cranberry sauce were set on the table to compliment the brisket. I looked over at Mr. Thompson, who flashed his wife a giddy smile as she completed the spread with a dish of white mushroom sauce.

I marveled at the china in front of me, taking in its intricate patterns as everyone settled in. The cloth napkins were held by silver napkin rings, and the silverware looked as if it had been polished earlier that day. But it wasn't the china or the silverware that attracted me—not even the candles that adorned the table—all of these things could be found at my own family home. It was the exuberant warmth; it was the sense of belonging I felt as we sat around the table.

"I would like to make a toast this evening. This is the first time in a long time that most of us have been together. And I'm happy to say that even the empty seat is filled," said Mr. Thompson, glancing in my direction with a smile. "To family."

We clinked our glasses around the table, and I soaked in the familial togetherness that I'd only ever dreamed about.

"Tell me about yourself, Lou. James says you attended the Teachers College?" asked Madora as we started in on our meal.

"I did. I'm interested in becoming a writer—a journalist, I hope."

"God knows there are plenty of things to cover right now," added Mr. Thompson.

"You could cover the vote," suggested Marceline.

"I'm sure you could tag along with Marcie and her secret society," joked Holden.

The realization hit me all at once. "You're a suffragette?"

Marceline nodded. "I am."

"I've always been so interested in the rallies, but my mother never allowed me to attend any."

"We'd love to have you along," she said.

I smiled, and the dinner table again fell silent as our forks scraped across the china.

"I was always envious of the boys at the front who were covering the war. I wish I'd done that instead," recounted Holden.

"What you did takes a lot more bravery," assured Mr. Thompson.

The lighthearted glint vanished from Marceline's eyes as they shot to Holden, who shrank back in his seat.

"I have to disagree," he mumbled.

"Pop's right," Jamie chimed in. "You should be proud."

Holden laid his fork and knife down gracefully next to his plate, setting his sights across the table. "Tell me more, little brother, about how I should feel."

"I'm sorry, Holden," Jamie replied unapologetically. "I forget that you're so strongly a pacifist now."

"If I wasn't a pacifist after the things I've seen, I'd be mad. There's nothing glorious or brave about it." Holden's voice rose with each word. "And do me a favor and keep your comments to yourself because *you* weren't there. *You* don't know."

"I would have gone if I'd been a little older."

"Fuck's sake, Jamie. Be glad you didn't, all right?"

Marceline turned to him. "Holden—"

"As if Richmond was any better with the flu? You think you're the only one who's seen death."

"You haven't seen it like I have."

"Right! Because no one has seen it how you have, Holden. Not the rest of us, fighting a war back home." Jamie lowered his voice. "You're *completely* unique."

"Forgive me, but which of us was laid up in the hospital with—"

"Enough, please," begged Madora, her voice weary. "I can't stand it."

Holden threw his napkin onto the plate. "I've lost my appetite."

Marceline looked at her father, pleading for direction.

"Who's ready for dessert?" asked Mr. Thompson, trying to smother the tension with caramel custard.

"I'm going to get some air." Holden excused himself, giving his mother a quick kiss before leaving the dining room.

Mr. Thompson looked across the table to his wife as the front door closed behind her.

"It's all right, dear, if he needs some air, let him have some air," she said quietly.

"I don't think he's used to sitting at tables for long periods of time, at least not anymore," mumbled Marceline. "There was no need to antagonize him." She shot Jamie a scornful look.

"Firstly, Marcie, *you* antagonize him all the time. Secondly, he's always been that way! Willing to pick a fight any chance he gets. Dane is a saint for putting up with him."

"Enough," said Mr. Thompson. "Let's have dessert."

I suffered through that caramel custard with my eyes on the door—watching, waiting, and wondering if Holden would return. I wondered if he was all right out there. I wondered what I might say to him when we spoke next.

Mr. Thompson and Jamie joined at the mantel for a nightcap after dessert, and Madora and Marceline began to help the staff clear the dinner table. I tried to follow suit, but Marceline stopped me.

"No," she pressed. "You're a guest. Why don't you go try to convince Holden to come back inside? It's freezing out."

"It seems like he wanted to be alone."

"I think a friend would do him good," Marceline whispered, before following her mother into the kitchen.

I walked over to the tree and looked out the window, sparkling with the reflection of Christmas lights. Holden sat on the edge of the portico with his back to a column, using the glow from the inside to light the pages of a book.

I stepped outside, bundled in my fur coat. "Marceline sent me to fetch you."

"That's why you're here, then?" He looked up, bookmarking his place. "Because my sister sent you?"

I didn't know what to say.

"And here I was hoping you wanted to sit out here with me."

I looked around. "Do you *want* me to sit with you?"

Holden leaned forward, patting the edge of the portico. He struck a match and lit a cigarette as I found his side, obliging him.

"What is this?" I asked, grabbing his book. It only took one flip through for me to realize I couldn't read it.

"Hermann Hesse. My brother sent it to me. Read it if you want."

"I can't," I admitted, handing it back to him.

He took a drag of his cigarette and smiled. "You can't read German?"

I blushed. "Only French."

"I can speak French, too," he replied. "Badly."

"I'll bet that made it difficult to get around Paris."

"I had a little help. Dane can speak both German and French fluently. Even a little bit of Italian too. German is the only one that ever stuck for me." He laughed to himself. "And it's hardly a romance language."

"You studied it in school, then?"

"I did. Almost as if I knew I would need it down the road." He paused to take a drag. "I read a lot of German books when I was in the trenches. We had plenty of time and not a lot to do, and they were the easiest to find."

I looked away, trying my best to hold back my questions surrounding the obviously sensitive topic.

"You can ask me about it," he said, "I promise not to blow a gasket."

"How long were you in France?"

"From May of 1918 until this past spring. I stayed on with Dane for a while in Paris after the armistice, but he thought I might do better back home."

"What do you mean by that?"

He smiled and shook his head, unwilling to elaborate. "I just need to save enough for Bette and me to live on for at least a year, then I hope to be on my way back."

"Your plan is to go back to Europe?"

"What's yours?" he asked. "Your plan—I don't imagine you want to work for my father forever."

"I suppose New York City is my hope. I think I may build a portfolio and see if any papers are interested in me."

"The city would suit you," he said. "But you can't leave until *after* I leave."

I laughed. "I'm honestly just happy to be out of my parents' house."

"Poor little rich girl," he snickered.

I managed a smile, dropping my eyes.

"I'm sorry." It was clear from his tone that he knew he'd struck a nerve. "It's not my place to say that."

"It's fine. My family doesn't understand me, that's all."

"Go on," he coaxed. "I'm interested."

"I used to write books when I was little," I recalled. "You know, just simple stories with illustrations. I kept them all in a green journal and would work on them when I was supposed to be practicing my embroidery in the afternoons. But I was *terrible* at embroidery and eventually, my mother caught on and figured out why. Anyway, I was punished and my stories were taken away. After seeing how upset I was, my father bought me an expensive new leather book, thinking I could just write new stories." I turned to see him smiling at me.

"You *are* a storyteller after all."

As he spoke, I felt something cold hit my nose, then again on my arm. I looked up and saw a few snowflakes floating gracefully to the ground. "Snow."

He grinned and took another swig from the flask he'd brought outside. "The last time I saw snow, I was sharing the world's tiniest flat with Dane, living off of wine and baguettes."

"You really miss it there, don't you?"

"I do," he admitted. "Especially since my problems seem to follow me wherever I go."

"What do you mean by that?"

He inhaled shallowly, casting his gaze across the yard. "I'm always running from something. I thought anything would be better than school at the time. But every place feels worse and worse."

"You can't outrun yourself."

He turned to me. "It's not myself I'm trying to outrun."

"'*Hell is empty and all the devils are here.*'"

Holden laughed, his dimple pronounced by the light streaming from the parlor window. "I do love Shakespeare."

"Maybe we have something in common after all," I remarked.

"We have more than Shakespeare." He eyed me dubiously. "We're cut from the same cloth, you and me. That's why we..."

"What?"

He shrugged. "It's why you insisted on hating me, I think."

"I never hated you."

"No?"

I rolled my eyes playfully and looked away, suddenly aware of how painfully handsome he was.

"'*We loved with a love that was more than love,*'" he quoted, shutting his book abruptly.

"Too easy," I said. "Poe."

He laughed. "Too easy, huh?"

"And predictable." I smirked. "So *tortured* you are."

"*And* she's funny." The gleam in his eyes dared me to challenge him. "Impress me, expert. You'll have a hard time stumping me."

"All right—" I held my finger up to him while I thought. "'*But O Heart! Heart! Heart! O the bleeding drops of red...*'"

"'*Where on the deck my captain lies, fallen cold and dead,*'" he finished, looking a little stunned. "How did you know that's my favorite Walt Whitman poem?"

"It's not!"

"*It is,*" he insisted. "Since I was a boy."

My cheeks rose with a smile. "'*O captain, my captain.*'"

"*Yes?*" he asked, his eyes glittering back at me.

It was there, against the softly falling snowflakes that I truly saw him for the first time—his playful spirit burning bright. But then the door opened, snuffing the flame.

"Come inside," said Marceline. "You'll freeze to death out here!"

Holden rose to his feet, offering his hand. "Let's go," he said, pulling me up.

Chapter Six

The sentimental Christmas feeling slipped quietly into the past as a new decade dawned on the horizon. A fresh start for a world plagued with war and sickness. Ultimately, only one thing was certain in the eyes of the majority: 1920 was coming full force.

Mr. Thompson's New Year's Eve parties that he held to build community with his clients were something of a town favorite. And now that the influenza restrictions had been lifted, he was ecstatic to continue the tradition.

Maybe it was the noise downstairs, growing louder by the minute, or maybe it was the fact that crowds made me anxious, but when Marceline finally came to knock, I'd been nervously puffing on one cigarette after another at my vanity mirror.

"Lou, are you coming down?"

"I'm almost ready," I called. "Come in."

Marceline walked in looking effortlessly pretty in a trim but modest maroon velvet dress. The scent of her honeysuckle perfume wafted in behind her. "It's a full house," she remarked, scanning the room.

The state of my apartment was clear evidence of my decision paralysis, scattered with dresses of all colors and styles. One look at Marceline had me second-guessing my black silk dress, embellished with decorative beadwork.

"Do you think Bette will come this time?" I asked, finding her in my mirror.

"I don't see why she would," she replied. "It's not that we don't invite her to things—she's always welcome to come with him. She just chooses not to."

"Why don't you like her?"

"It's not that I don't like her. I don't *know* her, and I don't think I ever will." Marceline dropped her shoulders. "I just can't understand how he could go off and marry some girl we'd never heard of, who seems to have no interest in getting to know his family. What am I supposed to think?"

"Is Holden downstairs?"

"Fashionably late as usual. A few of his old school friends are in town visiting, so who knows where he is."

"I suppose I'm as ready as I'll ever be." I motioned to the door. "Shall we?"

I took a deep breath, straightened my dress, and descended down the staircase into the thick, smoke-filled air with Marceline as my escort. Immediately turning the corner into the shop, we met Mr. Thompson at the desk, surrounded by a slew of clients.

"My favorite pair!"

The familiar refrain always brought a smile to my face, once again affirming my place in the family.

"Marceline!"

A group of women with large hats approached us.

"I have some friends I want you to meet," said Marceline.

"The suffragettes?" I asked excitedly.

"Soon," she promised, turning to them. "Ladies, this is Lou Morgan, our newest employee. Lou, these are my friends from church: Bethany, May and my cousin Mary Jane."

I observed the stiff group with their stale faces. Mary Jane, the most approachable, looked almost exactly like Marceline, only short and brunette.

"You're so *pretty,*" she gushed.

I laughed, suddenly feeling the weight of their collective attention. "Oh, thank you."

"Are you married?" asked May.

"No—"

"But you're getting on with Jamie, right?"

"Certainly not," I replied, humored.

"Marceline told us that you two were always writing, so I could only assume."

Looking past Bethany and May, I caught a glimpse of the face I'd been searching for. "We're friends," I murmured.

Holden ushered his two friends through the back door, meeting my eye from across the room. I waved, and Bethany turned around to look at him.

"I see Holden is without his wife tonight," she said dryly.

The girls all turned their heads to find Marceline's brother in the crowd.

"I for one am not upset," said May.

"It's obviously for show." Bethany fixated her gaze intently. "They've been married, what, half a year?"

"What do you mean?"

Bethany turned to me snobbishly. "What do you *think?* His reputation stretches from here to New York City."

I looked between them bewildered. "You mean, you think he—"

"A shotgun wedding," said Bethany.

"Ladies!" interjected Marceline. "Please."

"All I'm saying is" —Bethany leaned in toward me— "talk to him at your own risk."

My own risk.

I didn't want to believe Holden was that kind of man, but even the first time I'd seen him at Goolrick's, he was flirting with another woman at the counter. What Jamie had told me at Chenault's only confirmed it. I watched him dismally as he socialized, trying to remind myself that his personal life was none of my business.

"Have you met Holden's friends from Princeton yet?" Mary Jane asked, turning to me.

"I haven't. Should I?"

"They're something else."

I smiled, seeing the perfect opportunity to excuse myself. "Perhaps I'll introduce myself."

Promising Marceline I'd find her later, I cut through the empty foyer, glad to leave the gossip behind. At the end of the hall, the lavatory door swung open, completely blocking my path.

A husky man with glasses stepped out. "Sorry about that," he said with a wink.

In his typical fashion, Holden had vanished by the time I reached the back door. Assuming he'd gone outside, I slipped out to investigate, not bothering to go back for my coat.

Greeted only by an empty parking lot, I reached into my purse to pull out a cigarette.

And then—

The back door *slammed* behind me.

Losing my cigarette, I turned around to find Holden looking around in a frenzy. He pressed his finger to his lips, motioning for me to stay quiet as he stepped down the stairs. The doorknob wiggled, and he grabbed my arm, pulling me into the shop's alleyway.

"Holden?"

The voice sounded like Bethany's, but I couldn't be sure. With our backs to the wall, I watched the light from the opening door creep across the ground in front of us. Holden's fingers brushed across my bare skin, holding me in place. With no response, the door closed, and he released me.

"Who are you hiding from out here?" Holden asked, pulling out his flask.

"I'm not hiding," I protested, sounding more defensive than I'd intended.

He took a swig, then offered it to me.

"I was looking for you, as a matter of fact," I said, declining.

A large smile took hold of him. "You were looking for me?"

"Don't flatter yourself."

"Why not?"

"It seems you don't need it," I said coolly. "I've been warned to stay away from you."

He laughed. "Did you ever consider the gossip might be biased? People love to hold outdated versions of others in their heads."

"Why did you marry Bette?"

"Well, *that's* a personal question—" His eyes widened. Big and beautiful, even in the dark. "You're asking me why I married my wife?"

By some miracle, he spared me asking why I'd wanted to know.

"It's not for the reason you heard," he added, tucking a cigarette in his lower lip. "It's all right, no one likes Marcie's friends. Not even Marcie."

"Your cousin seems nice," I said, happy to move on.

"She is." He pointed his lit cherry at me for emphasis. "But she's the only one. The rest are leeches in Sunday clothes. Whiskey?"

"No, thank you. How did you get the script?"

"It's for depressive episodes and mania," he stated in a doctorly voice. "Are you sure you don't want any? You look like you need to relax."

"I don't take candy from strangers."

"Celebrate with me *a little bit.*" Holden flicked his cigarette ash. "It's a new decade. And I'm quite happy to leave the old one."

The door slammed again.

"Thompson, you out here?"

"Over here, Teddy," Holden called back.

Footsteps joined us in the alley. "You poor bastard, I figured you'd be out here hiding," the voice taunted. "You'd better go find your date before she gets ahold of Scott."

"Bethany Sinclair is not my date," Holden countered. "It was one time. We went out *one time* when I first got back!"

Bethany.

So *that* was why she wanted me to stay away from him.

Holden's friend walked into view, just enough for me to faintly make out his dark complexion and curly black hair. He was much bulkier than Holden, and next to me he seemed like a giant.

"This is Theodore Elliot. Theo is a former classmate and my very best friend," said Holden. "Theo, this is my new friend Lou."

Theo looked with amusement between Holden and me. "Is he boring you with stories of the golden years out here? If so, I apologize on his behalf."

"Lou was just asking me about my apparent over-active love life," Holden said, offering me a drag of his cigarette.

I almost took it. "No thanks."

"Suit yourself." He exhaled and looked at me, holding the cigarette to his lips. "What are you doing tonight?"

"I don't know," I replied. "This, I guess."

"No—what are you *really* doing tonight?"

I looked at him, confused. "Um…"

"My friends and I are throwing a private party across the river. I think you should come."

"I second that," added Theo. "You'll have much more fun with us."

"We can drink tonight to forget today," said Holden. "Not to boast, but it's kind of a specialty of mine."

"Will Bette be there?" I asked.

"You'll have to wait and see like the rest of us." He looked to Theo. "Let's find Scott before he hits it off with one of my sister's friends."

I hadn't realized how cold I was until we stepped foot back

inside. Leaving me with Theo, Holden took it upon himself to collect their other friend.

"Lou! There you are!" Marceline hurried over. "Theodore," she greeted.

"Marcie." He nodded back.

"Dearest sister," said Holden, finding my side, "will you be joining us tonight? You look in need of rescuing."

"Joining you where, and with whom?"

"Theo, Scott, Lou and I are going across the river."

I opened my mouth to object. "I didn't say I was—"

"Lou, this is my good friend Scott Cleary, Scott, this is Lou." Holden pointed to the man who had winked at me coming out of the restroom.

"Hello madame," he said, tipping his hat.

"*Someone* has to stay with Papa," Marceline said, turning to Holden. "And if anything happens to Lou—"

"No need for threats, Marcie" —his hand found my waist— "she'll be safe with me."

Caroline Street was littered with energetic locals, ready to ring in the new year as the four of us piled into Scott's yellow roadster, Holden riding shotgun, and Theo and I taking the back.

"Here we are," said Holden, laying a couple small bottles of whiskey on the back seat between Theo and me. "I told the doc I needed an extra prescription this week because my nightmares were worse."

"Is that true?" asked Theo.

"What does it matter?"

Scott and Theo both followed suit, each taking a bottle from their own coat pocket to add to the stash. Theo moved the bottles onto the floorboard as Scott began to pull onto the road.

"Where are we going?" I asked, spotting a lantern by my feet.

"Across the river," Holden answered.

"I know that. *Where?*"

"Patience is a virtue, Lou."

The shores of Chatham looked dark and dismal as we crossed

the bridge in the freezing temperatures. Aside from the glass bottles bumping gently by my feet and Holden chattering on, the ride was quiet.

"My friend is in the process of buying this place," he said as we turned onto a dirt road.

The light from Scott's headlights reflected the imprint of an old, decrepit mansion.

"I know it looks scary," Holden added as we pulled up in the field, "but I come up here all the time by myself."

I wrung my hands anxiously. "Oh?"

"I live just down the street," he replied, swinging his door open. "Theo, do you have a match?"

Bottle of liquor in hand, I climbed out of the car. The four of us began our walk toward the house through the tall, dead grass, with Holden lighting the way.

"What is this place?" I asked.

He was more than happy to explain. "It's called Chatham Manor. It was built in the 1700s and was overtaken by the Union Army during the Civil War and used as a hospital. When the owners returned, it was near ruin."

"And your friend is buying it?"

"A colonel I met overseas, Dan. He and his wife are planning to restore it."

The house towered over us in an unearthly fashion, its portico completely engulfed by vines.

"It's beautiful," I remarked, angling my head. "In a haunted kind of way."

"I thought so too," said Holden.

The lamplight revealed a flicker of a grin, and I couldn't help but smile back.

"You're both crazy," Theo scoffed. "This place gives me the willies."

Holden paid him no mind. "Just wait until you see the front."

I was careful to stay close as he led us around the side of the house.

"Those windows right there," he went on, pointing his lantern in the direction of the broken out frames, "they say there were so many amputees that the piles of arms and legs reached the window from the ground."

"I'm not listening to this." Theo turned to Scott. "Let's get firewood. Thompson, give me the lantern."

"Teddy is squeamish," said Holden, handing it off with a laugh. "Let me show you the best view in town."

He reached for my hand, and, reluctantly, I gave it, following him through the dark as Scott and Theo walked toward the edge of the woods. Holden pulled me forward, through the overgrown brush, until the house was behind us. The Fredericksburg cityscape looked like a little toy town with its windows aglow. Streetlights illuminated the sides of buildings and cars zipped along the river's edge, past the church steeples that pierced a blanket of stars. I felt a cold chill prickle the back of my neck.

Holden turned to me.

"You weren't kidding," I said, clutching my liquor bottle.

"This overlook is my well-kept secret. Well, one of them." He pivoted toward me like he might say something else, but his friends began to call for him in exaggerated, theatrical voices. "They always know just how to ruin a moment," he added.

We followed the lamplight to where Scott and Theo had started building a small fire.

"Won't people think it's odd to see a campfire up here?" I asked.

"They'll just think it's the ghosts," Holden joked.

The three men worked together to get the fire going while I looked around, taking in the bare winter trees, their branches stretched across the sky.

"Speaking of spirits," said Holden, opening the first bottle. "I'm parched."

We followed his example, each opening a bottle of our own.

"Terrible that you have to come all the way up here to have a drink in peace," he added. "I can't wait to go back to Europe."

"Why would you want to go there? You just got back," said Scott.

"The Volstead Act," said Theo, taking a sip. "That's enough reason for me."

It was a fair point. Virginia had been a dry state since 1916, but soon enough alcohol would be illegal nationwide, and the boys had plenty to say about it as we huddled around the crackling fire, reminiscing about the past year and what was to come. I was beginning to feel considerably drunk and cozy when Holden finally asked for the time.

Scott looked at his watch. "Fifteen minutes past eleven. Where's Bette?"

"I think it's safe to assume she's not coming."

The three of us all took sips from our respective bottles.

"Come on," Holden roused. "Don't get all silent—let's go inside the house. Anyone?"

"No," said Theo. "Absolutely not."

Holden turned to me. "Lou?"

"Okay," I hiccuped. "I'll go."

"I'll stay and guard Theodore against the ghosts." Scott grinned, passing the lantern back to Holden. "Have fun, you two."

He split a nod between his friends. "She's braver than the two of you put together."

Holden and I waded through the tall grass and through the rickety front door, which opened into the home's palatial foyer, a time capsule layered in dust. I felt another chill at the back of my neck as I stood at the entrance. "I think you're right about this place—that there are ghosts here," I whispered. My eyes followed Holden's lantern light around the room, revealing shredded wallpaper and pieces of broken furniture.

"What if it's the ghost of Walt Whitman?" he asked. "Would you want to contact him?"

"What are you talking about?"

"*Apparently* he visited this house when it was a hospital."

"How do you know?" I demanded.

He smiled at me and laughed just slightly before walking through a doorway to our left. "That's my other well-kept secret."

I chased the disappearing light, afraid to be alone in the dark. The next room was even more otherworldly, with torn curtains and fabrics littering the floors. I walked to the window, waiting for my eyes to adjust so I could read the writing on the frame.

"Soldiers," said Holden, holding the lantern to the graffiti. "They left their names on the plaster—just in case anything happened to them. That way, someone would know where they were."

"Did you ever leave your name anywhere?"

"Of course." Holden set the lantern in the middle of the room, lying down next to it on the floor. "I have an innate fear of being forgotten," he added, glancing at me with a subdued expression. "Do you really find me so ordinary?"

I laughed, taking a seat next to him in the dust. "No."

He pulled his flask out of his coat pocket and took a long sip.

"What was your favorite church in Paris?"

"None of them."

"You said you had a favorite," I pressed.

"I exaggerated." He looked up at the ceiling. "There was one I used to sit in from time to time when it was empty. I never went there to pray."

"Because hell is empty and all the devils are here?"

"Because no one who was at the Western Front could believe in God."

"You really don't believe in anything?" I lay down next to him. "It doesn't make sense for everything to just go black."

"I never said I didn't believe in *anything.*"

"Go on," I coaxed playfully. "I'm interested."

"I believe" —he sighed a heavy sigh— "that if you whisper to the universe, it will whisper back to you."

Our arms were just barely touching, but it was the only warmth I could feel in the numbing cold. I stared up at the old ceiling of the mansion, meditating on its peeling plaster medallions until my eyelids grew heavy.

When I opened my eyes, Holden was propped on his elbow leaning over me. A single curl fell across his forehead.

"Is this the part where you start reciting Edgar Allen Poe?" I teased.

His exhale was soft on my cheek. "I'm intoxicated enough."

"Then perhaps you'll romance me with your German," I whispered.

His lips parted in a boyish smile. "Is that what you want?"

I was certain he could hear my heart pounding as I tried to steady my breathing, our faces mere inches apart. "It's almost midnight," I murmured, looking up at him.

His nose brushed mine. "We should go back outside," he whispered back.

I tilted my chin, taunting him to do it, and then—

A burst of light filled the room with a *bang*, startling us senseless. I sat up among the raining shadows, looking out the window. "Fireworks!" I exclaimed, turning to Holden. "Happy New…" My smile vanished when I saw his face. His trembling body and worry-filled eyes made it look like he'd *actually* seen a ghost. "Holden?" I waved my hand in front of his eyes and found little recognition in them.

Another firework lit the room, its rumble causing him to take cover. Scott and Theo barged in, only needing to take one look at Holden to know something was wrong.

"Holden—"

He resisted as they tried to lift him.

"It's just us," said Theo. "We're your friends, remember?"

Holden tackled him to the ground in a state of fury.

"Goddammit, Thompson!" yelled Scott, pulling him off.

Holden went for Scott next, grabbing him around the neck. I could see that he was acting on pure instinct and adrenaline, completely blind to what was actually happening. Theo reared back and threw his fist at Holden, knocking him unconscious and freeing Scott from the chokehold.

I ran over and knelt next to Holden on the ground.

"Jesus," said Scott, finding his breath.

Theo rubbed his knuckles. "I shouldn't have hit him."

"It's probably best this way," Scott replied, reaching for the lantern. "He's all right."

"He doesn't *look* all right!" I snapped.

Both men glanced down at me.

"What's wrong with him?"

"Shell shock," Theo replied. "It's a flashback from the war."

"Loud noises send him right back to France," Scott added. "I'm sorry you had to see that."

"This isn't the first time, is it?"

"Far from it." Theo flagged Scott for a hand. "That's why his brother sent him back to the States."

"Why would he send him back in this condition?"

"He thought he might do better at home. You know, a change of scenery," said Scott, helping Theo lift him. "But it hasn't made much of a difference."

Holden's friends carried him to the car, laying him across my lap in the back seat before skipping off to extinguish the fire. Something in me wanted to reach out and stroke his hair as he rested on my knees, but I refrained. Maybe I was scared.

"How much did he drink?" Scott asked, reappearing in the front seat.

"I don't know. Half a bottle of whiskey if I had to guess."

"Plus, whatever he had before," Theo added, slamming his door.

Scott sighed and started the engine. "Let's get him home."

Holden winced in my lap as we drove down the bumpy bank of the heights, but he didn't open his eyes. Finally, I lifted my fingers to his hair, brushing the curls from his forehead.

"No one's home," said Scott. "There are no lights on."

I tried to look forward, but it was too dark to see anything.

"Well, we can't leave him here," said Theo.

"But we can't bring him into the hotel, either," warned Scott. "He doesn't need an alcohol offense."

They both looked back at Holden, who shuffled a bit in my lap.

"He can stay with me," I offered.

We pulled up to the shop around two and unloaded Holden from the car, trying our best to avoid any attention.

"I'm sorry I hit you," Theo whispered, shifting his weight so he and Scott could carry him up the stairs.

Holden half-consciously patted the arm of his friend, mumbling something we couldn't make out.

"I think I can take it from here if you both want to go. I know it's late," I said as they stretched him across my settee. "I don't think he'll give me any trouble."

Scott made his way to the door. "We'll stop by his place tomorrow and check on him."

"He'll be alright," Theo added, halting to look back at me. "But I wouldn't mention this to anyone if you can help it."

"I won't."

"Well, goodnight."

"Goodnight."

I turned my attention to Holden, who lay there in a pitiful state. In the light I could see the gash on his temple, and the forming bruise on his eye.

He peered up at me with a smile as I took a seat on the settee's edge, wet cloth in hand. "And here I thought you didn't like me."

"How are you feeling?"

"Fine," he murmured. "Theo hits like a girl."

"I don't think you'll be saying that tomorrow," I said, dabbing his eye. "Does this hurt?"

"*Fuck,*" he groaned.

Chapter Seven

Holden left without a word the following morning, leaving me to find an empty settee on New Year's Day. Figuring Scott and Theo would reach out like they'd promised, I waited for Tuesday with bated breath. Between the almost-kiss and his shell shock episode, I knew things wouldn't be the same when I saw him again.

When Holden strolled into the shop that Tuesday, late as usual, Marceline stopped mid-sentence at the sight of him. "What happened to you?"

He made no effort to hide the black eye and cut on his face as he hung up his coat.

"Did you get into a fight again?" she asked.

"Not that it's any of your business anyway" —his gaze found me— "but no, I didn't."

Marceline lowered her voice. "That's what you said last time."

"*I told you*, I didn't."

They glanced in unison toward the front of the shop where Mr. Thompson sat at the desk.

"You can't come in here like that," she mumbled.

"I have powder upstairs," I interjected quietly.

The siblings turned to me.

"We can cover it."

Marceline grabbed Holden by his sleeve, ushering him into the foyer toward the stairs "Don't let Papa see you," she whispered as we climbed to the second floor.

Closing the door behind us, I followed Marceline to my vanity, where she promptly sat Holden in front of the three-fold mirror. I opened the drawer, grabbing the powder and handing it to his sister.

"Are you going to tell me what happened?" she asked.

Holden closed his eyes, sporting an amused smile as she tilted his cheek to the window light.

"Theo and I roughhoused too hard," he said, grimacing as she applied the powder under his eye.

"This doesn't look like a friendly roughhousing."

"Well, it was."

"I worry about you," she admitted. The heaviness in her tone told me she was no stranger to his outbursts.

"I'm fine Marcie," he said, opening one eye to look at her. "I'm not made of glass."

"Could've fooled me." Marceline turned his shoulders. "How does he look, Lou?"

Holden opened his eyes, smirking just slightly.

"One more thing," I said.

Marceline stepped aside as I walked over to the vanity, directing Holden to close his eyes again. I reached for my black eyeshadow, taking a knee in front of him.

"What are you doing?" he murmured.

"You'll see," I replied, dabbing the ashy makeup under his opposite eye. "There..."

Holden opened his eyes, which glistened in the morning sun as he looked up at me. I shot to my feet and took a few steps back, attempting to smother the sudden heat between us.

"See?" I swiveled to Marceline. "Now it just looks like he got even less sleep than usual."

Holden's gaze snapped to mine in the vanity mirror. Dancing, flirtatious. I pursed my lips to keep myself from smiling back. I wouldn't give him that satisfaction.

Marceline nodded in approval. "Well, as much as I'd like to keep playing dress up" —she grinned at her brother— "I have a lot of work to do this morning."

I was following her out the door when Holden called after me.

"Lou—"

"What?"

"I need to talk to you," he replied, finding my side.

"All right…" I held my breath, waiting what felt like an eternity for him to speak.

"Thanks for not ratting me out to Marcie," he said finally.

I crossed my arms. "Is that it?"

"That, and…" He cleared his throat, raising his brows in an ambiguous manner. "I wasn't myself the other night."

"Right." I bit my bottom lip. "Me neither, actually."

His lips curled into a disarming smile. "Friends…?"

"Friends."

Holden nodded, squeezing past me in the doorway. "As your friend," he murmured, "I'm wondering if you have any plans on Sunday night?"

"Do you need a babysitter?"

"I'm having a little get-together at my place with Scott and Theo. It's their last night in town."

"I don't know," I replied hesitantly.

"They really like you. Plus, it would give you and Bette an opportunity to get acquainted."

I narrowed my gaze on him.

"*And* if it's any consolation, I'd like you to come too," he added.

"If you insist."

"I do," he said, making his way down the stairs. "I'll have Scott and Theo pick you up on Sunday."

Holden carried on that day apparently unaffected, as if the makeup had covered up more than just his face. The bitter cold, icy rain and post-holiday cancellations had us all looking for a way to pass the time. Mr. Thompson read the paper, Holden stared out the window onto the empty street, and Marceline paced over the threadbare oriental rug, anxious and bored. The only sounds were the ticking of the clock and the crackling of the wood stove churning out heat.

"I could use a cup of coffee," I said at last.

Mr. Thompson looked up.

"May I take a walk?"

"I don't see why not," he replied, turning back to his paper.

"Does anyone want to come?"

Holden looked at me flatly. "It's raining…"

"Will you melt?" I teased.

"I'm willing to brave the weather if you are," Marceline chimed in.

"Don't be too long, you two," Mr. Thompson added. "You're still on the clock!"

The three blocks felt like three miles in the stinging rain, but once we finally shed our coats and chose a table at Chennault's, the prospect of a warm cup of coffee made it worth the trek.

"It's a shame it's so ugly outside today," said Marceline, shedding her velvet gloves. "At least it's only up the street." She rubbed her hands together to warm them.

"Why didn't you ever live in the upstairs apartment?" I asked. "I've always wondered since you work below already."

"Well—"

She was interrupted by a staff member, who delivered two coffees and a little cup of creamer to our table. "On the house, Miss Thompson," he said.

"Thank you, David." Marceline smiled sweetly. "Your mother's dress should be ready by Thursday, if you'd like to pass on the message."

"Glad to."

She turned back to me with a proud grin. "Anyway, the apartment is a bit of a sore spot for my father," she began, treading carefully with her words. "You know of our older brother?"

I nodded.

She took a sip of coffee and lowered her voice. "Well, when my father was married to his first wife, Dane's mother, they lived upstairs. After she died, my father just kept the apartment barren. I think most of us just forgot it was up there."

"What happened to her?"

"Consumption. She died when Dane was two."

"That's terrible," I said, gripping the rim of my mug.

"The whole thing is just tragic. My father doesn't like to talk about it."

"I wouldn't either."

"But I *know* it makes him happy that you've taken up residence there! It's such a pretty space."

I had long assumed that Mr. Thompson's first wife had died when their half-brother was young, but I didn't know that they'd lived upstairs. I was curious to know more, but not wanting to pry, I simply smiled along.

"I'm glad to have a moment alone with you," said Marceline suddenly.

I was struck with a strange anxiety, a worry that she would inquire more about the nature of Holden's black eye.

"I know it's a bit last-minute, but there is going to be a suffrage meeting in the square on Sunday. We're preparing for a few speakers to come to Fredericksburg soon for a rally. Do you have any interest in coming with me and meeting a few of my ladies?"

"Oh," I said, relieved. "That would be lovely."

"Perfect!"

"Oh, wait." I hesitated. "You mean Sunday as in *this* Sunday?"

"I know, it's last-minute—you can still come with me to the rally. I just thought you might want to get acquainted with some of my ladies and see what it's all about. Maybe try your hand at some reporting?"

"Thank you for the invitation. I'd be glad to go, but Holden already invited me over for Scott and Theo's last night in town, and I already told him I would come."

"What?" Her large, baby blue eyes stared at me in wide astonishment. "He never invites anyone over."

"He doesn't?"

"I've never been to his house once," she admitted.

"Oh," I said, suddenly feeling a little uncomfortable. "I could tell him another time would be better."

"Honestly speaking, I'd feel better if you went." Marceline looked down at her mug, expelling a gentle sigh. "I try not to worry, Lou. But when I saw his eye this morning…I don't know how to help him. He's a mess and the company he keeps is no better."

"He was being truthful. I saw it happen."

A look of relief washed over her. "Scott and Theo are nice. They've known him since his school days, but he only sees them once in a blue moon. The rest of his friends are questionable, and certainly don't help his…condition."

"I'll try my best," I promised, reaching across the table to squeeze her hand. "To look after him in the ways you can't."

"And the suffrage movement will still be there after Sunday," she added gently.

To Dane from Holden
January 31, 1920

Hello brother! Many thanks for the Hesse book. You'll be both surprised and pleased to know that it arrived right on time for Christmas. In regard to you staying in Florence for a while, I think it's a great idea. I'm seething with envy. Make sure you tell me your new address this time—or we're going to be playing catch-up again with our letters.

New Year was rather eventful for me. Theo and Scott came to visit, so that was a respite from the general boredom. You know the old run-down Civil War hospital up at Chatham Heights? Well, an army friend just recently acquired the land and is planning on fixing the place up. Devore—he was a colonel I met in the hospital—I don't know if you'd remember the name or not. Anyway, I've been spending a considerable amount of time up there since I got back. I feel a whole new connection to the old place.

The boys and I went up there on New Year's Eve to celebrate with a few bottles we acquired. Lou came with us too—the one I mentioned before. I'm still not tempted, but I think I'm becoming quite fond of her and goddammit, that is so much worse.

I drank too much and made a complete jackass of myself and now I have a ripe shiner to prove it. I lost control again. You know how it goes. This time it was fireworks. Fucking fireworks. A solid knock from Theo put me out of my anxious misery, so I thank him for that but I'm sorry he had to do it. Like you, Teddy doesn't particularly enjoy hitting people.

No one knows about it and I don't plan on telling them. I don't want them to worry. Or worse, put me away. You shake your head, I know. But fireworks are a rarity around here and I'll be more careful next time. Don't be worried by my

LETTER. I'M DOING JUST FINE. THIS IS ALL ONLY TEMPORARY ANYWAY —I'LL BE BACK IN NO TIME. EVERYONE SENDS THEIR LOVE AND HOLIDAY WISHES.

HOLDEN

Chapter Eight

I was told that Scott would be by to pick me up sometime between five-thirty and seven, and even then, he still managed to show up late. I wasn't sure what to expect from the evening at Holden's, but based on my last experience, it was sure to be full of debauchery—and this time, I'd be ready.

About twenty minutes after seven, I heard the roadster's horn from below my apartment. I grabbed my short beaver coat to wear over my blouse and wool skirt, hoping that it would be warm enough. The horn blew again as I made my way down the stairs and pushed open the front door. Knowing that I wouldn't be home until late, I left the shop's outside light on.

"Evening, madame," Scott greeted, opening the door of his yellow car.

Theo turned to the backseat as I climbed in. "Nice to see you again," he said, looking cheerful. "How are you?"

"Cold," I replied, teeth chattering from the January air.

It was déjà vu—me and them in the car. The only thing missing was Holden in my lap.

"Where have you been staying in town?" I asked as we drove over the bridge toward Falmouth.

"We're right up the street at the Princess Anne Hotel," Theo replied.

"Oh, the brick one with the big white columns—I've been to the restaurant inside."

"That's the one."

I looked up, finding Chatham Manor hiding sullenly atop the cliff as Scott turned onto River Road. We drove swiftly along the Rappahannock and I was no longer sure where we were; even the lights from the city were beginning to fade into the background.

"Right there!" yelled Theo.

Scott took a sharp left turn off the main road, throwing me to the other side of the backseat.

Theo whipped around to me. "You all right?"

Disheveled, I fixed my hat and sat forward as we continued down the bumpy driveway. "Are you taking me somewhere to kill me?"

"Not today," Theo joked.

Scott cut the engine as the roadster rolled up on the grass. "Milady, we have arrived."

I squinted ahead, trying to get a better look at the small house on the right as we unloaded.

"A perfect night for stargazing and not another person in sight for miles," Scott remarked.

"Well, I do have one neighbor. An artist lives up the hill a way."

I followed Holden's voice in the dark, finding the red cherry of his lit cigarette.

"There he is," said Theo. "Waiting in the shadows as always."

"Would it kill you to get a sign?" Scott chuckled under his breath. "I can't remember that turn for the life of me."

"Maybe if you came to visit me more often," Holden countered. "Come inside and out of the cold."

Holden held back as they walked ahead to the cottage, lit by a dim porch light. "Bette's inside," he said, nudging my shoulder. "She's glad you could make it."

I was skeptical.

Entering the quaint home, I took notice of all the personal knick-knacks lying around: a Civil War bullet on the fireplace mantel, a postcard from France, books piled high. My curiosity immediately kicked in as I looked to his desk on the left, scattered with letters. Or were they remnants of *something else?*

"Clementine!"

I stumbled back, knocked off my feet by a chocolate-colored dog.

"Holden!" Bette shouted. "Get your—"

"Sorry." He took a knee, wrapping both arms around the dog's furry neck. "This is Clementine. My best girl."

"His best girl indeed," Bette added. "He likes to bring home strays."

I looked at his wife, who'd avoided eye contact with me since I'd walked in. The enigma was dressed in her usual black flapper ensemble, nursing a cigarette at the tiny kitchen table.

"She acts like she never gets any attention," Holden went on, sending Clementine on her way with a kiss. "Don't be fooled." He walked to his cupboard, snatching a mason jar of clear liquid from the second shelf. "Scott! Theo…I got my hands on something special for your last night before departure."

"What in God's name is that?" asked Scott.

"It's unaged whiskey from the mountains," Holden replied, passing it to him. "They say the alcohol content is so high you could blow fire with it."

"May I?" asked Theo.

"Be my guest, Teddy."

Theo silently toasted him before taking a huge swig and handing it to Scott.

I looked over to Bette, mirroring her timid smirk. Boys.

"Be careful with that," Holden scolded, seizing the jar from them.

He poured the contents into a pair of glasses, handing one to me and one to Bette. Thanking him, I made my way over to his desk, setting my sights on the writings that lined the top. Unable to help myself, I picked up a piece of paper and began to read.

I WRITE SO THAT OIL DOES NOT SPEW FROM MY MOUTH AS I SPEAK—SO THAT I WILL NOT COMBUST IF A MATCH COMES NEAR.

"No, no, no," said Holden, carefully removing the paper from my hands. "You can't read this."

"Why not?"

"I don't like anyone reading my writing. I don't even like reading my writing!"

"So much for being friends," I sneered.

"Please, just don't." He slipped the piece of paper under a stack, then glanced up at me with a playful, cocked eyebrow. "Besides, this is the burn pile."

"The burn pile?"

"That's right—try the whiskey, will you?"

I looked down at the lukewarm substance in my glass, sniffing it before reluctantly taking a sip.

"Be careful," he warned. "It sneaks up on you."

"No blowing fire, then?"

"Maybe leave that to us."

"Thompson!" Theo joined his side. "Are you ready?"

Holden turned to him, looking as excited as a child on Christmas morning. "I'll grab the map!"

In a flash, the three men had disappeared out the front door.

Bette sat quietly at the table, staring at her glass of whiskey. The silence was painful.

"What are they doing?" I asked, trying to make small talk.

"Counting the stars and getting drunk." She struck a match, lighting a cigarette.

I laughed. "Full of quirks."

"You're a writer like Holden, then?"

"I wouldn't know." I dropped my gaze to Clementine, who lay on the floor at my feet. "What kind of things does Holden write?"

Bette scowled at the faint sound of *singing* just beyond the wall. "Goddammit," she murmured, snuffing her cigarette.

Following her onto the porch, I spotted the trio in the yard, singing arm-in-arm.

"You're going to wake everyone within a five-mile radius!" she yelled.

I could tell by Holden's walk that he was already drunk, immune to his own advice.

"Holden, I swear to—"

He placed a finger to her lips. "No reason to get uppity, darling."

Bette snatched the half-empty jar from his hand. "Your singing is going to wake everyone up."

"Everyone?" Holden laughed, stealing it back. "Our *one* neighbor? Since when do you care about what anyone thinks?"

She glared at him with disdain. "I'd rather people not know you're an obnoxious drunk."

"I'm a mess," he said, taking another swig from the jar. "Believe me, I know."

"You *poor thing,*" she replied, taking her leave. "Enjoy your wallowing."

"Where are you going?" he demanded.

"To bed."

"I love you, too," he yelled after her.

I looked to Scott and Theo in the yard, unsure of what to do or say as Bette slammed the door.

"I'll catch up in a minute," Holden called out to them.

I looked down at my remaining whiskey, swirled the glass, and finished it.

"It never fails," said Holden, taking a seat on the step. "You always seem to see the worst of me."

"Tell me, what do you write about?" I asked, clumsily finding his side.

"Things." He took another sip, then turned to me with a grin. "Mostly short stories about the war," he said, offering the mason jar.

I hesitated.

"I'm not sick," he promised.

Warily, I took the jar from him, refilling my glass before handing it back. "Cheers."

"To what?"

"The whispers of the universe," I replied, clinking my glass against his jar. The whiskey burned like fire as it went down.

"You know there hasn't been a serious outbreak of the flu since last year, right?" Holden let out a low laugh. "What are you going to do if someone wants to kiss you?"

"I…" I snapped my gaze to his, unsure of what he was insinuating. "I'm only being cautious," I replied, turning front. "My history teacher did die from it, you know."

"So, if I tried to kiss you right now, you'd refuse?"

I took a sip of whiskey. "You're right—you *are* a mess."

"You really have no idea, Lou." A thick blanket of melancholia seemed to fall over him. A validation he didn't want.

"Why did you join up?" I asked.

"It's a long story and I'm not nearly drunk enough to tell you."

I bumped his shoulder with mine. "Drink up."

"I left Princeton because I was full of chaos and couldn't stay." It felt like days passed between his words. "Dane tried to dissuade me, but I wouldn't hear it."

"You could always go back."

Holden shook his head, looking more somber than I'd ever seen him. "I tried to hang myself a few months ago. I just wanted to sleep. To *really* sleep."

"Did someone…"

"The rope broke and I fell." His voice quivered as he spoke. "No one knows."

"Not even Bette?"

Desperation painted his face as he looked up at the glittering stars above us. Then, as if he didn't know what else to do, he leaned his head on my shoulder. I wanted to comfort him, to shield him with my wing like a mother bird. "Whatever you had going for you then, you still have now," I said, wrapping my arm around his shoulder. "The war can't take that from you. Nothing can."

"It took my humanity," he murmured.

"It doesn't look that way from here, Holden."

Between the moonshine and the conversation, my head was starting to spin.

"Do you think I'm crazy now?"

"No, of course I don't think that."

Holden lifted his head from my shoulder, looking anxious and unconvinced.

"I promise."

"You know," he said, sitting up, "the stars here look exactly the same as they do in Paris."

"Oh?"

Holden went on about his time with Dane and the Parisian cafés in great detail. How he and his brother would write and paint together on the street during the day, and hunt the constellations at night. But his words began to slur together, and not because *he* was drunk. I looked up at the stars, and through the haziness of the mountain-distilled whiskey, their twinkling seemed to double. Holden took another sip from the fast-emptying jar, then handed it to me, and against my better judgment, I indulged him.

"Look," he said.

The tail of a shooting star trailed across the sky above.

"Make a wish," he whispered to me.

"Did anyone else see that?" yelled a voice from the field.

"Uh, oh," said another, much closer. "She doesn't look so good."

"Lou?"

I turned to Holden, nauseous with the spins. "I'm just going to lie down for a moment," I said. On my back the stars seemed to triple, but when I tried to close my eyes, I felt even dizzier.

"Someone had a little too much to drink."

"I'm fine," I whispered.

Someone lifted me, and despite my struggle to stay conscious, everything went black—and thus ended my night of debauchery.

The next morning I was awoken by the slam of a drawer from my kitchen. Head pounding, I looked around the familiar walls of my room with no recollection of how I'd gotten there.

Humiliating. Absolutely humiliating.

"You're awake!"

I shot up in bed as Holden rounded the corner, looking especially chipper.

"May I ask why you look so horrified to see me?"

I clutched the blanket to my chin. "What are you doing here?"

"I brought you *food,*" he said, holding up a small paper bag.

Certain I'd be sick, I covered my face with a pillow. "What happened last night?"

"Do you really want to know?"

I peeked over the pillow's edge. "Don't do that."

His smirk was shameless, even by his standard. "Do *what?*"

I sighed dramatically into my pillow, falling limply on the bed.

"You were passed out on my sofa for a while until we brought you home. I unlocked the front door and we carried you upstairs. Nothing to write home about," he said. *"You're welcome."*

"What time is it?"

"Ten-thirty. Scott and Theo are on their way back to Baltimore." He took a seat on the end of my bed. "You should eat," he added, setting the paper bag between us.

Muffins. I could smell them.

"Why are you still here?" I asked, adjusting my cheek on the pillow.

"I stayed to make sure you were all right. You did the same for me a week ago, so now I've repaid my debt."

I reached for the paper bag.

"And assuming you can remember our conversation last night," he said, lowering his voice, "I'd appreciate it if you didn't tell anyone what I told you. I hope you won't hold it against me."

"No, of course not." I reached for the paper bag. "Thanks for looking out for me."

Holden grinned. "Now we're even."

THE LOVERS

union – choices – crossroads

July 1920 — March 1921

Chapter Nine

It was clear to me that Marceline had an admirer.

It wasn't the first suffrage rally he'd attended in the Square, watching from the edge in his top hat and eyeglasses. I'd seen him at the one in April, and then again in May. Now it was well into July, and Marceline stood beside me among the diaphanous layers and fancy hats with a twinkle in her eye, as though she knew she were being watched.

Despite the hundred-year fight for the vote being a stone's throw away from paying off, I couldn't focus on anything except the stranger trying to catch the eye of my friend. Maybe I *was* as nosy as Holden said.

"How's it going, Lou? Getting anything good?"

I turned to Molly, who'd found my side in the crowd. "We're close," I replied, using my fingers to bookmark the spot in my notebook. "She keeps saying so."

Molly rose to her tiptoes, casting her glance over the sea of hats. "Saint Adele," she mumbled. "Bless her heart."

I laughed under my breath, looking again to Marceline and the knowing smirk she wore. If Molly were half as observant as I was, she would have noticed it too. But nothing on God's green earth could distract her from the words of Adele Clark.

"Molly," I murmured in her ear.

She leaned toward me, but kept her eyes on the stage. "Hm?"

"That man over there…" I cocked my head left. "The one who looks like a politician."

"He doesn't seem like the type you'd be interested in," Molly huffed. "But it's nice to see a man at these rallies, wouldn't you agree?"

"No—I mean, what's his name?"

"Arvin Stanley. He works for the city."

I'd heard the name before, from Holden. He always had something or someone to complain about, but the thought of him still brought a smile to my face. My respective friendships with him and Marceline both had blossomed over the spring months, and I'd learned just how different they were. Where Holden's principles came from the pain of his past, Marceline's came from her vision of the future. With her, it was always about the big picture, while Holden got caught on the details like a fly in a spider web.

The Square erupted in applause, bringing me back to the present.

"What was that last part?" I asked Molly.

"We cannot be tame spectators."

"Oh, that's good," I replied, jotting it at the top of my notebook.

Marceline took a deep breath, clapping her hands together as she turned to us. "Dinner?"

Glancing over her shoulder, I noticed her admirer was gone. "Count me in," I replied. "Molly?"

Hands on her hips in her fitted blazer, Molly only stared longingly toward the makeshift stage as the crowd dispersed around us.

"Molly."

"Hm? Oh. Dinner—sure thing."

Marceline and I exchanged a look.

"Why don't you go talk to her?" I asked.

"Oh, no," Molly replied. "She..." Her eyes again found Adele. "She is merely a goddess I worship from afar."

"Next time, then."

"All right, all right," said Molly, hooking me in one arm and Marceline in the other. "Next time."

Molly charged ahead, pulling us along as we turned the corner from William Street. She was a bit older than both of us and more bombastic than a firecracker on the Fourth of July. I'd liked Molly from the moment she crunched my hand in her masculine grip, and was fully convinced that if Holden knew her, he might think differently of his sister's friends.

We walked up the half-moon terrace of the Princess Anne Hotel, glittering in the twilight. The warm glow of candlelit dining tables met us on the other side of the door. Molly held up three fingers to the host, and he led us to our usual round banquette with velvet cushion. It seemed like we'd just been there to celebrate Holden's birthday in June.

"How's the collection coming, Lou?" Marceline asked.

"Well, I think." I looked at my notebook, filled with four months of suffrage reporting. "Adele seems to think we almost have it."

"I hope my empress is right," Molly chimed in, scanning the menu. "If a man tells me one more time that my future husband can vote for us both..."

"I concur," I replied dismally.

"What are you going to do with them?"

"My papers? Well, I think I'm—" I halted.

Just past Marceline's shoulder, her admirer entered the restaurant.

"What is it?"

Molly turned over for a better look. "Hmph," she said triumphantly. "Arvin Stanley just walked in."

"Arvin?" Marceline gulped, nearly swallowing an ice cube. "He's here?"

"Arvin?" I asked.

A first name basis.

"He attends Saint Mary's with us," she added, anxiously fidgeting with her napkin.

"He's by himself. Don't look now, but he's coming over." I watched as he followed the host, taking a seat in the booth next to us. "I can tell you fancy him," I whispered across the table. "Does he know?"

"Of course not!" Marceline whispered back to me. "Besides," she said, her voice returning to normal, "there's nothing to know."

"Ah," said Molly.

I slipped my napkin under the table, dropping it to the floor. "Excuse me," I said, peeking at Arvin over my shoulder. "Do you have an extra napkin? Our waiter only gave us two."

He looked past me, finding Marceline on the other side of the table. "I'll fetch you one," he offered.

"Oh, no. You don't—"

Arvin Stanley rose to his feet in his top hat and silk vest. "Please," he said, holding his large hand to his chest. "It would be my pleasure."

I looked back to Marceline, whose eyes were full of giddiness and wider than the harvest moon as he found the side of our table.

"Miss Thompson?"

"Mr. Stanley!" she exclaimed.

The formalities sounded so wry I knew they were for show.

"It seems the waiter has seated us right next to each other," said Arvin, setting the rolled napkin on our table.

"What a funny coincidence," Marceline replied.

Molly shot me a proud look from across the table.

"I saw you at the rally earlier too," he went on. "I rather enjoyed her speech."

"Why don't you join us?" asked Marceline, scooting over in the booth.

"Oh, I wouldn't want to impose," he said, glancing at Molly and me.

"Not at all," I assured him. "There's plenty of room."

He nodded graciously and took a seat, filling the last open space. His kind eyes shone behind his spectacles as he smiled at each of us.

"Lou, we ought to be going anyway," mumbled Molly, looking at her watch. "Before the press shop closes."

"Oh—I completely forgot!"

Arvin began to stand.

"No, no! You two stay," I insisted. "We can handle it. Can't we, Molly?"

"Without a doubt."

Marceline's quiet smile told me she understood our ploy, and Molly and I slipped out of the booth, leaving the two lovebirds behind.

"So" —Molly brushed her skirt, turning to me— "dinner, Lou Lou?"

"That was nicely done."

"Compliments to us," she replied with a laugh. "Watch now, she'll marry that man."

Arvin and Marceline were a match well-made in the eyes of society. He was a respected city official and she, a notable bachelorette from a beloved Fredericksburg family. For the whole month of July, Arvin accompanied us to all the suffrage meetings, even going as far as to drive us to Richmond for the rally at the Capitol. As for Marceline, not only could she keep her sense of independence, but she'd found a partner who would make sure of it.

However, as smitten as they were, they kept their courtship private, and I found myself the guardian of another secret. Marceline insisted that Arvin not meet her brothers until she was ready to introduce them—and knowing Holden, I couldn't blame her.

It wasn't until the ratification of the 19th amendment that August, when we gained the vote at last, that Jamie and Holden met Arvin Stanley.

"Where is the queen of the hour?" Holden asked, fanning himself with a newspaper. "It's unlike her not to be three hours ahead of schedule."

"I'm sure she's on her way," I replied, absent-mindedly leafing through an issue of *Vogue.* "We'll be sure to tell her that you were concerned."

Holden picked up a small sofa pillow, tossing it at my head. Sweat beads rolled from Jamie's temples as he glanced up from his own paper to look at us. Dressed for the Thompsons' luncheon in our best white summer dresses and suits, we were all feeling the heat as the house swarmed with guests.

"Marcie's here," Jamie announced.

Holden and I turned just in time to see Marceline walk through the front door with her special guest.

"So this is what you're always whispering back and forth about at work," Holden whined, whipping around to face me. "I'm always the last to know anything."

"Lou, you knew about this?" Jamie asked.

"She wanted to be the one to tell you! Both of you."

"Well, at least I know you haven't told any of my secrets, then," Holden added, throwing the pillow at me again.

"Holden, isn't that Arvin Stanley?"

"Holy shit, it is." Holden slid closer to me on the sofa. "Dirty politicians."

I hushed them as Marceline approached us with her beau. "Behave."

Jamie spoke first. "Who's this?"

"Arvin Stanley. Pleased to meet you."

"James Thompson," said Jamie, taking his hand.

"You already know Lou..." Marceline grinned. "And this is Holden."

Holden offered his hand so naturally it made me nervous.

"You must be Marceline's eldest brother," said Arvin, grabbing on. "I've heard a lot about you both."

"I am the eldest. Now, that is," Holden replied. "God rest his soul."

Arvin's brow knitted in confusion.

"Oh, I see...Marcie didn't tell you," he continued somberly. "Our eldest brother, Dane, was lost to us in the war. He's in France now."

"Holden!" Marceline screeched.

Arvin's face drained of its color. "Please forgive me. I beg your pardon," he said, turning to Marceline. "You said that you had a brother who served, but I didn't know he..."

Holden collapsed into Jamie's arms and the two of them held each other, trying to stifle their laughter into believable sobs.

Marceline stamped her foot. "That's because our brother isn't dead!"

"She's right," said Holden, trying to catch his breath. "She's right."

Arvin's gaze darted between Jamie and Holden. "Your brother didn't die in the war."

"Dane is very much alive," Holden replied, looking smug as can be. "Though he does live in France."

"Arvin Stanley! Good to see you!" interrupted Mr. Thompson. "Glad to see everyone is in such good spirits! Come in, come in! Let me introduce you."

"I'm sorry," Marceline murmured as they followed her father. "My brother's humor is detestable."

"You're so predictable," I scolded, punching Holden in the arm.

"Ow, Lou!"

"No wonder she didn't want you to meet him!"

"I couldn't help myself! It was too easy—"

I rolled my eyes.

"Don't be mad," he begged. "It was funny. Even Jamie thought it was funny!"

"You're ridiculous."

"You're no fun."

"I'm plenty fun," I countered, flicking the center of his chest. "I just—"

Holden scooped me up, throwing me over his shoulder.

"Holden, put me down!"

He laughed. "You were saying?"

Jamie shot me a look from across the room—a reminder that people were watching.

"Holden," I urged, softer. "Let me go."

He obliged, releasing me. I reached to tuck a strand of fallen hair behind my ear as I slipped down his chest, only for my hand to clash into his. When I looked up, Holden was *blushing.*

What was *this?*

Had *he* been moving to fix my hair?

"Sorry," he murmured, taking a step back.

To Dane From Holden
October 12, 1920

I got both of your last letters at the same time, so I am going to combine as much as I can into this one and hope it reaches you intact.

Things with Bette aren't the best. Before you say anything, this has nothing to do with Lou. I've kept my wandering tendencies in check and she's only been a good friend to me. Ironically, I have a suspicion that Bette's affections have fallen on someone else. Even before this, I was beginning to second guess myself on whether or not I made the right decision by getting married so quickly. It astounds me how much she and I have both changed. Regardless, I've made a commitment and feel the need to stick with it.

Arvin Stanley told me he plans to propose to Marcie after dinner on Christmas Eve. He's a nice enough fellow. Not that this will at all surprise you, but I had my way playing a joke on him when we first met, a joke you surely would've enjoyed if it didn't have to do with you, but I'll wait to tell you that one in person.

As much as I wish I were back in Europe with you, things are not so bad here. I figure that prolonging my stay in the States gives me time to work things out with Bette, as well as stay for the wedding. It's too bad you'll be in the middle of your ceiling commission come spring.

To answer your other questions, yes, I have been writing and yes, I am still having nightmares, though fewer of them. I did get an invitation recently to a reunion for Great War veterans, though I doubt I will go. For now, my daily distractions and friendships seem to be enough, and I am staying afloat just fine. Anyway, I need to get back to work. All my love.

Holden

Chapter Ten

The shop was filled with the feeling of change that fall. The kind of change that blows in with the wind, vanishing just as quickly as it appears, but not without consequence.

Spending nearly all my free time at my typewriter, I was beginning to feel more confident in my essay compilation. Holden, ever curious, asked more than once to read them. At first, I found the idea unnerving. By the end of December, it *petrified* me.

But Holden had his ways.

"Are you coming to Christmas Eve dinner this year?"

I sat at the desk, eyes glued to my draft. I'd long lost count of which one. "If I'm invited," I murmured. "And if I don't visit my parents." I could feel his dissatisfied stare. "What?" I asked, finally meeting his gaze. "It's not for another few weeks."

"I was just wondering."

I grinned, turning back to my reading.

"What are you going to do with those?" he asked, pulling the packet down with his finger. "Are you sending them to New York?"

"They still need a last revision."

"Which papers did you decide on?"

"I was going to send them to the *Herald* and the *Sun,* but I learned recently that they merged—saves me postage, anyway."

"This is the last time I'll offer my services," he warned. "I *did* attend one of the most prestigious schools in the country..."

"You have never let me read anything *you've* written," I reminded him. "Besides, my own eyes work just fine."

Holden whipped around, facing away from the desk. "You're probably right," he said. "Your eyes are perfectly adequate..."

"All right," I said, handing my packet of papers over reluctantly. "Just please, be kind."

"Wonderful." He snatched them with a handsome smile. "I'll give them back to you on Christmas Eve."

"Christmas Eve?"

"I want to be thorough," he said, licking his thumb to turn the page. "I guess you'd better clear your schedule."

Christmas Eve came quickly.

Holden offered to drive me to dinner, claiming that it was *on the way, anyway,* and predictably late, he pulled up closer to six-thirty than our agreed-upon six. He tried to muster a smile as I opened the car door, but I wasn't fooled.

"What's wrong?"

"Nothing," he mumbled.

The ride was eerily quiet as we drove to his parents' house. I wanted to pester him about my essays, but he looked far too gloomy for me to attempt it.

"Tonight's the night," I remarked.

"What?"

"Arvin and Marceline."

"Oh," he replied sullenly. "Right."

"It should be nice."

"Mhm."

Trying to cheer him was like pulling teeth, and I was relieved to see the lit tree from the Thompson's parlor window as we approached the driveway. But suddenly, Holden took a swift right turn, steering us off our path.

"What are you—" I clutched the door and looked over at him, waiting for an explanation, but he gave none. "Holden!"

"I'm sorry, Lou. I can't."

"You can't *what?*"

"I can't go to dinner."

"What are you talking—"

"It's Bette," he snapped. "She's leaving."

Taken aback by his admission, I wrinkled my brow at the sight of his bare ring finger.

"She told me earlier today. I thought I could manage the dinner, but I can't—not with Arvin proposing and…"

"All right, then where are we going?" I asked timidly.

"If it's all the same to you, I'd rather not figure that out quite yet," he replied with his dark eyes on the road.

We rode around in companionable silence for a few miles, and I kept my eyes on the moon, shining full and bright behind wisps of clouds that covered it.

"Did she say why she's leaving?" I asked finally.

"She told me we didn't want the same things. The perfect thing to say if you have someone else lined up—I would know."

So there *was* some truth to that reputation of his.

"Well, what do you want?"

Holden thought to himself. "What everyone wants—a place to belong."

"Maybe you don't belong with Bette."

"That's pretty apparent," he snickered, turning to me. "Don't you think?"

"I'm sorry," I murmured. "Sincerely."

"Let it be a cautionary tale." He almost smiled. "Don't marry someone you've only known for two months."

"What makes you think I want to marry at all?"

"One day you'll meet someone who will change your mind," he replied.

"You sound like my mother." The light of my sparked match flickered over the car's interior. "I don't think we can ever truly know someone, at least not completely," I said, lighting the end of my cigarette. "It seems irresponsible to promise forever when you don't know what forever looks like."

"That doesn't mean it's not worth trying. Where's your sense of adventure?"

I looked him over with a grin. "You're not helping your case."

"The moon is huge tonight," he said, drawing my attention to the view as we cleared the wood line. "Let's stop for a minute. I need some air."

I wasn't sure where we were, only that we were somewhere in Spotsylvania, when Holden pulled off the road. His chiseled face looked like porcelain in the moonlight as he stared forlornly ahead, across the miles of open field. I wondered if they reminded him of France.

"Tell me," I began, "why *did* you marry her?"

He shot me a reluctant glance as we stood side by side with our backs to the coupe. "Because she made me feel alive," he admitted. "Like an everlasting summer."

"In what way?"

"The first time I saw her, she was reading Nietzsche in an illegal bar. I was in a bad state. I'd just gotten home. When I tried to talk to her, she ignored me. Naturally, I kept trying—"

"*Naturally*," I teased.

"Nothing worked. Until one night I finally walked in and ignored *her*."

"And she walked over and talked to you?"

He smiled. "We went for a walk along the river. Eventually, we came across this house and there was no one home, so she insisted we stay the night. I broke the window so we could climb in."

"And you slept there?" I asked, amused.

"Only until the homeowners arrived. I almost broke my ankle climbing back out the window and it was the most fun I'd had since I got home. She was between places…and I'd just bought the cottage." He paused. "I thought settling down would give me what I needed...a reason to stay."

I knew what he meant.

I followed his example and tilted my head to the sky, to the moon that illuminated our faces. My eyes drifted to the right and caught on a star. "I'm glad you did." My voice was softer than I'd intended. "Stay. We wouldn't have met otherwise."

"I suppose you think it's a good thing we met, then?"

"Don't get ahead of yourself."

He sighed, crossing his arms over his chest. "But I'm so damned good at it."

"Venus is out," I said, pointing up.

"How fitting. I..." Holden thought to himself for a moment, as if his own words had struck a nerve, and then he turned to look at me. "I'm much less miserable than I was a few hours ago. I suppose I have you to thank." Before I could reply, he smacked the top of the car and walked around to the driver's door. "But I've held you hostage long enough, haven't I? We should get going—you can bring your stars and moons with you."

"What are you going to tell your family?" I asked, climbing back into the car. "What are you going to tell *Marceline?*"

"Eventually I'll tell them the truth. But *tonight,* we got a flat tire." He started the engine and pulled back onto the road, empty of any other cars. "You're not a terrible writer, by the way."

"Thanks."

"What I mean to say is that you're excellent." He'd never looked at me so earnestly. "I'd love to see what you could do with a real project. Something more creative."

"Journalism gives a voice to people who can't speak."

"And what about your own stories, then? The ones flowing through you?"

"I don't have anything like that," I argued. "No stories *flowing through me.*"

"I have a hard time believing that."

"Holden," I said, finally understanding him. "Fiction is your cup of tea, not mine."

"Says the one who writes short stories in her letters."

"*Jamie,*" I scoffed. "Those are just for fun."

"He says they're remarkable."

I rolled my eyes. "It's because I'm writing about real people."

"But no one ever *knows* that." His eyes blazed with that burning enthusiasm I'd seen once before. It was flammable. Contagious, even. "Don't you know the best characters are always real people?"

The town was deep in slumber when we finally pulled up outside of the shop. I'd completely lost track of time, carried away by our conversation.

"Before you go—" Holden reached into the back seat, handing me an extra paper in addition to my essays. "Here."

"What is this?"

"You said you've never gotten to read anything that I've written."

The Captain and The Reckoner
By Holden Thompson

The captain swears this has happened before. It all seems so familiar—the damp earth, the smell of old fabric and gunpowder, the sound of boots on faulty wooden ground. It's been days since he's slept. He holds a lantern, leading his men through the empty tunnel, filled with German debris. He can't shake the sensation of dread—a feeling that something is about to happen.

A shot in the dark. Something warm splatters his face. The familiar taste of a friend's blood. The captain's eyes burn in the glow of the lantern light. His best friend has been hit, and groans under his feet.

He can see the German is only a boy, younger than his own brother. A certain deserter. The boy says the shot was an accident, his own clumsy fault.

The captain's best friend lies in the mud. His best friend that he led to death.

He's led all his friends to death.

He only had two shots, says the Jerry boy, as he turns the gun on himself. Before the captain can stop him, he pulls the trigger.

He can't even do that right.

A figure looms in the corner, beckoning the captain. Is it the soul of one of his friends? Or the Devil come to claim him?

When he turns back, he sees the body of his friend is gone, replaced only by ashes. The captain grabs his gun and alerts his men. There is no one there, they say. It's a trick of the eyes, a shadow on the wall.

It's then that the captain realizes he's alone in the tunnel, just him and the Reckoner.

Chapter Eleven

The days following Christmas were a bitter time and Holden's emotional landscape seemed much like the winter weather—dark, bleak and cheerless. It was a stark contrast to Marceline's excitement over cake flavors and guest lists. With 1921 on the horizon and her wedding set for February, everyone was distracted and it felt like I was the only one who noticed him slipping.

"What do you think about violets, Lou?"

I tore my gaze from Holden, who stared absently out the window at the dull gray sky. "Sorry?"

"Violets," Marceline repeated. "For the wedding."

"Oh, sure. Violets sound lovely."

She scribbled something in her notebook as my eyes again drifted off to the window.

"I haven't heard back from the florist yet," she said, tapping her pen against the top of the desk. "Papa said he might be at the New Years party tonight. I may just ask him, if so. I'm just a little worried with them being out of—"

"Marcie," Holden mumbled. *"Stop."*

"Excuse me?"

He squared his shoulders. "It's not the end of the world if you don't get the flowers you want. Some of us have *real* problems."

"Indeed," she snapped back. "Both real and imagined."

"Yeah? Well I'd rather not listen to—"

A loud thump against the window silenced him.

"What was that?" asked Marceline.

We toppled each other trying to get to the front door.

Marceline gasped, reaching around my shoulder as I opened it. "Oh God..."

"Oh no," I whimpered, leaving her and Holden behind on the stoop. Soft on my approach, I knelt beside the contorting bluebird that lay beneath the window. I scooped it delicately into my hands.

Holden took a knee. "Its wings are broken."

I could hardly make out his features through my tears as the bird twitched in my hands.

"We can't let it suffer."

"I don't want it to die," I whispered.

"Everything dies, Lou."

His voice caressed my heart like a gentle ocean breeze. And I wondered how anyone could be so accustomed to death, so willing to lead even the tiniest soul to its door.

"Let me see," he whispered. Gathering it gently in his palm, he stroked its feathered head with his thumb, as though he knew what it felt like to have broken wings.

I was in awe of him.

"Go," he said.

I brushed my fingers against his rolled sleeve in protest.

"Go." Softer this time.

Marceline had already gone back inside, and was likely giving Mr. Thompson a play-by-play. I stumbled into the alleyway, unleashing a spring of hot tears. I didn't hear the deed between my sobs, nor did I hear Holden walk into the alley behind me.

"Are you all right?"

I whipped around, wiping my eyes. "Mhm."

In his hand, the bluebird lay wrapped in an old pocket silk. "I'm going to take it home and bury it," he said.

"I'm sorry you had to."

"I've done much worse, believe me."

"It isn't fair," I breathed. "I..."

"What?" he asked, stepping closer.

"I don't want you to be sad. Ever."

His amused grin only confirmed the ridiculousness of my statement. Still, it was the first time I'd seen him smile all week. "Happy New Year, Lou," he said, sliding past me. "Have a good time tonight."

"Where are you going?"

"I'm leaving early," he called over his shoulder.

"You're not going to stay for the party?"

Holden halted at the other side of the alley. "Do you *want* me to stay?" Apparently, my hesitation was all he needed. "That's a no," he said, clearing his throat and looking away.

"Why wouldn't I want you to?"

"You know what I mean," he murmured. "Don't pretend that you don't."

I could see he was embarrassed by the way he rubbed the back of his neck, and I knew he was really asking if it was *him* I wanted.

"Stay," I said.

The word seemed to light a fire under him. "I don't need your pity."

"And I don't need your stupid tests!" I yelled.

He only turned his back to me, murmuring over his shoulder. "Then we're better off apart."

If I hadn't been so preoccupied with the chance of Holden changing his mind about the party, I would've excused myself to bed with a headache instead of sulking through the festivities that night. A small sliver of me held faith that he would show up at the stroke of midnight, having known all along I wanted him there. But he didn't, and I hated him for it.

The other side of the new year began with a startling crash downstairs.

I wasn't sure what time it was, but it was still dark outside, so I turned on my lights and climbed out of bed. Wondering if someone had forgotten to lock up, I cautiously opened my door, peering down the staircase.

There he was—the intruder with a key—sitting on the bottom stair, slumped against the wall.

I let out a low, irritated laugh. "You're a little late, Holden."

God, I hated him.

Holden looked up to me, standing at the top of the landing in my pink floral nightgown. "Fuck," he whispered under his breath. "I didn't mean to—"

"I waited all night for you!"

Disheveled and lacking a coat, he leaned his head back.

"You're drunk," I said, walking down the stairs to examine him. "Really drunk." I knelt down, counting the smudges of maroon lipstick that dotted his neckline and collar. "Eventful evening?"

He glanced at me. "Why do you care?"

"I don't."

"It didn't mean a thing to me."

I thought if I stared at him long enough he might explain why he was sitting at the bottom of my staircase, or where he'd been all night, or *who* he'd been kissing.

"I don't think I can drive," he said at last.

"You sleep on the sofa," I demanded, snapping to my feet.

I boiled beneath my clean, white sheets as I thought of him sprawled across my settee.

I hated him.

I really, really did.

But I wished him a silent goodnight, and sleep found me all the same.

I was awoken not long after by the sound of coughing. Holden hadn't looked sick earlier—just drunk. But my feet found the floor anyway. I needed to know he was all right. Coughs and groans ricocheted down the hall, leading me to where he lay on the settee, broken out in a sweat.

Struck by the degree of his distress, I dropped to the floor next to him. "Holden," I whispered.

His body erupted in violent shivers.

He was *dreaming.*

I'd seen the consequences when Scott and Theo had tried to touch him at Chatham, and if I'd had any sense, I would've kept my distance. But against my better judgment, I reached out and gently stroked his face. "You're safe," I whispered.

Holden's eyes shot open in fright, and the look on his face was nothing short of horror-stricken.

My hands found his cheeks. "It's all right," I hushed. "It was just a dream."

His voice trembled as he tried to catch his breath. "Did I hurt you?"

"No."

"I didn't?"

"No," I assured him. "You wouldn't do that."

His palm, cold and clammy, found mine against his cheek. Water brimmed over the edge of his bottom lashes. "It feels so real," he whispered. "So viscerally, unapologetically real."

"It *was* real," I replied. "But you're safe now."

Covering his face with his hands, he started to cry. "I'll never be safe."

I knew, without having to ask, that it was far more than lost illusions and nightmares that plagued him. It was his dead friends and absent brother. A questionable marriage and an even more questionable future. But what haunted Holden most was the light that flickered over him from time to time. The ghost of whoever he used to be.

I knew that about him, somehow, and I think he sensed it.

He relaxed under my touch as I brought him to me, and

caught in this bizarre act of intimacy, pressed his lips to mine. I was the first to pull away with a gasp.

"I'm sorry," Holden whispered, mirroring my dumbfounded expression.

I touched my lips with my fingers, trying to process what had just happened. Having danced around each other for a year, it shouldn't have been a shock, but it was.

I stood up, fumbling my words. "Can I make you some tea?"

"No—thank you. I'm fine."

"Will you be able to get back to sleep?"

"I think so, yeah."

I looked to my desk, remembering the half-melted candle sitting in my top drawer. "Do you…want me to stay with you?"

"I'm all right," he whispered.

We both knew it was a lie.

"Just until you fall asleep." I opened my desk drawer and grabbed the candle, then reached for the brass holder on the fireplace mantle. "It's no trouble," I added, promptly lighting the wick with a match.

I took a seat on the floor, settling in with my back against the settee. The heat from the wood stove downstairs was long gone, leaving the foyer drafty and cold. Holden wrapped half of his blanket around me, and, grateful for the warmth, I brought the heavy quilt to my chin. We sat in silence, watching the flame of the candle dance wildly as it sat on the floor in front of us.

"I'm sorry for today," he whispered.

I turned my cheek. "Me too."

"You passed my stupid test with flying colors, by the way."

That got a laugh out of me. "And the bird?"

"I buried it at the edge of the woods. Wildflowers grow there in the spring."

"What's your favorite flower, Holden Thompson?"

"I'm partial to bluebells." I could feel him readjust himself on the settee behind me. "But there was a yellow flower that grew in France. It always caught my eye when I saw it."

"What was it called?"

"Great Mullein. Most people think of red poppies when they think of the front, but it wasn't only poppies. There were varieties of types and colors that grew there...all over the place." He sounded far away as he spoke, tucked deep within his memory. "I swear sometimes they'd pop up the day after a battle."

"And this one yellow flower sticks out to you?"

He leaned closer to my shoulder. "I'd go back to France just to pick one for you."

"Maybe you can think about that when the bad thoughts come on. Try to replace it all with something less scary."

"Sometimes it's not a thought at all. It's a feeling."

"What does it feel like?"

"A sudden darkness that closes in," he whispered sleepily. "All-consuming panic with no relief."

"And now?"

I felt a sigh against the back of my neck in place of a response, and turned my head to find Holden fast asleep.

Stirred by the sound of birds outside, I lifted my head from Holden's arm, which he'd wrapped around my shoulders at some point as we slept. He hugged me to him as if to say *good morning* before moving his arm and releasing me.

When I turned to face him, he smiled. "Sorry," he murmured, looking rather sheepish.

"No more bad dreams, then?"

Holden rested his chin on his forearm and looked up at me. "Do you want to have breakfast with me?"

"Right now?"

"Right now." His gaze slipped past me, to the packaged essays on my desk. "Whether you want to spend time with me or because you need a reason to pass the postage box, it's all the same to me."

I grinned, tucking a piece of hair behind my ear.

Chapter Twelve

The warmth of the winter sun on my cheeks was a familiar comfort, despite the cold temperatures. Holden and I strolled side-by-side down Caroline Street beneath a cloudless sky, neither of us brave enough to mention the spontaneous moment we'd shared—an unorthodox New Year's kiss, with only the crescent moon as our witness.

He let out a deep sigh. "I'm going to be apologizing to you for the rest of my life."

"Breakfast will suffice."

"I owe you more than breakfast," he replied, coaxing me across the street. "My first real night of sleep in nearly a month. What did you do to me?"

"You don't mind that I'm a witch, do you?"

Holden looked over at me, tracing my face with the watery pools of his eyes. "It would make a lot of sense."

Feeling my cheeks turn hot, I held tightly to my envelope of essays as we passed Goolrick's. "I thought the whiskey was supposed to help with the dreams," I said.

"It does if you drink enough."

The tiny cafe he chose was teeming with churchgoers, eager to fill their bellies after a morning of worship. With no available tables, we were seated together at the counter, in full scope of the cafe's patrons. Holden had a way of attracting the gaze of every man, woman and child in an establishment—it didn't seem to matter if he wanted it or not.

The waiter behind the bar poured us two mugs of coffee. Nodding thanks, I turned to Holden. "The story you wrote really happened, didn't it?" I asked, cautiously probing.

"More or less." He watched as I sipped from one of the mugs. "When you write about something from your own life, it doesn't belong to you anymore. The experience, the feeling…it belongs to who's reading it."

"Then I imagine writing a novel might be as cathartic as reading one."

A smug grin. "It is," he whispered. "Even if no one ever reads it."

"Even if it goes to the burn pile?"

Holden chuckled. "Even then."

"Then, the story in the tunnel—it's all true?"

He gave a dispassionate nod. "The kid was a lousy shot and the bullet went through his jaw."

"Jesus."

"He was still cognizant enough to hit me with his knife when I knelt down next to him," he said, pointing just above his collarbone. "He was much better with a knife than a gun. At the time, I hardly felt it—I pulled out the blade and threw it aside…and he just looked at me. You see, dying is strangely intimate."

A chill prickled the back of my neck.

"I told him *Denken Sie an zu Hause.*"

"What does it mean?"

He rubbed his brow, fixating on the counter's edge. "Think of home."

"And your friend?"

"He died a few days later," he replied, looking unspeakably sad.

Holden declined any food as we continued to talk, content

with a second cup of coffee for breakfast. I, on the other hand, was ravenous, and ordered enough for the both of us.

"I told Marcie about Bette a few days ago," he said.

"How did she take the news?"

Holden's eyes rolled back. "How do you think?"

I grimaced playfully, dipping my toast in the egg yolk.

"No, she was sympathetic enough." His eyes found mine as he ran his fingers across his jaw. "I was right, by the way, about there being someone else."

"Oh, Holden. I'm sorry."

"It's fitting that I should finally know how it feels. All those years of doing whatever I wanted with whomever I wanted—I guess it's my *karma,* as the eastern sages say."

"The truth comes out."

"It's not something I'm proud of, believe me."

"Is there anything you *are* proud of?" I regretted the question as soon as it left my lips. How it stunned him into silence. "I didn't mean…"

"I know," he assured.

"But is there?" I asked, urging him to take a piece of toast. "Anything at all?"

Without argument, he obliged me. "My relationship with my brother," he mumbled, taking a bite. "To know him."

"Dane."

Holden nodded, looking satisfied with his answer.

"I'm sure he's just as proud to know you," I added, scooting the remaining plate of toast over to him. "I know I am."

I thought I saw him blush as he turned his cheek and asked for the check.

After breakfast, Holden walked me to the postage box, where I gave my package a small hug before sliding it in, never to be seen again.

"Wish me luck," I said.

"You should have told me it was *luck* you wanted from me this morning," Holden joked. "I thought it was charm."

I cupped my hand over my mouth, succumbing to a flurry of giggles.

"There *is* something else I'm proud of, actually," he added.

"What?" I asked between my laughs. "Finding four-leaf clovers?"

"I *am* good at that, but..."

My heart jumped in my chest as he stepped closer. "Then what is it?"

"The way I can make you laugh like that," he breathed, holding my eye.

I smiled up at him, big and candid. "It is admirable."

Holden took a deep breath. "Would you be my date to Marcie's wedding? I know we're both already going anyway, but I—"

"Yes."

He raised his brows. "Yes?"

"Like you said" —I swiveled away, back toward the shop— "we're both going anyway."

To Dane From Holden
February 3, 1921

Why must every letter to you start with a confession? I've done what I said I wouldn't do. I've fallen in love with my best friend and I'm not sure what else to say, except that I'm not exactly sure how it happened. How can I be in love with someone I've hardly touched?

You say I move on fast, but this is a different thing entirely. It's all the great poets have written about and has hardly to do with desires of the flesh. She's my heart outside of my body—a moving, breathing extension of myself. And speaking frankly, if you knew her, you would understand.

Does she feel the same? Fuck, I don't know. I think she might, but you know how that goes. I made the mistake of kissing her impulsively and she looked more stunned than anything—though, for a moment I swore she kissed me back. We ended up falling asleep snuggled up together in her foyer, and now I'm stuck wanting to relive that moment each time I go to bed.

Imagine the girl of my dreams living a county or two over, and all these years, never crossing paths until now. If I could have any wish, it would be that I'd met her earlier. Before the war, before school. All of it. And I know I hardly deserve her now, but it would shatter me all the same if she didn't love me back.

She's agreed to be my date to Marcie's wedding, so if all goes well, I will tell her how I feel afterward. Say a little prayer to Venus for me.

Holden

PS. Thanks again for helping with Marcie's gift. I'm sure it will be appreciated.

Chapter Thirteen

Holden arrived nearly on time to pick me up for the wedding, and his reaction was exactly what I hoped for when I opened the front door in my velvet dress. It was a twenty dollars well spent, patterned with earthy colored flowers and threaded vines weaving in between. I'd even found the perfect mink hat to match the fur-lined bottom and sleeve cuffs.

"Look at you," he stuttered.

"Look at *you.*" I motioned to him, standing before me freshly shaven in his crisp AEF uniform, complete with hat and ribbons just above the left pocket.

"Tonight, I am merely your accessory," he said, offering his arm.

My fingers ran over the stiff wool of his tunic. I'd never seen him in his captain's uniform before, despite trying to imagine it. *And my God,* he looked handsome.

"Where did you park?" I asked.

"In the back," he replied. "I figured I'd leave it here since it's just a short walk up. We can come and get it to drive to the reception."

"Whatever you say, Captain."

Holden reached in his pocket and pulled out a small photo,

handing it to me as we began our walk up Amelia Street. "I found this last night, packed away with my uniform."

I studied the portrait of him in his old sergeants' garb. He looked so much younger.

"I had it taken before I went to France," he added. "Some friends and I ducked into a studio last minute while we were in New York."

"Can I keep it?" I asked, turning to him.

"You want to?" There was surprise in the way he laughed. "Please—take it."

I pocketed it as we walked past the piles of snow that had been preserved by the temperatures.

"I think we're going to be a few minutes late."

I looked over to see Holden frowning at his watch. "We can't be late to your sister's wedding—you'll never hear the end of it."

He raised an eyebrow. "What makes you so certain *I'd* be the one to blame if we were late?"

Grabbing him by the hand, I bolted ahead. It was a three block sprint, which was a grievous mistake in heels. When we finally reached the entrance of St. Mary's, Holden was out of breath from carrying me on his back for the final block.

Jamie was ushering the last of the guests into the church when we walked up. "You lucky son of a bitch," he teased. *"By the skin of your teeth."*

Holden grinned, pushing his hair back under his hat. "Don't swear in the house of the Lord, Jamie."

I slid down from his back, trying to fix what I could of my upswept hair before limping inside. "Says the man who might spontaneously combust once he walks in," I teased.

Holden's hand snaked around my waist. "She *is* funny."

Jamie closed the doors behind us, following close. "Did you bring the—"

"See me at dinner," Holden whispered back, holding me steady.

Holden halted just beside the sanctuary doors, squeezing us into the back pew.

"Don't you want to sit in the front with everyone else?" I asked.

"Not particularly," he replied, removing his hat.

I looked around at the nameless statues and lit candles. "This is your church, right?"

"It's my *family's* church," he corrected. "Not mine."

"I see."

Holden leaned back in the pew, as though he were preparing for the longest hour of his life. It was only a few minutes before a priest adorned in robes took to the dais, directing us to rise.

"Pray for your knees," Holden whispered in my ear over the organ chimes.

Under her ivory veil, Marceline wore a serene smile as Mr. Thompson walked her down the aisle. Her dress was remarkable —cut just below the knee, with a lace embroidered tunic covering her shoulders. The beads on the dress sparkled as she passed by with the veil trailing behind them.

Marceline glanced over her shoulder, finally finding Holden and me in the crowded sanctuary before turning to Arvin at the altar. She'd been pleased to hear that we were attending together and even thanked me for helping to raise his spirits. Whether she believed there was anything more between us, I don't know. My relationship with her brother was the one thing I couldn't really confide in her about.

Holden was right to pray for our knees as we sat and stood our way through the long, Catholic ceremony. My ankle was no better for it, either, aching and swelling beneath the wooden pew.

I turned to Holden as we watched guests flood the aisle. "When was the last time you took mass?"

"A long time ago," he replied. "I stopped coming when I was old enough to have a say."

"How come?"

He shrugged, taking a moment to think about it. "I don't

know. After my grandad died, I just didn't see the comfort in it anymore."

I wrung my hands in my lap. "Why don't you go up?"

A sly, humored smirk. "For shock value?"

"For Marceline."

Holden looked to the overflowing aisle, then back to me. "Come with me."

"I'm not Catholic."

"Neither am I."

I raised my eyebrows at him playfully.

"All right." He stood up, inhaling deep. "Pray for me."

It was clear from the astonishment on his family's faces as Holden joined the line that he had not been exaggerating. And yet, he seemed to take the wine and host so naturally, as if actually *wanted* to.

"Did you hate it?" I asked as he slipped back into the pew.

As usual, his answer bordered on comic relief. "Best wine I've had since I got back."

The vows were poignant, heartfelt, and even more so with Holden's fingers interwoven in mine. He'd grabbed my hand without warning, looking at me with a gaze that seemed to ask permission. I had rubbed his hand with my thumb, only letting go when it was time to clap.

We followed the procession out the church doors, cheering and throwing handfuls of rice all over the newlyweds. I leaned on Holden's arm to keep the weight off of my ankle until the crowd cleared, and he led me to a nearby bench.

"I'll get the car," he said. "If you're still up for it."

"I'm fine," I assured. "It's feeling a little better already."

The sunshine glinted off of the metal pendants on his uniform as he stood there, peering down on me with a smile. "Then I'll be right back."

• • •

We arrived at the reception site early, parking right outside the brick colonial that had been rented on the end of Caroline.

"What was Jamie talking about earlier?" I asked.

Holden cut the engine, sliding his gaze to the backseat. "Go ahead." He motioned for me to lift the seat cushion.

Four bottles of whiskey hid under it. *Large* bottles.

"I don't think I want to know how you managed this," I said, turning to him.

"European imports." His grin was puckish as he reached back to grab one. "It might help your ankle," he added, filling his flask. "And it will definitely help me with my speech."

"The last time I accepted liquor from you—"

"*I told you* to be careful that night." His eyes twinkled as he wiped the flask with a handkerchief and handed it to me. "I think it all turned out all right. Don't you?"

I raised it up to him in a toast.

"To the whispers of the universe," he said.

The finest silver lined the tables in the dining hall with crystal glasses to match. White roses and cedar bows hung over each entrance, and countless arrangements of violets surrounded us at every table. I followed the glow of the fireplace to our table, where I found our names on cursive place settings.

Holden pocketed his hands, as if he were scared he may break something. "I'm afraid to move in here."

"Surely that won't stop you," I poked. "We know how you love to be the center of attention."

He pulled my chair from under the table. "I love *pretending* to love it."

"There's Molly." I nodded to the door as I took my seat. "The one I told you about."

Molly hurried over in her best vest, looking relieved to see a friendly face in the fast-filling room. "Please tell me one of those place settings has my name on it."

"Right next to us," I replied.

Molly looked me over, then turned to Holden. "Who's this?" she asked. "Did you go out and get yourself an army captain?"

"I'm Holden."

"*The* Holden?" Molly's eyes found mine, lively and sharp. "I've heard a lot about you."

He took his seat, appearing especially smitten. "Have you, now?"

Dinner began at five o'clock sharp. Dungeness crab salad, curried cauliflower and smoked salmon tartare with caviar were brought to every table, followed by potatoes au gratin and vegetables with hollandaise sauce. We waited our turn to greet the couple as they circled the room, combing through the few hundred guests.

Holden lunged to his feet, meeting them halfway from our table.

Marceline held her hands up in protest. "Holden, *no!*"

Stretching his arms around her wide, he lifted his sister off the ground, spinning her around. She beat down on his shoulder, demanding he put her down, but Holden only spun faster, until she erupted in laughter and he was dizzy.

"Arvin," he said, passing her off to his new brother-in-law, "take good care of my sister."

Molly and I abandoned our table to join them, sandwiching her in a hug. "You look beautiful," I murmured, squeezing her tight.

Holden whispered into her other ear. "There's something in my car for you." He pulled back with a wink. "Dane's treat."

The way she giggled told me she already knew what it was.

"Why didn't Dane come?" I asked Holden as we walked back to our seats.

"He's painting a ceiling right now in Italy," he replied. "You know what that means, right?"

I shook my head.

He grinned from ear to ear. "We'll have to go see it."

It didn't matter that Holden didn't want to be the center of attention. People young and old—men and women alike—gravitated to him like flies to honey. Whether it was to chat about his service or the weather, they hovered around our table, waiting for a turn to talk to him.

Jamie took a knee, hanging an arm around each of us. "There you are."

"There *you* are, little brother," said Holden, handing him the keys to his car. "Get it from the one I've already opened and be discrete."

"Yes, Captain."

"And bring the keys back when you're done," Holden added.

Jamie slipped past the jazz band, beginning to set up.

I nudged Holden with a low giggle. "Almost time for your speech."

"Will you reward me with the first dance when I'm done?"

"My ankle hurts."

"You can lean on me."

"I shouldn't."

He eyed me dubiously. "That sounds like an excuse."

"It's not."

"I'll bet I can change your mind," he murmured, sliding his gaze to my lips.

I smiled to myself with a certainty that he was right.

"That is a good-looking man," Molly remarked, motioning toward my date as he walked off. "If I liked men, I'd find myself one just like that."

"He is one of a kind." My heart pinched in my chest. "The three of us should get together this weekend," I added, turning to her.

"Can't. I have plans in Richmond."

I laughed. "Would these plans involve a certain Saint Adele?"

Molly only leaned back in her chair, grinning like a shot fox.

The mingling crowd slowly quieted and I turned around in my seat to watch Holden at the front of the room.

'"If only those treasures were not so fragile as they are precious and

beautiful.'" He lowered the paper with a shaky hand. "I underlined this passage in Goethe's *Sorrows of Young Werther,* which I read more than once while passing time in the trenches. Surrounded by the chaos of man, one either seeks comfort in thoughts of love, or balks against it altogether. It is a precarious thing, after all–love. It requires vulnerability in a world that is unjust and unsafe. It's for this reason I saw fit to armor myself against it for so much of my life. But the love of a sister, and for a sister, is something that can bend even the strongest iron." A grin. "It's not easy for a girl to grow up in a house of all brothers, and if you *know* us, then you can attest to Marcie's resilience. Surely, she wasn't born with that will." He laughed under his breath. "For those who don't know me, or remember me, my name is Holden. I am the middle brother of the family. I was two years old when Marcie was born, the first and only daughter, and she's been stealing my glory ever since. From letting me lean her over a well to see her future, to bribing her silence with one of our grandfather's coins when she caught Dane and me stargazing on the roof —*sorry, Ma*—our relationship has always been one of extremes. But even still, she would have followed me to the end of the earth when we were young." He looked to her. "I would do well to remind her that the admiration is mutual. My sister is everything I am not: she is a humble champion, willing to sacrifice her own comforts in the name of reform. And she's looked out for me more than a younger sister should ever have to. For that, I am forever indebted. Congratulations to the newlyweds. You've found it, Marcie—the holy grail, the elixir of life. Take good care of it." He cast his gaze across the crowd, finding me as he raised his glass. "I hope I can be as happy as you, someday."

The way the room applauded was *almost* enough for me to reward him with that dance when he made his way back to me.

"I took mass for you today," he said, reading my mind as the band began to play.

"That was for Marceline."

"On *your* suggestion," he said, offering his hand.

I shook my head, motioning to my ankle under the table. It really did hurt like hell.

Holden took a knee in front of me. "One dance."

I narrowed my eyes on him.

"I'll support you the entire time. Unless, you're *scared* to."

"Why would I be scared?" I shot back. "Because you're so irresistible?"

Perhaps it was the sudden heat between us that startled him to his feet. "Let's just see about that," he said, offering his hand again.

Reluctantly, I took it.

I took notice of all the girls looking at Holden as I limped on his arm to the middle of the floor. He stepped closer to me, placing his hand around my waist as the band began to play, carrying us into a soft and slow melody.

"See?" he said as we began to waltz. "It's not so bad."

"Don't let me fall."

"I won't let you fall."

He was sturdy against me, holding my weight as I studied the colored ribbons above the pocket of his uniform, wondering what each of them meant. A whiff of tobacco and vanilla tickled my nose.

"Can I tell you a secret?" he whispered in my ear.

"Another one?"

He pulled away, just enough to rest his chin to my temple. "I can't remember the last time I felt this happy."

Now my *heart* was throbbing along with my ankle. It was a feeling I didn't recognize, a bittersweet ache—as if it had been filled to the brim and might burst. I closed my eyes and leaned onto the scratchy green wool of his uniform, feeling my own heartbeat synchronize with his. And in that moment, caught in a net of something unexpressed but ever-present, I wondered what *we* were.

Feeling suddenly weak in the knees, I slipped, dropping my

weight back on my ankle. I must have let out a whimper, because Holden hoisted me up again with a gentle tone.

"Let's get out of here."

Holden helped me into the passenger seat of the car, handing me the flask. "May I?" He lifted my dress, revealing the swollen ankle.

I grimaced. "That doesn't look good."

"I don't think it's a sprain." He reached down the side of the car, grabbing a handful of snow. "I think you just twisted it," he went on, packing the snow into a ball. He pulled out a handkerchief, crafting a makeshift ice pack. "There you go." He pressed it to my ankle—it was cool and soothing. "Keep it on like this until we get back."

Within a few minutes, Holden pulled into a spot right outside of the shop. With much maneuvering on his part, he carried me gingerly up the stairs. It was a funny thing, he and I, working as one entity to turn the knob and open the door.

"Thank you," I said, adjusting my compress as he slid me onto the sofa. "You didn't have to."

The relaxed smile on his face faded just slightly. "Yes, I did."

A canyon of unspoken feelings separated us in my empty foyer. The inevitable was coming, and I wasn't ready for it.

"There's something I need to—"

"I know what you're going to say."

"All right," said Holden, taking a seat next to me, "what am I going to say, then?"

"Don't say anything you can't take back."

He leaned in, close enough for me to feel the whisper of his words. "Why would I ever take it back?" he asked, closing the distance between our lips.

I thought I saw a glint of a smile as he pulled away, back to his side of the settee. And then it happened, he said what I knew he would.

"I love you."

The words burned in my throat—as if I was on the precipice of eternal joy but unable to reach it. "I…"

Holden kissed me again, drawing me in with his hand on the nape of my neck. I hardly noticed the pain of my ankle or the ice pack hitting the floor—only his thick curly hair, the warmth of his lips on mine and his long eyelashes brushing against my cheek. Our eyes met briefly as he lay over top of me. *We can't come back from this,* I cautioned, looking up at him.

He reached for the brass buttons on his tunic, and piece by piece, the olive-green uniform ended up on the floor beside my velvet dress.

I sat up in my slip, running my fingers over the raised skin just below his collarbone.

He looked at me with such softness that it frightened me, and, delicately, he unfastened my hair, allowing it to fall down my back.

His heart was throbbing so intensely that it seemed he could hardly catch his breath, and carried away in his smoky, sweet scent, I turned my cheek and closed my eyes. I listened for the faint sound of him unbuckling his belt as his lips again found mine. "I'll be gentle," he promised, following the length of my neckline. He slipped his hand up my back.

Then, all at once, a single thought stopped me in my tracks.

What happens after this?

"Holden," I murmured against his shoulder. "I can't."

He lifted himself off and looked at me with a sense of bewilderment.

"Why are you looking at me like that?" I asked, suddenly feeling exposed.

"Forgive me if I'm a little *confused,* Lou."

"It wasn't my idea."

"Of course it wasn't!" he scolded. "If it was left up to you, nothing would ever happen."

"Nothing should happen, Holden! *You're married.*" I crossed my arms over my chest. "Your everlasting summer. Remember?"

He re-buttoned his pants. "You know me well enough to know I've always preferred autumn."

"I wonder how many women you've said that to."

"None," he countered. "This isn't just some conquest to me—I want *you.* All of you." He turned away, lowering his voice "And I thought you wanted me."

"Holden, please." My voice cracked. "You're my best friend."

"What about all of this, then?" He motioned to the clothes on the floor. "You weren't going to just…*let* me, were you?"

"No! Of course not."

"Then tell me *why,"* he demanded.

"Because we're friends." I blurted out the first thing that came to mind. "Because I might be going to New York."

"You think I wouldn't follow you to New York?" he asked, grabbing his tunic from the floor. "It doesn't make a difference to me."

"There are a million other reasons this would never work."

Holden dropped his shoulders, falling silent.

"Then make it easy for me," he said finally, heading for the door.

"You don't have to go."

"That would make us both feel better, wouldn't it?" he asked, peering dismally over his shoulder at me. "Stay off the ankle, all right?"

Chapter Fourteen

I'd thought about following him out that night as I peered down at the street from my foyer window. I thought I might chase him down the stairs and stand on the edge of the stoop, yelling after him—*Holden! Wait!* And he would turn around and ask what I wanted, his breath visible in the February air. Then I'd say *I don't want you to leave,* and he'd look at me in that smug way.

I saw him look over his shoulder, back toward the shop's door, clearly wrestling with a similar notion. Maybe he'd charge back up the stairs to find me still on the sofa, and say *I just couldn't leave.*

But he did leave, and I watched him like a coward from behind the safety of the glass.

He was the last thing I wanted to think about, and he was *all* I'd thought of since he walked out the door. I traced his face in the photograph he'd given me a dozen times through the night, focusing carefully on those beautifully pensive eyes. I'd wanted to tell him how I felt, but I'd hardly admitted it to myself.

Having left things on such a raw note, I was afraid to see him again. Afraid of what he would say, or what he might think of me. Afraid that despite it all, he might want me anyway, with all my fickle moods and imperfections. That's what scared me most.

I was making a much-needed cup of afternoon coffee the next day when a folded piece of paper slid underneath my apartment door. Holden had returned for the last word. Stepping over it, I hesitantly approached the wooden threshold that separated us.

I imagined him on the other side, undecided on if he should stay or go while he hoped I read it. Setting my coffee on the windowsill, I reached for the paper on the ground, opening it up.

Dear Lou,

I still wouldn't take it back.

Meet me outside around two if you want to talk.

Holden had started back down the stairs when I swung my door open to find him looking as sleepless as me. I leaned my shoulder on the doorframe, waiting for him to speak as his eyes snapped to my striped French linen skirt. I'd worn it the first day we met.

"Do you want to go for a ride?" he asked finally.

Neither of us said much as we crossed the Rappahannock in his coupe. Bits of lime-green lined the trees across the river, promising the beginnings of spring. I knew where we were going without having to ask, so it was no surprise when he pulled off the road onto the overgrown driveway. With its freshly painted bricks and portico removed, I hardly recognized Chatham Manor as we pulled up next to the newly constructed outhouse.

"The Devores say the restoration will likely take another year or two," said Holden, cutting the engine. "But it's a process worth appreciating."

I opened my door, in full view of the newly established gardens. They'd been modeled in Greek revival style, with concrete busts of Pan and Demeter to guard over the baby shrubs. A tall, brick perimeter lined the yard, concealing the owner's slice of Eden from the rest of the world. It would be beautiful one day.

"It's not haunted anymore," I said, wistfully looking up at the pristine estate house. "It makes me a little sad."

Holden slipped his hand in mine. "You always did see the potential in damaged things."

"Should we really be walking in their yard?" I asked.

"They haven't moved in yet," he said, as we retraced our old path around the side of the mansion. "They told me I'm welcome to come up anytime and walk the gardens. How's your ankle?"

"It's better," I replied. "The swelling is almost gone."

What had once been untamed brush was now a landscaped lawn, and reaching the edge of the bank, we found ourselves in the same place that we'd once stood as strangers. Holden sat down in the grass and I followed, plopping beside him.

I sighed. "Holden, last night was..."

"We don't need to talk about it," he assured.

I laid my head on his shoulder as he gazed out at the skyline. "I'm sorry," I whispered.

He turned his cheek to me. "Marry me."

"What?" I replied, snapping to attention.

"I mean it."

I'd hoped that my gaping expression might bring him back to reality, but he plowed ahead. "I don't mean right this second. Bette came by last night to get some of her things and I told her how I felt about you."

"You *what?"*

"It will only take a few months for us to clear it on paper," he explained. "She wants it as much as I do."

"Holden, I don't want to get married. To you or to anyone!"

"I know you've never felt close to your family," he said, taking my hand. "We could be that for each other. We could have our own family someday."

I gazed into his eyes, feeling as though I might drown in them. It was everything I didn't want for myself, at least not at the age of twenty-two. And yet, I could picture myself in a white silk gown with a train to the floor, and him standing before me in his uniform. I could imagine the nervous excitement—our hands intertwined, the feeling of eyes all around us—but I couldn't see his face. My vision was hollow.

"That can't possibly be what you really want."

"You know it is," he said under his breath. "One of us has to be the one to admit it."

Provoked, I stood up, brushing the grass from my skirt. "What does that mean?"

"That you've been stringing me along for months because you can't make up your mind," he said, equally quick to rise.

"You're not even divorced and you're talking about getting married! What am I supposed to think?" I demanded. "What if this whole thing is just another illusion? Another case of your clouded judgment?"

"I think I know all about illusions," he countered. "Certainly, better than you do."

"Your passions come in and out with the tide! You say that you're a different man now, but you play with people's hearts all the same." I turned to walk away but he grabbed onto my hand, pulling me back. "What do you want from me, Holden?" I asked, yanking myself free. *"You already know how I feel."*

"Do I?" His stare was hard as ice. "Because you haven't told me."

I shoved past him, making my way down the bank.

His laugh was sharp with irritation behind me. "You're so afraid of being loved—truly *seen*—that you never let me in for more than a few fleeting seconds. And you know what, Lou? It's a goddamn cop out!"

My eyes burned as I glanced over my shoulder at him, knowing he was right.

"I of all people would know," he added weakly.

I stepped off the steep bank, into the tangle of weeds.

"Where are you going? Lou—"

"I'm walking!"

I heard him swear as I began my downward climb. "What about your ankle?" he called after me.

"I'll risk it!"

"Well, don't call me if you break it!"

My legs were scratched and bleeding by the time I reached the road at the bottom, but I was too wound up to notice. I'd left him there on the bank, and broken my own heart in doing so. Holden had his problems, and plenty of them, but I couldn't deny his tender heart. He was decent and kind with emotions as deep as the sea. And as much as I wanted to write his feelings off as an exaggeration, I knew he was telling the truth.

It was I who was the liar.

I brushed the twigs from my linen skirt as I walked along the edge of the road, shivering in my light coat. Twilight was quickly approaching, and as my temper cooled and my heart ached, I began to wonder if he would bother looking for me.

When Holden finally pulled up alongside me in the coupe, it was clear I'd been crying. I kept my gaze forward, following the car's headlights.

"I *still* don't take it back," he said. "But I can accept it." The coupe followed closely next to me. "I'd rather have you as a friend than not at all."

I turned to him, teary-eyed and mute.

Offering a weak smile, he reached across the seat and opened the passenger door for me.

We sat quietly in the car as darkness fell over the back parking lot, neither willing to budge first. We'd exchanged as little as three words on the ride back, more a side effect of defeat than anger. But I could have sat in there all night with him, not saying a word.

"Maybe it's best this way," Holden said finally. "I'm not some sort of model of happiness. We both know that."

I could sense an unspeakable sorrow in him, latent with dashed hopes. More broken dreams.

"Why?" I asked, swallowing hard. "Why do you want me?"

He shifted in his seat to face me.

"You could have anyone you want." I didn't try to stop the words as they tumbled out. "Why me?"

Holden dropped his lashes under a furrowed brow, as if to study the stitching on his sport coat sleeve. "Because you see me," he said, glancing up. "Whoever it is I am, under all of this broken glass."

Bewilderment washed over him as I slid closer on the seat, hoisting myself up onto his lap. His fingers snaked around my hips, pulling me closer as mine found his cheeks.

"You are my favorite person in the *whole world,*" I whispered.

He started to smile but his eyes watered, as though he were afraid he might wake up from whatever this was.

"I love you, Holden."

One tear fell, then another, synchronizing with the words he'd wanted me to say. That he needed so desperately to hear.

"I love you," I hushed, wiping under his eyes with my thumb. "I love you, I love you."

As if the stars had finally aligned just so, he pressed his lips to mine in perfect harmony. I wrapped my arms around his neck as he pulled me further onto his lap, bumping the horn on the steering wheel. He only laughed between our kisses, losing his fingers in my hair.

I hadn't expected to find anyone in the shop when I finally walked through the back door, dizzy on the comedown. A dim lamp glowed in the corner of the room, lighting the fabric Marceline cut with her scissors.

"It's about time," she said, meeting my gaze from beneath her mauve hat, brimmed with blue grosgrain.

"I…" I reached to touch my hot cheek, burned from her brother's stubble. "I didn't realize…"

"Playing catch-up after the honeymoon." Marceline cocked her head with a knowing smile as she laid the scissors on the table. "I saw the parked car."

My mouth went dry. "Believe me," I breathed. "I never intended for any of this."

It was the truth. That somewhere along the way, in between our arguing and teasing, my feelings for Holden had grown like an invasive wildflower.

"Rarely is the path we imagine for ourselves the one we take," she replied, walking over to me. "At least, that's what my father always says."

I looked her over, feeling my pulse slow. "You aren't angry?"

Marceline's brow twitched in an amused confusion. "You two weren't fooling anyone but yourselves," she said with a laugh.

"You are more intuitive than you let on," I admitted.

"I've always felt like you should be part of our family—I knew it the moment you walked in that day that he'd found his match."

"This won't change anything," I assured.

"Oh, *it will.*" Marceline laughed again, straying toward the door. "But it's all right," she added over her shoulder with a wink. "I've always wanted a sister."

THE TOWER

upheaval – catastrophe – awakening

May 1921 — July 1922

Chapter Fifteen

"*There* you are."

Holden stood in the alleyway with his back to the siding, cigarette in hand. Delicate white blooms from the pear tree above had landed in his dark hair, and blanketed the ground, carried by a warm May breeze.

"I've been trying to catch up with you all day." Finding his side, I wrapped my arms around his neck. "Just to do this," I added, kissing those lips I'd come to love so much.

His smile seemed worn, as if it took everything in him to manage it.

"What's wrong?" I cooed, picking a petal from his hair. "Bad night?"

He met my eye with the faintest nod.

I knew he was withholding something, as he often did, even with me. And I knew not to push it. I'd learned that about him in the months we'd been together—that the harder I pushed, the more he would retreat. So, I did what I could for him on those hard days.

"I love you," I whispered, snuggling up to him.

He wrapped his arm around my shoulder, pulling me in. "I love you too."

I closed my eyes with a sigh against his firm chest. Spring had been a whirlwind of long walks, root beer floats and stargazing by the river. Discussions of the future—*our* future—splintered in all directions, from New York to Europe. We'd even considered staying in Fredericksburg, but Holden was eager to leave, and truthfully, so was I.

"It's not fair to you," he murmured. "These moods I get in."

I knew what he meant. Lately I'd wondered where he was when he stared absently out the window, as though he were watching life happen from behind a glass.

"Holden," I said, tilting my chin to him.

"I wish you'd known me before."

Before. He always talked like that.

"I'm glad to know you now," I replied.

He exhaled a breath of smoke, looking to the sun-lit blossoms above us as he squeezed me to him. "I think I need to take some time," he said.

"What do you mean?"

His lips pressed to my forehead in a kiss. "Go back to Paris for awhile, maybe."

I could hear the restlessness in his tone—a desperation to claw himself out of whatever pit he'd fallen into.

"I know you miss him." I slid my hand down his rolled sleeve, slipping my hand in his. "As soon as I hear if the *Herald* has interest in me, which I doubt they do, we can go."

"I don't know if I can wait. I…"

I pulled back, but he wouldn't look at me. "Holden?"

"I don't feel like myself, Lou," he said, at last meeting my eye.

The sapphire of his irises was dulled; the bombastic blue replaced with crystalline slate. There was no trace of the little flame behind them.

"It will all be all right when the dust settles," I said.

Holden lifted my chin, kissing me fervently, as if time itself were running out. We held still, eyes closed.

"Lou," he whispered.

"Yes, Holden?"

"Without a doubt, you are the greatest highlight of my life."

He brought his lips to mine again, even more tenderly, as if it were the first time, or the last. My fingers found the hair just above his ears, tucking them back into place.

"I had a feeling I might find you two out here…"

We turned in unison to see Marceline hanging around the corner.

"You know," she added, "there *is* a second floor."

I grinned, burying my face in Holden's chest.

"I just finished up for the day and I'm meeting Arvin at the Princess Anne for dinner. Would you like to come along?"

It was the perfect opportunity to cheer Holden—a night out at his favorite restaurant.

"I don't think so," he said.

He must've seen the confusion on my face when our eyes met. "I'm going to head home," he added.

I glanced to Marceline, then back to him. "You don't want to come?"

"Go on." A little smirk. "You don't need me."

I let out a puzzled laugh. "Who says I don't?"

Holden only kissed my forehead, murmuring softly, "I'll see you in the morning."

I grabbed his fingers as they slipped from my hand, not willing to let him go.

He laughed, shaking the remaining petals from his hair. "*Go.* Have a good time."

"Don't be late tomorrow," I ordered, releasing him.

Marceline found my side as he walked back through the alley. "Is he all right?"

I watched Holden blow us a kiss as he rounded the corner, and my stomach sank.

"He's been acting peculiar all day," she added.

"He's all right," I lied, unwilling to think otherwise. "He had something he needed to take care of."

Marceline, looking satisfied, turned back to me. "Shall we, then?"

Holden was late.

As I opened up that morning, greeting the early risers on the street from the desk window, I thought of all the ways I might scold him for making me wait. But fifteen minutes passed, then thirty. *Everyone* was late. Even Marceline, the most punctual of us all.

I walked to the telephone hanging in the hall, swiping the receiver. "Hello, operator? Thompson residence, please. Norwell 341."

The line began to ring. I imagined Madora Thompson in a nighty set picking up on the other end, asking sweetly why I'd rung so early in the morning. I waited, gripping the piece to my ear, but no one answered on the other line.

"I'm sorry," the operator chimed in. "I don't think anyone is home."

I was still clutching the telephone when the front door swung open and I whipped around, expecting to find Holden and Marceline talking over each other, each trying to explain the reason for the tardiness.

"Good morning, Lou," said Mrs. Robinson.

"Was there a traffic accident on the bridge?" I asked, hanging up the receiver.

"Not that I saw, dear. Is everything all right? You look a little…"

Pale. I could feel it. The color draining from my face.

"Everyone is just running a little late this morning," I said. "I'll fetch your coat."

I searched for the finished garment, hung up in the back. I told myself it was just another day. Just another morning. I had to do my job.

Mrs. Robinson waited for me at the desk.

"Here you are," I said, handing the coat off to her.

She made her way to the front door. "Tell everyone hello for me."

"I will."

I listened for the door to close as Mrs. Robinson left me alone in the empty shop, with only the ticking clock for company. Grabbing a pencil, I opened the appointment book, drawing a check mark next to her name. And then I saw it.

All seven of Holden's appointments had been rescheduled for the day. All initialed by him.

You are without a doubt, the greatest highlight of my life.

My blood ran cold.

The sharp ring of the telephone echoed through the shop. A foreboding, daunting ring. I didn't want to answer it.

When I picked up the receiver, the line was eerily quiet. Marceline's voice crackled through the sound waves, breaking the silence.

"It's Holden."

I wanted to object but the words stuck to the back of my throat. I could say, feel, think nothing, except for a roaring surge of *needing* to get to him. To see him, to touch him. I would accept nothing less, not from any fate or any God.

I bolted for the door. I would get to him. I'd find him. I'd hitch a ride, I'd run across the bridge if I had to—

I ran directly into Jamie, who caught me in his arms.

"Lou!"

"Let go of me, Jamie!" I yelled. "I need to—"

"He's *dead,* Lou," he pressed. "Holden is dead."

I screamed and I fought for him to release me, until the rage turned into sobs, and we collapsed into an embrace. Holden's blazer was still on the coat rack. Everything was still in place. Nothing had changed, and yet, everything had disintegrated in a single moment. He'd never walk through the door again, he'd—

I thought of the last time I'd seen him in the alley, petals in his hair. And I wept. I pleaded to the skies like a broken record. But God was silent.

"He can't be," I cried, clutching Jamie tight.

"Bette found him this morning." His voice was weak as he held me in his sturdy arms. "We lost him."

The Thompsons' driveway was already full of cars when Jamie and I arrived. Mary Jane sat on the edge of the portico, leaning against the column the same way that Holden had done two Christmases ago.

Wiping a tear from her eye, she slipped down from the edge as Jamie and I approached. "I'm sorry, Lou," she said, folding me gently in her arms.

I could have fallen apart right there. I wanted to.

"Where is Marceline?" I asked.

"She hasn't come out of her old bedroom since we found out." Mary Jane pulled away and turned to Jamie. "Theo and Scott are on their way. They should be here by tomorrow morning."

"Jamie," I added hesitantly. "Where is Bette?"

"Not here."

My gaze slipped past Mary Jane to the front door of the brick colonial.

"I want to talk to her. If she isn't here, how can we know if she—"

"Lou..." Jamie dropped his voice, exchanging a quick glance with his cousin. "He died in the night. The coroner confirmed it..."

My heart stung. He'd died in the night, while I was sound asleep in my bed. Alone. Without me. And I hadn't felt a thing. No premonitory dream, no feeling to jolt me awake. Nothing.

"Come inside," Jamie pressed.

I looked into the dining room as we walked through the front door, almost able to imagine Holden leaning in the doorway. Marceline met us with red-rimmed eyes on the stairs, Arvin following close behind. Just last night we'd been at the Princess Anne having dinner, gossiping over shrimp cocktail.

Life would never be so carefree again.

"Marcie," I whispered. It was all I could manage as I reached over to hug her.

We slumped together to the bottom step.

"Scott and Theo will be here. They're on their way," said Mary Jane.

Marceline dried her flushed cheek and straightened her back, as if she were determined not to shed a single tear more. "When he was in France, I wondered every morning if that would be the day," she said.

"I'm going to check on Ma," Jamie murmured.

Arvin squeezed past where we sat on the stairs. "I'll join you."

Marceline stared into the empty foyer, as if she might be imagining him there too.

"He was acting strange yesterday," I said.

"In the alley, you mean?"

"He..." I looked into his sister's reddened eyes; how closely the blue resembled his. "I thought the mood would pass. I didn't want to worry you."

"I see," she said.

There was an undercurrent of anger in those two words. Betrayal, even. I opened my mouth to speak, but the words wouldn't flow.

"Honey, you should eat something," said Arvin, reappearing by the staircase bannister. "It doesn't have to be much."

Marceline shot to her feet without another word, leaving me on the stair.

In the kitchen, a few unrecognizable family members surrounded Madora, who sat at the kitchen table, face buried in her hands. I caught the eye of Mr. Thompson as I stood in the doorway, unsure if I should enter.

"Come in, Lou," he said, in a welcoming but tired tone. "I'm sorry we left you waiting at the shop."

I tried to smile, but my eyes filled with tears. "Jamie and I left a note at the shop." I again saw Holden's mother at the table. "I can't tell you how sorry I am," I whispered.

"You don't need to, dear," Mr. Thompson reassured. "I already know."

"Let's go outside," said Mary Jane, finding my side.

Jamie and I followed her to the back porch, where we met Marceline and Arvin.

The mood was somber as the summer skies darkened above us, and the leaves flipped over with a promise of rain. We spread out over the porch, watching the clouds plunge the backyard into shadow. A crack of thunder rumbled in the distance. In an attempt to outrun the storm, Arvin and Marceline left quickly, promising they'd return in the morning. And I watched through the window as guests began to depart, returning to their own, untouched lives.

Mary Jane scooted to the stair's edge, hugging her knees as the rain began. "Do you think he…meant to do it?" she asked, gazing out into the darkness. "It seems unlike him to not leave a letter."

"Of course he meant to do it."

I looked to Jamie, a little pained by the certainty in his tone.

"What do you think, Lou?" asked Mary Jane.

"I don't know," I admitted. There was no use in telling them the plans Holden and I had made. They had all turned to dust.

Dust.

One of my last words to him. Not *please don't leave me here,* or *I'd die without you.* Just *everything will be all right when the dust settles.* Empty, useless words.

I watched the lightning dance in the distance, rupturing the thunderheads. Through the pounding rain, the door creaked open next to me.

Mr. Thompson managed a frail, exhausted smile when he met my eye. "This is where everyone is, then," he said, walking out to join us. "How are you all holding up?"

"We're all right, Pop," said Jamie.

Mr. Thompson turned his attention to the rainfall. "Even God is crying tonight," he remarked.

Any man who was at the front could never believe in a God, Holden had once said. Maybe he'd been right.

I wrung my hands, turning to Mr. Thompson. "Do you need me to do anything when I go back home tonight?"

"We'll tackle that in the morning," he replied. "Tonight, we mourn."

"There's plenty of space here," Jamie added. "You can take my room."

I looked to Mr. Thompson for confirmation.

"I insist," he said. "Stay."

"Could I..." I bit my bottom lip to keep it from trembling.

"You may," he whispered, reading my mind. "Jamie will show you where it is."

There were two beds in the wallpapered room that Holden and Dane had shared growing up, with a single lofty window in the center. A few Princeton banners decorated Holden's side above his bed.

"Here you are," said Jamie. "If you change your mind—"

"I won't," I whispered back. "Thank you, Jamie."

He turned to leave but I grabbed onto him, bringing him in for a hug. "I'm sorry."

"I never thought I'd be the only brother left," he mumbled.

I knew better than to prod in a time like this.

The blankets on Holden's bed held none of his scent, just the must of an inhabited bedroom. I brought the quilt to my chin, trying to imagine him sleeping there as a boy. What he'd been like, who he'd been *before.* And Dane, the elusive brother who'd known him so well. My tears stained the pillow as my eyes found the dark window, knowing there were no answers to be had—with or without God's help.

Chapter Sixteen

If it weren't for the headache from crying, I would have never fallen asleep that night. A hint of tangerine light trickled in from the window, illuminating Holden's boyhood room and the things he'd left behind. More pieces of him for me to collect. I reached down to the small pile of books against the wall, plucking *Leaves of Grass* off the top. It was a well-loved copy, with dog-eared pages and countless annotations. I opened it to a random page, and found a section he'd underlined.

And what I assume you shall assume
For every atom belonging to me as good belongs to you

The heartbreak flooded back into my body. The nightmare scenario of my waking world—that he was gone, and I was here.

Rays of morning light bled into the hall when I opened the bedroom door, drawing my attention to the collection of portraits. One was a larger picture of the one Holden had given me. The dull, colorless portrait could capture his perfect features but not the iridescent sapphire of his eyes. The thought I might one day forget their color was more than I could endure.

Among the portraits of Holden, Jamie and Marceline, another face hid in the background of the group photos. A light-haired boy with a shy look, who appeared to be no older than fifteen.

Dane.

Jamie was deep in slumber on the parlor settee when I reached the bottom of the staircase. Figuring he must've given his room to Mary Jane, I slipped past without waking him.

I could see Mr. Thompson writing a letter on the porch through the stained glass window of their kitchen, and I wondered how long he'd slept, or if he'd slept at all.

"Morning," I said, closing the door behind me. I wouldn't dare say it was a *good* one.

Mr. Thompson motioned to the opposite chair. "Why don't you join me?"

Obliging him, I took a seat.

"I'm writing to my son," he murmured.

"Dane?"

He picked up the letter, inspecting it closer. "That's right."

"Has he heard yet?" I asked timidly. "About what happened?"

"Jamie sent a telegram yesterday." Mr. Thompson removed his glasses. "But he deserves a more thorough explanation."

I'd never considered asking *how* Holden had done it. Then again, I didn't need to.

Without knowing Dane, my heart ached for him. "I understand they were very close," I said.

"He's the only person Holden would listen to," Mr. Thompson recalled with a faint smile. "When the episodes began, Dane and I thought he might do better back home. Had I known this would be the outcome…"

"You couldn't have known."

Mr. Thompson paused for a moment and looked out into the

yard before folding the letter and sticking it in an envelope. "No, I suppose not."

I tucked a piece of stray hair behind my ear, not knowing what else to say.

"I'm going to close the shop for the week," Mr. Thompson said at last. "There is far too much to do."

It only just occurred to me that the world was, in fact, still turning, and if it were any other Saturday, we would've opened the shop an hour ago.

"I'll come with you," I said.

Jamie was sitting up when I walked back inside, looking like he'd aged significantly in our ten hours apart. "Morning," he said.

I took a seat on the settee next to him. "Morning."

"It doesn't feel real..." His eyes followed the room. "To wake up here, like this."

"I offered to go with your father to the shop to help him close for the week."

"The world spins madly on," he murmured. "Will you come back?"

"I don't know," I replied. "But God knows I need to change my clothes."

Mr. Thompson opened the back door and walked inside, slow and sluggish, like a shadow hugging the walls. "Are you ready, Lou?" he asked, peering into the sitting room.

I looked back to Jamie with a nod.

Whispers of what felt like another lifetime greeted us as we entered the dimly lit shop. The appointment book was still open to Holden's initials when I took my seat at the desk.

"We'll move all appointments this week to next week," said Mr. Thompson. "I will call everyone who has a home telephone if you compile a list."

"What about the rest?"

"I'll have our pastor pass the message along to the rest of the community."

I could hardly feel the pen between my fingers as I began to write, scratching meaningless numbers across paper. Mr. Thompson paced as I wrote, examining every detail of the shop as if he were searching for a clue he'd somehow missed.

"Lou," he said the moment I laid down my pen, "you should go pack some clothes."

I understood he was asking for privacy, so I headed for the stairs, but not before glancing back at him to be certain.

"I'll be all right," he assured.

My apartment felt cold when I opened the door, despite it being nearly June. I pictured myself at my vanity on New Year's Eve, and Holden lying across my settee with his black eye. The two of us fast asleep in my foyer next to an extinguished candle. Our clothes all over my floor.

This place, this beloved apartment of mine, was not *home* anymore.

It was just an empty building.

I could imagine Holden sitting on the edge of my bed, paper bag of muffins in hand. His infantry portrait watched me from its place on my nightstand as I threw clothes into my open suitcase.

I wanted to tear it to pieces.

"You've killed me too," I wept, tucking it between my clothes.

I could hear Mr. Thompson mumbling into the phone from the top of the landing. Over and over again, I listened as he broke the news to each person on my list.

"He passed suddenly yesterday morning…mhm—yes, thank you. We appreciate your prayers…of course."

And I wondered if it pained him as much to say it as it did for me to hear it.

When Mr. Thompson finally hung up the receiver for good, he found me waiting on the stairwell with swollen eyes, suitcase at my side.

"We're finished here," he said quietly.

I followed him out into the vacant parking lot, scattered with puddles from the storm.

"I told them it was wound complications," Mr. Thompson muttered, shutting the driver's side door.

There was truth in that lie. Holden's wounds had been mostly invisible, but no less lethal.

"He deserves a proper funeral." Mr. Thompson eyed me from behind his glasses, looking especially forlorn."I believe that our God is a loving one, despite what others want to say."

"I won't tell a soul," I promised.

"I'm..." He sighed. "I'm very sorry, Lou. I know how much he will be missed by you."

I knew that Mr. Thompson was returning to a road traveled years ago with the death of Dane's mother. He was no stranger to loss, and the way he thought of *my* feelings at such a time was clear evidence of that.

My voice was raspy as I spoke. "Does it ever get any easier?"

"Just different," he said, turning to me. "It just becomes different."

Scott's yellow roadster waited in the Thompsons' driveway when we returned, eliciting an anxious sting in my stomach. I hardly knew them both, and most of what I *did* know of Holden's friends was based on the anecdotes he'd shared. I could only assume Scott and Theo felt the same way about me.

Marceline's eyes seemed to glaze over me completely when I walked through the door.

With Scott and Theo nowhere to be seen, I made a beeline for the staircase. I lugged my suitcase down the length of the hall, jarred by my own reflection as I passed the mirror on the wall. How frail and dejected I looked. If I'd cared at all, I would have pinched my cheeks to bring some color back to them.

Afternoon sunshine streamed through the window of Holden's room, bringing me an unexpected feeling of relief. I was glad to be there again—in his room, among his things. I climbed into his bed, burying my face in the pillow and pulling the blanket over my head. I wanted to lie there all day, undisturbed in my quilted crypt. The only place I could still feel close to him.

A knock on the door.

"Lou, are you in here?"

"Come in," I replied, peeking out from the covers.

Jamie opened the door to find me cocooned. "Scott and Theo are here."

"I saw Scott's car outside."

"Theo asked after you." Jamie looked over his shoulder, back down the hall. "I needed an excuse to escape from everyone for a moment."

"Who are all of these people?" I asked.

"I wish I knew," Jamie replied. "Should I tell Theo you're asleep?"

Yes. That was what I wanted.

"No," I murmured, propping myself up. "I'll come down."

I could hear Theo's voice downstairs as I followed Jamie back down the hall.

"Jamie" —I halted next to a family photo— "is this?"

"Dane," he replied.

"Why aren't there any newer portraits of him?" I asked.

"He left for New York right after our grandfather died. We haven't seen much of him since." Jamie turned away from the photo, as if it hurt him to look at it. "I was quite young…to be honest, I don't remember him terribly well."

I nodded in understanding, slowly untangling the threads of the Thompson siblings. As much as Holden had proclaimed himself the black sheep of the family, I could see that he'd modeled himself in Dane's image. Or perhaps the line of where one brother ended and the other began wasn't entirely clear, not even to them.

"I'm going to go find Marcie," Jamie said as we reached the bottom of the stairs.

I met the gaze of Scott and Theo, who stood in the foyer to our right. "We'll catch up later," I said, patting his arm.

It was immediately clear to me that Holden's friends were as nervous to see me as I was to see them. But as I walked to meet them, I noticed something else between us.

A quiet, curious camaraderie.

"I guess Thompson's whole family is here," Theo noted.

"It's been like this since yesterday," I replied.

Theo's eyes watered just enough for me to notice. "It's good to see you."

"It is," Scott added.

The lump in my throat disappeared as I reached to hug them both. "I'm glad you're here," I whispered to them.

"Theo! Scott!" Mr. Thompson appeared at our side. "Thank you boys for coming."

"Hello, Mr. Thompson. I..." Theo stopped mid-sentence, looking unsure of what to say as the three of us separated. "Please, let us know if we can help in any way."

Mr. Thompson looked between him and Scott. "How long will you two be staying with us?"

"We're staying at the Princess Anne in town," Theo replied. "We didn't want to impose."

"No imposition at all—any friend of Holden's is a friend of ours."

"We want to be of use however we can," Scott added.

"Thank you, boys." Mr. Thompson managed a smile as he split a nod between them. "Now, I'm afraid I have more people to greet."

"Of course," said Scott.

Theo turned to me as Mr. Thompson moved on. "Are you staying here, Lou?"

"In Holden's room," I replied. "I'll stay there as long as they'll allow it."

"When you head home, let us know if you'd like any company." Theo leaned in, lowering his voice. "I think he'd want us to look after you, you know?"

"*If* you'd have us," Scott added.

"Yes." Theo nodded to him. "If you'd have us."

Chapter Seventeen

"Your turn."

I glanced down at the checkerboard between Jamie and me on the floor. We'd been playing all evening, with nothing else to do but sit around and wait for something to happen. The days had blurred together, separated only by a quiet gloom each night.

"There," I murmured back.

Mary Jane brushed Marceline's hair on the settee next to us. No one had bothered to turn the parlor lights on, opting instead for the low light of the oil lamps scattered about.

"Jamie. It's your—"

In unison, we turned to the car headlights shining through the parlor curtains.

Mary Jane rose to her feet. "Who would be calling at this hour?"

"It's probably someone dropping off a dish," said Jamie, turning back to our game.

Flowers and covered dishes had accumulated on all available surfaces in the days following Holden's death.

"It's Father Breen," said Marceline. "He's come to talk about the wake."

Mr. Thompson swept through the parlor, opening the front door just in time to greet their pastor.

"My deepest condolences, James," I heard him say. "I've been praying for you all."

"Come in, Father."

Father Breen glanced into the parlor, nodding in acknowledgment.

"Hello, Father," said Marceline.

"How is everyone?" he asked, removing his hat.

Jamie kept his eyes on the checkerboard.

Marceline answered for both of them. "As well as can be expected."

He looked at each of us with large, sympathetic eyes, patting the back of the settee before joining Mr. Thompson in the kitchen.

"That was rude," Marceline scolded, looking toward her brother. "You could have said something."

"Forgive me if I'm not in the mood to talk, Marcie."

"I'm going to make tea," I said, shoving the checkerboard away.

"Tea would be wonderful," said Mary Jane.

The large house felt eerily empty around dusk, even with the small communions in various rooms. I listened for the low chatter between Father Breen and the grieving parents as I made my way toward the kitchen.

"May I make some tea?" I asked, halting at the doorway.

Mr. Thompson perked up from the table. "Be a dear and make some for us too?"

"Of course." I walked into the kitchen, turning my back to them.

"I have listed Holden's death as an accident," said Father Breen. "Using the account we've discussed."

Wound complications.

I'd overheard enough from guests to know the gossip mill was churning at full speed in town. Everything from foul play and alcoholism to the Irish mob were floated as possible theories for the real reason behind Holden's untimely death. No one seemed to buy that a wartime wound was what did him in.

"Thank you, Father." Madora's voice was hoarse.

I remembered back to my first Christmas Eve with them, how she'd been worried sick while Holden was at the front and how happy she was to have him home, only for it to come to this. My heart broke for her, and for all of us.

"I'll do everything in my power to ensure your son has a proper funeral, but I can't promise it will be any grander than necessary since he wasn't an active member of the church."

"We appreciate everything you're doing for us," said Mr. Thompson.

As I waited for the water to boil, they went on to address the fate of Holden's body—where it was, what was happening to it, and lastly, whether or not to do a closed casket under the circumstances. I wondered as I poured their tea where he had gone, if he was no longer in his body. I'd wondered if he might be floating around us, like pollen on a spring day. Everything that made Holden who he was—his snarky words, his sensitive soul—had to have gone *somewhere.* And in the moment before sleep, I tried to imagine him as the blanket around me.

"We'll plan to do the rosary at the wake," Father Breen went on as I brought the cups to the table. "Have you requested military honors?"

"A friend of his has volunteered to be the overseeing officer," said Mr. Thompson, nodding to me in thanks.

Filling four more cups with English breakfast tea, I carried the silver tray into the parlor. The only movement in the room were the dancing shadows of the lantern's flame. Marceline and Mary Jane were just as I'd left them, but Jamie had relocated and was looking out the dark window blankly.

"Oh, tea," said Mary Jane. "Doesn't tea sound nice, Marcie?"

Marceline only stared ahead impassively.

Setting the tray down, I brought one of the teacups over to Jamie.

"What are they discussing in there?" he asked.

"Arrangements," I said quietly. "For the wake and the funeral."

"What about them?"

"Father Breen said he recorded Holden's death as an accident."

"They want us all to lie," said Marceline.

"We've been doing it already," said Jamie. "It's just on paper now."

"That doesn't make it right."

"Don't you see? The truth is bad for business."

Marceline snapped to attention. "Lying means that we're ashamed of him."

"You think we shouldn't be?" asked Jamie coldly. "He gave up—let them make him look better for the sake of our family."

"Jamie!"

"Why are you upset, anyway? He still gets to be the hero as always. Even after all that he's done."

"That's not fair, Jamie," I interjected.

"This is between *my brother and me,*" Marceline snapped.

Taken aback, I silenced myself.

"We could have helped him if we'd known how bad things were," she argued.

"It's our fault, then?" Jamie scoffed. "As far as I can tell, it's a one-man show to put a noose around your neck and hang yourself."

"I can't believe you—you would say such awful things about our brother!"

"It's the only way he'll have a proper funeral and you know that," he mumbled, turning away from his sister. "Think of Ma."

Marceline's eyes overflowed with tears that wouldn't fall.

"He's the only one to blame, Marcie," Jamie added in a low tone. "And I for one will be *damned* if I let this ruin my life."

"Envy doesn't suit you," she snapped back.

Jamie shook his head, then made his exit, slamming the front door behind him.

I scanned the portico, lawn and surrounding woods, finally landing on the faint glow of a cigarette inside of Jamie's car. I was certain he saw me coming as I made my way down the walkway in my cream-colored dress, with only the lights from the house to guide me. Cicadas chirped all around us, reminding me that through our all-consuming pain, it was still just a Virginia summer night.

Jamie took a drag of his cigarette before leaning over to open the door. "If you've come to argue his case, I don't want to hear it, Lou."

"I wanted to make sure you were all right," I replied, climbing inside. "Did you really mean what you said in there?"

"Why wouldn't I?" Jamie turned forward, wiping his eyes. "He's shattered everything and all anyone can think about is *Holden's* suffering? What about everyone else? What about my poor mother?"

"Jamie—"

"He had *everything* going for him! He had everything going for him and he threw it away."

"I won't encourage you—I loved him and you know that," I said. "But I understand."

"You can't understand." He sighed. "I've spent my whole life in his shadow, and his shoes will be impossible to fill."

"Jamie, you don't need to fill anyone's shoes but your own."

He wiped his eyes again, then crossed his arms over his chest.

"He had his reasons," I added softly. "As painful as it is for the rest of us."

Jamie stared into the night with a stoic expression. "I hate him for it."

Days later, I studied Holden's tweed sport coat from my place in the bathtub.

It had been a pleasant surprise to find it on the foyer coat rack when I'd finally returned home. Sleeping in Holden's bed, amongst his belongings, was the only thing that had brought me any semblance of comfort, and I'd grown so accustomed to his wallpapered room that it felt like a second death to leave it. But the familiar, sweet musk on his lapels had brought him back from the grave. I wanted to bottle it, to keep with me always.

Stepping out of the claw foot tub, I examined my thin frame. I'd lost about five pounds since Holden's death, subsisting only on biscuits, tea and the whiskey of my newly-acquired room-mates. I pulled Holden's blazer over my summer dress, returning his portrait to the pocket.

Thunder erupted from the stairs on the other side of my wall.

"We're back," Theo called.

With the funeral set for Saturday, we were left with far too much time to think. The company of Holden's friends had made everything a bit more bearable in his absence.

Theo met my gaze with sullen eyes as I walked into the foyer, ringing my wet hair.

"How is everyone?" I asked.

Theo glanced at Scott, who paced as he held a cigarette at arm's length. "Somber as hell. About what you'd expect."

I walked to the window, my familiar roost, where I'd watched countless clients leave flowers and sympathy cards on the shop's stoop day after day. The orange wings of a Monarch butterfly caught my eye, fluttering in perfect figure eights among the pear blossoms outside. The sight of it almost made me smile.

"I'm so damn fidgety," said Scott. "Whiskey?"

"Hardly any left," I admitted, turning to him.

Scott stared at me, wide-eyed. "You drank it all?"

"*We* drank it all," I clarified.

"Where can you get a drink around here?"

"I know a place," Theo interjected. "What do you say, Lou?"

When I turned back to the window, my butterfly friend had vanished. "I think it would do us all good to get out."

It didn't matter that Holden's blazer was three sizes too big; I wore it over my black flapper dress. We'd been in the roadster no more than ten minutes when Scott pulled off of Edward Street and parked on the curb. It was a quiet part of town, surrounded mostly by row houses.

I read the sign that hung outside of the shop's entrance: *Jonesy Books.*

"A bookstore, Theo?" I asked.

"Wait until you see the collection," he replied over his shoulder. "It's quite impressive."

I had never heard of *Jonesy Books,* even in my college years.

Scott turned to Theo. "Are you sure this is the right place?"

"Thompson brought me here once. I'm positive."

I watched from the backseat as the two men stared at each other; their profiles silhouetted by the streetlights like a silent film.

"All right, then," said Scott. "I'm thirsty."

The shop was notably tiny, only opening up to a singular, smaller room in the back. With its dusty shelves and titles, it was the strangest bookstore I'd ever seen.

The man behind the counter, who looked to be absorbed in paperwork, watched us with suspicious eyes as we walked in. "Can I help y'all with something?"

Theo approached the counter, leaving Scott and me behind. "I'm looking for a particular title. Is this the right place?" he asked.

The man lowered the glasses on his pointy nose, raising his eyebrows. "Young man, this is a *bookstore.*"

"Right, of course." Theo leaned over the counter. "It's called *High Moon.*"

The man seemed to drink in Theo's words as he lifted his chin, knocking twice on the bookshelf behind him.

A voice protruded from the wall of piled, bound pages as the shelf shifted from the wall.

The man held up three fingers. "We got room for three more?"

Scott and I exchanged a look, unable to make out the answer.

"All right." The man pulled the shelf out further, until it opened into a door. "Come on now, ain't got all night," he said, urging us in.

We trickled through the narrow doorway, one at a time, into an underground world just on the other side of the bookstore. It was common knowledge that bootleggers ran moonshine over the Falmouth Bridge into town. One only had to know where to look. Deviants sat at the makeshift bar along with small tables, chairs and loveseats. Some leaned against the wall, completely content to forgo a seat. The room echoed with hushed giggles and slurred chatter as we walked through, following Theo to a small table in the middle of the room.

"Welcome to Jonesy's," called the bartender. "What'll it be?"

The barman, who'd introduced himself as Paul, returned quickly with two whiskeys for Scott and Theo, setting them on our table before going back to retrieve my gin drink.

"I was wondering why I'd never heard of this place," I said. "How did you know about the password?"

"I asked the bellhop at the Princess Anne," Theo replied. "It pays to make friends."

I'd never been so happy to see alcohol as when Paul returned with my drink.

"To Holden," said Scott, raising his glass to Theo and me.

"Wait" —Paul turned back— "Holden Thompson?"

I looked up at him, feeling the warmth of the gin grip my heart. "Did you know him?"

"Yeah, I knew him—he used to come around here a lot. I heard about what happened…it's a damn shame. He just had a way about him."

I hugged myself, suddenly reminded of his blazer I wore.

"We're friends from out of town, here for the funeral," said Theo.

Paul pointed to the back of the room. "His wife is here, you know. She's sitting in the back."

Bette?

I almost didn't believe it, and by the look on Scott and Theo's faces, they didn't either.

"Anyway," said Paul, tapping the table, "just holler when you need a refill."

"Make it a double for me!" Scott called after him.

"Fuck, do you see her?" Theo asked.

Between their heads, I could see her at the back of the room, visibly drunk and surrounded by questionable company. "It's her," I confirmed.

Theo grimaced. "Do you think she saw us come in?"

"What's she doing?" asked Scott.

"She's with a group of men."

"Standard Bette," murmured Theo. "Just ignore her."

While the boys got lost conversing about old times, I focused all my attention on the blonde-haired beauty, looking at once rapt and bored. Her new companion, a slick man in an even slicker suit, grabbed her face, turning her toward him.

"I don't remember you dating anyone by the name of Lorraine. How can you prove you didn't make her up?"

She was the one that looked like she got kicked by a horse," added Scott.

A glass slammed onto the table. "Ah, *Lorraine!*"

My gaze snapped back to them, meeting Theo's flat stare.

"I *said* ignore her, Lou. You're not ignoring her."

"I think she might be in trouble," I mumbled, looking past them.

The pair turned over their shoulders in unison, just in time to see her beau release her.

"I'm going over there," said Scott.

Theo shook his head. "That's a terrible idea."

"Wouldn't Thompson want us to defend her honor or something?"

"What is there to defend? Fuck's sake Scott, Holden's body isn't even in the ground and she's already out boozing about with somebody else." Theo glanced over his shoulder, then turned back to Scott. "What do you expect to do anyway, just waltz up to him and introduce yourself as her dead husband's friend and tell him to keep his hands off of her? I'm sure that would go over *very* well with a group like that. Not to mention, we're severely outnumbered."

"Theo's right, at least about that," I interjected. "You'll end up in a fight if you say anything."

"And I'm not getting kicked out over *her*," he added.

Maybe it was the gin, or maybe I was a glutton for punishment. "I'll go," I said.

"Why?" Theo pressed. "I can think of a hundred reasons why you shouldn't talk to her."

"And I can think of one reason that I should." I nodded to him. "Holden would want me to."

As if by design, the man left the table only a few moments later. Figuring a better opportunity wouldn't present itself, I downed the rest of my gin and stood up.

Theo grit his teeth. "Lou..."

I shot him a cutting glance. "Stop me, Theo."

Bette sipped on her drink, eyeing me sharply as I approached the table. "They didn't want to come with you?" she asked.

I must have looked surprised.

"Tell Scott to be a little less obvious next time." Her eyes followed the length of Holden's sport coat as I stood next to her. "I remember that blazer," she said. "Though, if I recall correctly, it was usually on the floor."

I swallowed hard.

She inhaled, placing a limp cigarette in between her lips. "Have you come to gloat?"

"Gloat?" I straightened my shoulders. "You left *him.*"

"Perhaps because he was in love with someone else," she replied. "I knew it long before he did."

An arm appeared with a match to light her cigarette.

"Hello, who do we have here?" asked the man from earlier, squeezing in next to Bette.

"I'm an old friend," I said.

"Old friend?" A flicker of distrust passed over his gaze as he turned to Bette. "How'd you two meet?"

"Through a mutual friend," I stammered.

He turned to me, looking amused as he fiddled with the toothpick between his teeth. "I've heard your friend was quite a lucky fella with the ladies—you were right Bette, she is *quite* comely…"

Bette locked her jaw, diverting her eyes to her lap.

"I suppose you have me all figured out," I said.

He said something under his breath, knocking back the rest of his drink. "You're a lousy actress." He stood, yanking Bette to her feet. "And *we* are leaving."

"I'm not ready to leave," Bette countered.

"I told you—I *told* you not to talk to anyone associated with him," he scolded. "And here you are, doing just that. You don't listen."

I stepped forward, blocking their exit. "It was me who walked over. Besides," I taunted, meeting his eye, "are you so threatened by a dead man?"

The man chuckled, shoving past me with Bette in tow. She fought as he dragged her toward the exit, causing everyone in the speakeasy to turn their heads.

"Let go of me, Roy," Bette hissed.

He only gripped her frail arm tighter, and then—

Bette did exactly what I'd *wanted* to do, with all the bravery that I'd lacked. She spit clear in his face.

"You're going to be sorry you did that," he growled, grabbing her by her platinum locks.

Scott and Theo stood up to intervene but found themselves surrounded by his henchmen, and we watched helplessly as he shoved her out the back door.

Suddenly, I was sober.

Chapter Eighteen

A flicker of sunshine lit the inside of my eyelids. It was morning. The day of the wake. I reached for my sheets only to feel the distinct texture of grass beneath my palms. A bright sky hung above me, bluer than I'd ever seen. For as far as the eye could see, yellow wildflowers covered the mysterious landscape. I rose to my feet and brushed off my dress, feeling at once not alone.

Following the current of a soft breeze, I turned around instantaneously. It took only seeing that familiar smirk to fill my eyes with happy tears.

Finally managing a whisper, I spoke. "Are you real?"

I held my hand up, and without speaking, Holden did the same. A solid, human touch.

I gasped, seizing him. "You found a way back!"

He hugged me tightly as I buried my face in his shoulder, unwilling to let go.

"I'll marry you," I whispered. "I'll marry you. I'll marry you. Just so long as I never have to live without you."

Feeling a tickle across the top of my forearm, I peeked over his shoulder to see a pair of orange wings. Holden looked up and smiled as another butterfly landed on his shoulder, and then another. Soon enough, we were surrounded by hundreds of marigold wings, glistening against the cloudless sky.

"I still don't take it back, Lou," he said, speaking at last.

A twinge of panic accompanied his words, and I squeezed him tighter, feeling he may slip away.

"I'm sorry—I don't have much time," he said, kissing my forehead in the same manner he had the last time we'd seen each other.

I begged him not to go. I anchored onto the sensation of his form beneath my fingers, the density of his chest against my cheek—but it was no use. I fell into the dark, unable to stay there any longer.

I awoke in my bed, head pounding and alone, with only the fading scent of his sport coat.

Theo looked up from the sofa as I walked into the foyer, nauseous with hopeless longing. "You look awful," he joked.

I took the chair opposite of him and sat down, squinting at him through the morning light. "You don't look much better."

"Gin not agreeing with you this morning?"

"Something like that," I replied. "Where's Scott?"

"Probably helping the Thompsons get ready for the wake tonight."

I grimaced. "The wake."

Theo was quiet, draped across my settee that was much too small for him to lie comfortably. His arm covered his face, shielding the light of my reflective white walls. "There had to have been some combination of words I couldn't uncover," he said finally. "To keep him here."

"You think we could've stopped him?"

"I don't know." Theo lifted his arm, showcasing the way the sunlight turned his brown irises tawny. "But I'd rather live with the burden that I didn't do enough than to think he was doomed all along."

"He was acting strange the last time I saw him." I thought

back to him in the alleyway as he stood beneath the pear blossoms. It was the most beautiful he'd ever looked, even in his sadness. "Marceline hates me now."

"She doesn't hate you. She's just in pain—it's easier to be angry."

"Is that how you feel about Bette?" I asked, recalling his reaction at the bar.

He rubbed his face with his hands. "She didn't make his life any easier, I'll say that. But I don't hate her."

"You're just in pain."

"Precisely. She..." He paused. "I don't know if Jamie told you, but I was the one she called when she found him."

"He didn't," I replied.

"She called from the neighbor's house. I don't even know what the hell she was doing there that day."

I was hit by a sudden pang of jealousy, remembering Bette's comment about his blazer. "Things ended rather amicably," I said, trying to smother it. "At least, that's what he told me. Now I'm not so sure."

"It was nothing," Theo assured. "Nothing like that, anyway. He only ever spoke of you as a beacon of love and as a symbol of getting his life back on track."

I turned away, feeling the familiar sting of tears. "I tried."

"I know," he replied, looking up to the ceiling. "We can't let anyone convince us that it was our fault, *or* that we had no ability to change it. For Thompson's life, we are the children in the middle."

I didn't hear the footsteps on the stairs and was startled when Scott opened the door.

"You're exactly where I left you," he said, pointing at Theo. "But you, my dear, are not."

"You're alive," Theo remarked.

"Unlike some of you, I can handle my liquor."

"Where were you?" I asked as he walked in.

"I was helping Jamie at the house. The house is full of flowers now. Stupid fucking flowers that stink up the whole place." Scott lit a cigarette and walked over to crack the window. "And Thompson's old man is fretting because no one has heard from Dane."

"You're joking," said Theo. "He doesn't know yet?"

Scott shrugged. "That's the problem, Teddy. No one knows."

"Jamie sent a telegram the day he died and Mr. Thompson sent a letter right after that," I chimed in. "That was earlier this week."

"Let me get this straight." Scott gripped the windowsill. "Our best friend is dead, his widow is being held hostage by a slimy brute, and now his brother is missing in action?"

"It would seem."

"And now we have to get ready for the wake," Theo added, throwing off his blanket.

The inside of the Thompsons' house was stuffy with the cloying smell of decaying flowers and phony merriment. Platters of food stretched across every surface, attracting mourners like fruit flies. I didn't recognize most of them, and I wondered if they'd known Holden at all. Each mirror in the house had been covered by a sheet, only adding to the morbidness of it all.

"The clock," I noted, inspecting the walnut grandfather clock. "It's stopped."

"The ways of the Irish," said Scott. "They stop all the clocks at the hour of death."

I swallowed hard at the sight of it—the hands moved to midnight.

"I don't like that," said Theo quietly as he turned away. "Time feels frozen enough already."

Jamie appeared out of nowhere at our side, wrapping a friendly arm around my shoulder. "Could I enlist you to help me move something?" he asked Scott and Theo.

"Absolutely," Theo replied. "Just show us the way."

And like that, I found myself alone in the hall, swarming with nameless people. Feeling for Holden's portrait in my skirt pocket, I pulled it out to meditate as the wake-goers talked, laughed and danced.

How strange it felt to be an outsider.

It seemed just as strange that Dane and Bette were nowhere to be found.

I glanced up from the photo, casting my gaze down the hallway toward the drawing room, where Holden's body lay. I wanted only to climb the stairs unnoticed and hide the rest of the day in his room.

"Have you tried the tarts?"

Bethany and May stood to my immediate right, gorging themselves on appetizers. "I'm sorry, what?" I asked.

"The tarts," said May. "They are delicious."

"I'm not hungry."

"Oh," Bethany cooed. "Of course, you're not."

"Terribly sorry to hear about Holden."

"I could have told you this would happen," Bethany added, reaching for another tart.

"His wound?" I asked.

"Sweet Lou" —she covered her mouth— "you know as well as the rest of us that's not what happened."

"I heard he fell in with a bad crowd," May added, popping another tart in her mouth.

"Have you talked to Marceline?" I asked.

They glanced at each other and then back to me, looking rather uncomfortable.

Bethany eyed the half-empty plate of tarts. "We did the best we could."

My face soured in disbelief. "Did you, now?"

"This whole thing isn't really our forte," May added. "That's why she has you, right?"

I almost laughed. What was it Holden had called them? *Leeches in Sunday clothes.*

"But it really is such a shame."

"An absolute tragedy," Bethany added.

I grabbed the plate of tarts from beneath her grubby hand. "I'm suddenly very hungry," I said, splitting a glare between them.

"Excuse—"

I nudged my way past them, spotting Theo in the hall.

"Have a tart," I said, extending the plate to him.

Theo held up his hand. "I'll pass."

"Where is Scott?"

"He went to see him. Have you gone yet?"

"No," I replied, setting the plate of tarts on the nearest buffet. "I haven't."

Theo wiped his brow with a handkerchief. "I'm quite nervous, if I can be frank with you."

A somber wave washed over me, as they did every so often, with the realization that this was waking life, and Holden was dead.

Theo and I stood in the doorframe as we waited to enter. The closed casket was draped with a flag, surrounded by lilies and lit candles. Pails were situated beneath to catch water droplets from the ice preserving his body. The portrait of Holden in his military uniform sat on display.

Scott, on his way out, stopped to give Theo a solemn pat on the shoulder. "Don't forget to smoke the pipe. It's a tradition for all men who visit the body."

Theo nodded, wide-eyed.

"Teddy," I whispered, "are you all right?"

He turned to me, looking like he might faint. "Splendid."

Theo and I waited until the room emptied before we walked up to the casket, my throat tightening as I looked the solid oak box over. I wondered if I might feel his spirit there—whatever a spirit might be—if only I focused hard enough.

Theo picked up the tobacco pipe from the silver tray, taking a reluctant puff. "Where do you think he is now?" he asked, his dark eyes fixated on the casket.

For the first time since I'd woken up that morning, I thought of my dream and the sensational realness of it. "I think he's where the yellow flowers are."

Chapter Nineteen

Of all my memories of Holden's funeral, the most predominant was that it was dreadfully hot. The earthy stench of the Rappahannock clung relentlessly to the humid air, with no inkling of a breeze.

"How do you think he's able to keep it together so well?" Scott motioned to Mr. Thompson, who was accepting condolences outside the church with Jamie.

"Dane's mother," I replied, absently studying the arched windows.

The last time I'd been to Saint Mary's was for Marceline's wedding, the reminder of which left me gutted. The unexpected pain of losing her alongside Holden had cut like a knife.

"I always forget that they're half-brothers," Theo added. "They look the most alike, in my opinion."

"You've met him?" I asked.

"Just once. It was a long time ago." Theo wiped his brow. "It's terrible he can't be here."

Ladies patted their foreheads with cool, dampened cloths and the men loosened their ties to combat the heat in the crowded sanctuary. Sliding into the back pew, I motioned for Scott and Theo to go ahead.

"Wouldn't you rather sit closer to the front?" asked Theo.

In a sore echo of the past, I shook my head. "I'm fine here."

I could almost envision Holden there next to me.

Fanning myself, I scanned the packed church, stuffed with clients, classmates and Great War veterans of all ranks as Scott and Theo claimed a seat in a middle pew. Just past them, I could see Marceline and Madora sitting near the casket at the front.

Theo glanced over his shoulder as folks began to settle; his eyes sliding to something behind me. She was the last thing I expected to see when I turned around.

Wearing a black lace mourning veil, Bette slipped into the back pew opposite me. As the organ began to play, Theo rose to his feet. The look on her face told me that she was as surprised as I was when he took a seat next to her.

Perhaps there was hope for us all.

Most of the funeral was in Latin, and I spent a great deal of it gazing up at the ceiling rafters, expecting Holden to pop out like Tom Sawyer at any moment, as if the whole thing was just another one of his jests. Young men joined the communion line, just as Holden had the day of Marceline's wedding, which gave me an unexpected ache. But it was the thought of what came next…

The thought of laying him in the ground. In the pitch black earth.

Suddenly aware of my inability to breathe, I clutched the back of the pew in front of me. It was as if the floor were quicksand beneath me, and I was falling—

As if it were no longer real.

As if *I* were no longer real.

I needed to stand—get air, *escape.*

I sprung from my seat, avoiding Theo's gaze as I pushed the sanctuary doors open into the sunny, bright afternoon.

The empty, iron bench beckoned me outside the church. My chest felt so heavy I was sure the pressure would crack my ribs as I took a seat, faint from the heartache and the heat. An explosion of tears followed, attracting the stare of every pedestrian who walked by.

I couldn't watch him be buried.

I couldn't.

My lips trembled as I placed a cigarette between them and struck a match. I closed my eyes, welcoming the smoke that filled my lungs. When I reopened them, it was to the sight of a man studying the church from across the street. A rather ordinary fellow, middle-aged with dark, raven hair. A studious type. I could imagine him as a classmate of Holden's had he been a touch younger.

The sound of leaves rustling above me seized my attention, and following my smoke stream, I looked up. There was nothing unique about the bluebird in the maple tree, other than its apparent interest in me. And I wondered if it was Holden in a new body with repaired wings.

We watched each other, the bluebird and I, until the church doors flung open, scaring it away.

"I'd ask if you're all right, but I think I already know the answer," said Theo.

"I'm afraid Holden has passed his ailment onto me," I admitted. "I lost myself for a moment in there."

Theo squinted at something across the street.

I followed, but saw only an empty sidewalk. "What?"

"I thought...ah, never mind." He offered his arm. "The procession is about to start."

No sooner had he spoken the words, than the doors opened a second time, and an officer in uniform stepped out.

"We can do this," Theo promised, urging me to my feet. "It's just another day."

At the end of the block, mourners were beginning to congregate outside of Saint Mary's cemetery gates. Theo and I followed the designated path through the grass to the burial site. It must have been a hundred degrees outside, similar to the day Holden and I first met—the day I'd walked through the Thompsons' front door. The sun beat down on us as we gathered around the large hole in the ground, with only a small locust tree for shade.

I did not hear the words of Father Breen as he spoke.

Men in uniform marched across the grass, holding the heavy, draped coffin with care. Unable to tell sweat from tears, I watched the water drip from their faces as they set the casket on its stand. I wondered if they'd known him in France.

Theo stood next to me, still as a statue with his arm linked in my own. I wanted to be as stoic as he was, as outwardly unbothered, but I *was* a lousy actress, and I couldn't fake it even for a moment.

"Please prepare for military honors."

I jumped at the discharge of the first rifle, regardless of the warning. The shot echoed through the air with a splitting crackle. Another followed it. I shut my eyes violently with no other wish than to disappear completely. Tears flowed down my cheeks as the remaining nineteen shots fired in sequence.

The bugle began to play as the men folded the flag. But it was Bette watching from outside the cemetery gate that caught my eye.

"Mrs. Thompson," said an officer as he approached Madora.

I observed the man, and unsure of his rank, I peered at his name tag.

Devore.

I thought of New Year's Eve 1920, how I'd once lain with Holden on the dusty floors of Devore's Chatham Manor, and how it all felt so painfully full circle.

Madora accepted the flag and the men stood aside so the family could visit the coffin and speak their last words. I looked back to the gate and let go of Theo's arm.

"Hurry," I whispered, walking briskly toward the edge of the cemetery. "They're about to bury him."

Bette glanced at me from under the black lace. "I can see that."

"I'll stand with you if you want to say something," I said, grasping the iron rods that separated us.

She dropped her eyes to the ground. "Just tell him that I'm sorry, would you?"

"I will," I promised.

Her request rang in my ears as I walked back to the crowd, unwilling to meet any of their eyes.

"She's not coming in?" asked Theo.

I shook my head, turning my attention to Marceline and Jamie at the casket. In another life, they could have been my brother and sister. If only I'd just said yes that day at Chatham when he'd proposed the idea of our *own* family. I might have come around one day, if he had stuck around long enough to see. I could have been a wife and a mother. I'd certainly loved him enough.

"Godspeed friend," said Scott, placing his hand over the solid wood. "To the stars."

Theo stepped up next, breathing steadily. "I'm glad I got one good punch in. If you were here right now, I would punch you again."

Holden would've laughed.

Along with Bette's apology, I only said one thing. Gently kissing the shined oak exterior, I whispered one last promise. "I won't let anyone forget about you."

"Are you sure you don't want us to stay one more night?"

I looked to the dark shopfront from the backseat of the roadster. "I'll be all right, Theo."

Ready for an early bed, I'd released myself from the events of the day.

"Until next time, then," Theo replied, though both of us were uncertain of when that would be.

"Until next time."

Unlocking the front door, I walked inside. Come the following week, I'd be back to work at the desk. Scott and Theo would be back in Baltimore, and Jamie back in school. Life would resume. And to me, the only thing worse than the permanence of death itself was having to return to a ruptured world where things were otherwise normal.

Halting in the doorway, I noticed Holden's shears on the back table, right as he'd left them. Walking over to examine them, I noticed for the first time how large they were. I picked them up, tracing the sharp blades with my finger.

All-consuming panic with no relief.

I'd felt it in the church that day, the claustrophobic darkness he'd described. I'd wanted so badly to ease his pain, and now that I finally understood it, it was too late. It wasn't death that he'd desired. It was escape by any means necessary.

I reached for the pin in my hair, letting my long tresses tumble to my ribcage. I'd acknowledged it on the church bench with the bluebird—that a part of me had died along with Holden. Who I'd been was buried with him, six feet under.

So, I lifted his open shears to my jawline and snapped them shut, shedding my old identity with each lock that hit the ground.

To Holden From Lou
June 17, 1921

Happy birthday, my love. I know you'll never get this letter, but I'll pretend for the sake of pretending this once. I miss you terribly, and no string of pretty words could adequately capture a feeling so desolate. Each day feels no different than the last—I've hardly slept since the hour I found out you were gone. I took one of your blazers from downstairs and have been wearing it in your absence; it still smells like you and I dread the day when the scent finally fades.

I wish you hadn't done this—and perhaps I am selfish for asking you to suffer so that we wouldn't have to. Please forgive me.

I am shredded.

Chapter Twenty

It was a hot and rainy summer, and all the time spent indoors only added to the collective anguish at work. Marceline was especially irritable, avoiding me at all costs, while Mr. Thompson tried to busy himself as much as possible. The whispers of our regulars were ever-telling—even they could see how the grief had absorbed into the walls. The air was ripe for conflict, and still, no one had heard from Dane.

"He got the letter as well as the telegrams! Arvin and I have been in touch with his landlord—he's been there *the whole time.*"

I looked up from my books, following Marceline's voice into the vacant hall.

Mr. Thompson spoke next. "Why wouldn't he write if he's heard the news?"

"I don't know!" she yelled irately. "Because he blames us for what happened—which would be ludicrous since it was *his* idea to send him home in the first place."

"Lou?"

"Yes, Mr. Thompson?" I called back.

"You have a letter."

I peeked into the hallway, seeing the shuffled postage in his hands.

"We all agreed about Holden coming home,"he said, extending my letter. "It wasn't only Dane's decision."

"He suggested it."

Careful to avoid their verbal bullets, I reached across the hall to grab my mail.

"Have you ever considered that he just doesn't care to respond?" asked Marceline.

"Even if he's received the news, it's unfounded to assume his silence is malicious."

I turned the letter over in my hand, my eyes widening at the return address.

New York Herald-Sun
New York City, NY

I'd hardly thought of my essays since Holden's death. With shaky hands, I tore open the envelope. My heart skipped as I read it over, concentrating on each word.

"Why do you always take up for him?" Marceline demanded. "You *always* do."

"Because they've been through this already with his mother," I murmured under my breath.

Marceline turned her blazing stare on me. "Your opinion is the last thing I want to hear. In truth, you're not a part of this family—no matter how you feel."

I glanced up from my letter with an equally provoking glare. "I wonder what Holden would have to say about that."

"He's not here—I'm talking about you and me."

"I knew it."

"That's enough," Mr. Thompson commanded.

"Yes, you did. You knew how I worried sick over him—"

"You know how he was! He wouldn't have wanted me to worry anyone more than they already did!"

"I didn't realize I was just *anyone*," she countered, becoming teary. "It's comforting to know you valued his trust so much more than mine."

"This is about that day in the alley, isn't it?"

She clenched her jaw, in the same manner Holden did when he was angry. "I'm sure there's more."

"You're right! There's more—do you want to know everything so you can hate me properly?"

"I don't need any help hating you."

"Then you'll be happy to know I'm leaving." I looked to Mr. Thompson, holding up the letter. "It's from the *Herald*. They want to work for their European edition in Paris."

"Paris," Marceline whispered, clearly in shock.

"You get your wish."

"I never said—"

"You didn't have to," I snapped.

Her face turned to stone. "I certainly won't stop you," she said, straightening her hat.

My eyes found the cherry wood planks as she slammed the back door, leaving Mr. Thompson and me alone in the foyer. "I'm sorry," I said, hanging my head. "That's not how I meant to tell you."

"Grief has a way of speaking for us in the early days," said Mr. Thompson. "I would know."

A tear slipped down my cheek. "I miss him so much."

"So does Marcie."

My lip began to tremble. "I don't know what to do with this —*feeling* inside of me," I stuttered. "It feels like I'm going to burn up from the inside out."

"You go to Paris," he said. "For him, and for you."

I wiped my eyes.

"Have I ever told you about my first wife? Dane's mother?"

"No," I breathed.

"Her name was Celia." A flash of recognition washed over him. "She was born in the spring, with curly blonde hair and hazel eyes. She loved to paint watercolors and plant flowers. I proposed to her with a sapphire ring and I lost her far too young." He sighed softly. "It's been over twenty years and there isn't a day that goes by that I don't still think of her. Do you understand what I'm saying?"

"I think so."

"You won't ever be who you were," he added. "But if you're lucky, you'll be better."

"Surely not," I said, surprised by his words.

"Do we not love more intensely after a loss? Do we not cherish every second?"

"I don't know," I admitted.

Mr. Thompson only smiled at me kindly. "You will."

Holden always said New York would suit me, and I only needed to walk into Grand Central Station to see that he was right.

Leaving his blazer on my bed upstairs for someone else to find, and telling no one where I was headed, I'd boarded the *Fredericksburg to New York,* a new woman entirely. I scanned the alluring atmosphere as I stepped off the train with two suitcases and my Corona typewriter, completely awestruck. I noted the women in their flashy summer fashions and haircuts that mirrored my own as I tried to keep their pace on the stairwell.

In the main terminal, sunshine spilled from the arched windows onto the sparkling marble floor, lighting the way for hundreds of men in business attire. My eyes followed the columns upward, to the cyan mural above me. I counted the various constellations—Orion, Gemini, Cancer, Pegasus—that stretched across the ceiling, dropping my suitcases at my side. "Stars and moons," I whispered.

"Excuse me."

I was jarred back to reality when a woman bumped into me,

almost sending me flying into someone else. Having learned my first lesson of the city, I made my way to the clock in the center of the room, where I'd been directed to meet my escort.

"Miss Morgan?"

A bald man in a linen suit found my side.

"Joe Heany," he said. "I'm here to take you to the *Sun*."

"How did you know it was me?" I asked, out of breath from dragging my luggage around.

He looked me over with his yellow-green eyes. "You can usually tell when someone's never been to New York."

"Fair enough," I replied, following him to the main exit. "Are you a journalist, Mr. Heany?"

"I'm an editor. Ever been to Paris?"

I let out a nervous laugh. "I've never been to Europe."

"I hope you like nightlife." He held the door open for me with a laugh. "Paris is full of it."

"I don't sleep well these days, anyway," I added, greeting the exhaust-filled street with a hopeful smile.

Chapter Twenty-One

Paris, nine months later

Empty glasses and half-full champagne bottles littered every surface of my Lenox Hotel apartment, including the marble-topped desk that housed my typewriter. It had come fully furnished in art deco style when I'd signed the lease. Along with its balcony, which promised fine views for people watching, it had been the *location* that sold me, only a few blocks down from the Montparnasse crossroads.

Such an atmosphere had proved both conducive at times and distracting at others.

It had been a long night.

And as for the illustrious socialite sprawled across the edge of my bed, she'd proclaimed herself my new best friend.

I'd been minding my own business under the awning of the Café du Dôme, waiting for the downpour to cease, when she'd joined me outside. I had seen her before—the tearful, blonde vixen from the Lenox—always walking the street below my balcony, dripping her wealth all over the cobblestones.

"Don't I know you?" I asked.

Her dark eyes, blackened from her running makeup, glanced up at me through her golden locks. She sniffled. "Pardon?"

Despite sharing a building for over half a year, she and I had never exchanged so much as a wave. "I live next to the Lenox Hotel," I said louder, realizing that she couldn't hear me over the thunderous rain on the awning. "We're in the same building."

"How quaint," she replied in a soft, diluted New York accent.

I offered her a cigarette, which she grabbed promptly and lit with a match. I was blown away by her beauty as she pulled out a small mirror and began to piece herself back together. Her full lips were shaped in a natural pout, the perfect complement to her arched brows and doll-eyes.

"They're only gin tears," she said to herself, wiping her under eyes with her thumb. "Do you have a sweetheart, love?" she asked, turning to me.

"Not anymore."

"Not *anymore*, hm?" She took another inhale, eying me doubtfully. "Look at you," she said, blowing the smoke between her plump lips. "I wish I had that problem. It's been one after another for me."

"Why do you put yourself through it?"

"It started with my fiancé." Her smile was nothing short of wistful. "I followed him here years ago after he turned up missing after the war, but I've had no luck, and there's no reason a girl should be lonely in the meantime."

The cynic in me wanted to laugh. "You're a romantic, then."

"Aren't we all?" she asked, flashing a gorgeous smile.

Amused, I cast my gaze to the flooding streets.

"What happened with your sweetheart?" she asked, scooting closer to me.

"You'd have to ask him."

Beneath the expatriate role I'd assumed, and its lifestyle tapered with gin and sweet vermouth, the streets of Paris were haunted. When I'd imagined traveling to France, I never imagined it would be alone—*he* was supposed to be there with me. And many times, I was certain I'd caught a glimpse of his face in a crowd or busy café.

After awhile, I'd begun to question if *I* were the haunted one.

"Have you ever considered that it wasn't meant to be?"

My gaze found the puddles, forming rivers among the cobblestone. "Trust me when I say that it was never meant to be."

She nodded, looking intrigued. "Well, you know what they say, love. Everything happens for a reason."

"No," I said, turning to her. "Things just happen. And then other things happen."

"What was it that brought you to Paris, then?"

"I'm a journalist."

"Oh? Who for?"

"The *Herald*."

"*Everyone* works for the *Herald*." A sly smirk. "Aren't they in some sort of trouble now?"

"The paper is probably going to be sold."

"To the *Tribune*, yes?"

"How did you know?"

"I've dated a journalist or two," she said, puffing a smoke ring.

"Frankly, as long as I get to keep my job, I don't care who I'm writing for."

"A working woman."

I clenched my cigarette between my teeth, freeing up my hand. "I'm Lou," I said, reaching to shake.

"Edie Cohen," she said, taking my palm within her manicured red fingernails. "All right, Lou from the *Herald*—have a drink with me. I'll buy."

"I have a piece due tomorrow."

"What do you write?"

"Fashion and lifestyle."

"*My specialty.*" Edie eyed me like a cat. "Consider me your source."

I was tempted, and she could smell it on me.

"Come on, neighbor," she coaxed. "I'm in desperate need of a friend. Just one drink."

It was *not* one drink.

In one night, Edie had spewed her entire life story—that she was an heiress, born to the owner of a hotel chain in Manhattan. That she'd been happily engaged to an American officer who had turned up missing after the battle of Belleau Wood. She'd sworn up and down that her fiancé was still alive—that one day, he'd find her in Paris, and she would drop whomever she was with at the time in the name of true love. She'd spent the whole night telling me about herself, never once asking me about my life.

All the better.

I rose to my feet like the living dead, feeling my way to my desk. Plucking a glass from the sticky marble top, I emptied the remaining champagne from the nearest bottle into it and took my seat.

"Lou," Edie groaned.

I sipped the lukewarm bubbly as I gazed ahead at my typewriter, hoping it might starve the hangover long enough for me to write my piece.

Edie flopped onto her back on the bed behind me. "*Lou,* are you going to ask me about fashion?"

Chapter Twenty-Two

I walked briskly through the puddles in my powder blue raincoat, notebook in hand. I'd stumbled upon La Closerie a few days prior —a smaller café, happily tucked away in the 6th arrondissement —and thought it might be a nice change-up from my apartment balcony and the Dôme. I needed fresh scenery that morning. Somewhere unfamiliar, and full of distraction.

It was June 17, 1922. Holden's birthday.

Greeted by the rich aromas of coffee and wine, I posted up at an empty window seat in the café. With a summer shower on the horizon, I knew it would only be a matter of time before the rain drove in stragglers from the street. A group of Bohemians sat behind me to my left, and by the look of their cluttered table, they'd been camped there awhile. The ladies had just had their hair waved, and thought the whole café should know.

It had been fortuitous on my part to chop off my own locks. Perhaps I'd wave mine too.

"Mademoiselle?"

I met the eye of the waiter as I shed my coat. "Café au lait, s'il vous plaît."

I opened my notebook and tapped my pencil against it, waiting for the inspiration to strike me.

"Lou...?"

I paused in recognition of the voice. *"Theo?"* I asked, whipping around.

His hair was long and curly, soaked by the rain, but the face was unmistakable, despite how it had thinned around his dark eyes.

"I thought that was you," he said.

"Teddy!" I looked to the table of Bohemians, and the empty seat he'd abandoned. "I didn't even see you sitting there—what are you doing here?"

"No, sit. I'll sit," he assured, pulling the small wooden chair out from the other side of my table.

"You're in *Paris,* Theo," I said again, unable to believe it.

He leaned over, smiling gleefully. "I know, me in Paris! I don't think anyone could have seen that coming. How the hell are you? Are you still working for the *Herald*?"

I held up my notebook. "Well, it's the *Herald Tribune* now. What about you—how'd you end up here?"

It was as if he didn't quite know, himself. "I just couldn't stay anymore. Everything felt too bleak."

"I can understand that."

"I'm renting a flat in the Latin Quarter," he went on. "Finally laying down some roots after traveling for the last six months. I've been to Florence, Venice, Tuscany. Spent a bit of time in Switzerland..."

"Sounds like an absolute adventure."

He motioned to my bob. "The hair suits you."

"You as well," I replied, doing the same.

I knew it was only a matter of time before the unnerving subject came up. It was, after all, the only thing we really had to talk about.

"Tell me," he said, "have you talked to anyone?"

"No. Have you?"

A solemn shake of his head. "I thought about stopping by the shop to see Mr. Thompson, but I just couldn't do it for some reason."

I cleared my throat as the waiter delivered my coffee. "You *do* know what today is, don't you?"

"Listen" —Theo leaned back in his chair, crossing his arms— "should we get some *vin?*"

I looked to the waiter. "S'il vous plaît."

With record speed, a bottle of Cahors arrived.

"Goddamn, I'm glad to see you, Lou," Theo gushed, pouring me a glass. "But it's downright odd that I run into you today of all days."

"I'm sorry I never wrote. I meant to."

"I thought about writing to you once or twice myself, but I didn't have an address. Jamie said you left in a hurry." He paused as if to catch his tongue.

"He was right," I said, sensing his discomfort. "How is Jamie? Do you know?"

Theo shook his head. "I'll bet he's managing. I'm sure he'd love to see you when you get back."

"Get back?" I asked, chasing my words with a hefty sip of wine. "I have no intention of going back."

Theo laughed, filling his own glass.

"I know it may sound wrong," I confessed, "but I just want to leave the whole thing behind."

"I don't think anyone would blame you for feeling that way. I certainly don't."

"How is Scott?" I asked.

"Old Scott has made his way out to Colorado. We weren't the only ones who needed..." Theo's eyes drifted over my head, widening with astonishment and wonder.

"There you are!" Edie scolded, hustling to our table with a bright smile. "I positively thought you would be at the Dôme—you will not *believe* what happened to me this morning—oh, who's this?"

Chivalrous as a knight, Theo rose to his feet, taking her hand. "Theodore Elliott," he said. "An old friend."

"Charmed." Edie's eyes dropped down to her hand, resting in his. "Are you from—where are you from, again, Lou?"

"Virginia."

"Yes! Are you from Virginia, Theodore Elliot?"

"Baltimore," he replied, at last releasing her.

"I'm from Manhattan, but I've been living in Paris since just after the war," she said. "My name is Edith Cohen, but you can call me Edie."

"Here—please. Take my chair."

I sipped my wine, unnerved by their immediate chemistry. Edie had no shortage of men interested in her, preferring whirlwind romances to commitment. She would eat Theo alive.

"Tell me, Theodore," she said in a low, sultry voice, "what are you doing this evening?"

"I was actually about to ask you two the same thing."

Edie raised her perfect brows. "Oh?"

"We're going out." He motioned to his table of friends. "I'd love it if you joined us," he added, turning his attention to me. "I have some friends I want you to meet."

Edie shot me a mischievous grin, and I shook my head *just* enough to decline—

"We can hardly wait!" she exclaimed.

I pursed my lips.

"You must tell me how you met Lou," Edie went on, lighting a cigarette. "She is dreadfully private, Theodore."

"Well," he began, "I met Lou through Holden—"

"Let's get another drink," I suggested.

"Holden?" Edie turned to me. "Who's that?"

I swallowed hard. "Holden Thompson. A friend of ours…my…"

Edie's eyes turned soft. "The sweetheart."

"He died," I said, shooting Theo a guilty look. "Rather tragically."

It was true that I'd made Holden a promise at his funeral—that I wouldn't let anyone forget him—yet I drowned his memory in late night aperitifs and the company of strangers with true dedication.

Edie sighed. "Oh, Lou."

Reaching into my raincoat pocket, I pulled out his infantry portrait. "I don't normally carry it," I said, handing it to her. "But it's his birthday today."

Her eyes studied the picture. "What a pretty fellow," she said, returning it to me.

"Theo! Are you coming?"

Theo turned over his shoulder, to his group of friends who were waiting to leave. "Let's go."

By the time we left La Closerie, the rain had passed, leaving behind a light fog and humidity, which did my hair no favors. Edie and Theo lagged behind me as we made our way down the left bank, following his group of nameless acquaintances.

"Where are we going again?" I asked.

Receiving only silence, I turned around to see Theo's full attention on Edie, who was whispering to him.

"It's just right up here," answered one of Theo's lady friends. "Listen!" She cupped her ear over her waved, ebony bob. "You can hear the music."

I *could* hear it. Jazz music, blaring loudly.

Theo's friends charged the tiny door of the smoky Bal Musette in an excited frenzy as soon as it came into view.

"Here we are," he said, following suit.

"And where exactly is that?" I called after him, having fallen behind.

But walking through the door, I could see that Edie had pulled Theo to the dance floor right away.

Daunted at the prospect of standing alone in an unfamiliar place, I squeezed in at the bar. I managed to spot my friends soon enough, due mostly to the fact that the entire bar was looking their way. Much like Holden, Edie had a talent for attracting attention, and every man in the room watched as she shed her blush raincoat, revealing a shimmering, sequin-encrusted slip of a dress underneath. There they twirled, a juxtaposition of my past and present.

Holden had told me of the Bals Musette and how much fun they were—unless you lived above one. Perhaps in an afterlife of his choosing, he'd be a fly on the wall in a place like this.

"Mademoiselle?"

I followed the voice over my shoulder to the bartender. "Oui?"

He slid a stemmed glass of red wine to me, nodding toward the other end of the bar. "Du monsieur au manteau brun."

I looked around for the man in a brown coat, weaving my eyes between the patrons until I at last landed on a young man in a worn, tawny blazer. My admirer stood quite tall with mousy-colored waves almost to his shoulders, and a wallflower demeanor.

"Merci," I mouthed, toasting him.

Filled with a nervous, *gripping* excitement, I turned forward, returning my gaze to Edie and Theo in the crowd. I hadn't felt even a spark of interest in anyone since Holden had died. But this one…

Something about him was particularly alluring. Enchanting, even.

"Bonsoir, mademoiselle," said the stranger.

I grinned, giddy to make conversation with the lovely Frenchman who'd appeared at my side. "Bonsoir," I replied, turning to him.

He was even taller up close, and I felt my heart begin to beat rapidly under his gaze.

"Parlez-vous français?"

"Oui, je suis Américaine."

"Hello, then."

I laughed. "You're not a Frenchman, but you could have fooled me," I said, taking a sip.

His eyes narrowed on me, a striking green. "Have we met before?"

"I don't believe so."

"Are you sure?" he inquired again. "I feel like I recognize you from somewhere."

"I'd certainly remember you, if we had."

He pursed his lips in a grin, revealing a matching set of dimples on each cheek.

"Thank you for the wine," I added.

"I couldn't help but notice you standing over here alone."

"I'm not alone," I said. "I'm just not in the mood for dancing much tonight. Or any night, really."

"What do you know about that? I'm not either." He leaned in closer. "Is that your friend out there?"

"Edie." I laughed. "Yes."

Of course he would notice her.

He pointed into the crowd. "And that's my friend, dancing with her."

"You know Theo?"

He turned around, setting his pint down on the bar behind us. "He was a good friend of my brother's."

"Your—your what?"

I felt as if I were the bluebird that had just hit the shop window.

"Theo was a friend of my brother's," he said, pivoting back to me. "Would you like another glass?"

All the wine in the world wouldn't have been enough.

"I see you two have met," Theo interjected, back from the dance floor.

My admirer's smile dissolved, and it was immediately clear that he'd been just as clueless as me.

Theo looked between us. "I'm awful at introductions—"

"Dane! Why didn't you write?"

The words tumbled out of my mouth.

"Well." Dane reached for his beer. "I suppose I should have asked your name."

"I thought you were in Italy," I stammered.

Holden's brother cocked an eyebrow at me. "I *was* in Italy."

Now that I knew, I couldn't *unsee* the resemblance.

"Why didn't you write home?" I asked again.

His gaze was impressively tranquil, which only made my blood boil more.

"It was pretty easy to forget about him all the way over here, wasn't it?"

"I could say the same for you," he said, finishing the last of his beer.

"I was there when it mattered."

"And I am grateful to you." Dane looked to Theo with a solemn nod, saying nothing more to me before he turned to walk away.

"How predictable!" I called after him through the thick crowd.

"Well done," said Theo, wiping the sweat from his brow. "*Well done,* Lou."

Edie joined his side, out of breath but full of smiles.

"You could have warned me, Theo!"

"I was going to introduce you—it's not my fault that out of everyone in the goddamned bar you ended up finding each other first," he argued. "I thought you'd want to meet him."

"I told you I wanted to move on—"

"Move on, fine! But you can't just pretend that the whole thing never happened," he countered.

"I was doing just fine until I ran into you!"

"*Doing just fine.* I don't buy it."

"Well, Theo," I said, seething and teary, "I don't know what to tell you. I'm a lousy actress."

My friends were no match for the force welling inside me. My heartache had turned to blind rage—to *fuel.* Pushing my way through the horde, I ran down the riverbank until I couldn't feel my legs.

I *had* wanted to meet Dane—when Holden was alive, and life made sense. Now, the only thing Dane and I had in common was his dead brother.

I turned onto a sleepy street, pitiful and exhausted. I'd long lost my sense of direction, and utterly defeated, I collapsed onto a small patch of grass outside of a few duplexes. Tear after tear slipped down my nose as my mind flooded with memories of Holden. Some funny and warm, others dismal—but all of them poignant.

"Please," I prayed to him under my breath. "Please help me find my way back home. You owe me that much."

Hearing the approach of footsteps on cobblestone, I wiped my face.

"Dare I ask what you're doing out here?"

I turned to meet the figure. "Some answered prayer," I said, rolling my eyes. "What do *you* want?"

Dane motioned to the building behind me. "I live here."

I glanced at the duplex behind me in disbelief.

"Come inside," he suggested.

I looked up at him combatively. "Why would I want to do that?"

"Because you're lost," he replied. "Unless you sought me out on purpose."

I shot to my feet. "I did nothing of the sort."

"If you're lost, then come inside." He stepped onto the grass to meet me. "You've had too much to drink and you're alone."

"All reasons not to trust a stranger."

"Do I feel like a stranger?" he asked. "You don't feel like a stranger to me."

"You don't know me at all," I protested.

"Of course," he said, eyeing me intently. "No one ever really knows anyone."

The glow of the full moon shone through the large window,

lighting his humble flat as I followed him in. It was hardly lived in, with a few open suitcases and countless jars lying about. The only art he had appeared to be his own, stacked haphazardly against every wall. Even in the dark, I couldn't help but notice that many of the paintings looked incomplete.

Dane lit an oil lantern, splashing the warm light of flames over his desk and some letters scattered about. Or rather, the beginnings of letters—as if they too had remained unfinished.

"You can sleep in my room," he said.

I blushed. "In your bed?"

"I'll sleep out here." He motioned to the sofa in the corner. "It's right there to the left."

I bundled myself in the unfamiliar bedsheets, which smelled nothing of Holden or their childhood room. I wanted to sleep, to end the day, but my eyes burned when I tried to shut them. I watched the light dance through the crack of the door, trying to remember all the things Holden had told me about his older brother, which wasn't much.

I awoke in the shabbily furnished room, forgetting at first where I was. But the recollection flooded back to me as my eyes adjusted to the blue shades of twilight.

It was the last place I'd ever dreamed I'd wake up.

Wrapping myself in the blanket, I slipped down from the bed, peering through the cracked door. Dane lay curled up on the sofa, fast asleep. A dozen paintbrushes rested in a jar of water on the floor next to him. I tiptoed my way to the large window, unlatching it. With just enough room on the ledge to sit, I climbed up. It was an exceptional view of the quarter below, with its staggered buildings and uneven rooftops, all washed in the colors of sunrise.

Light on his feet, Dane found my side, leaning his shoulder on the opposite side of the window frame.

I couldn't help but look over at him, standing with his arms crossed. In the daylight, his tousled waves were only slightly darker than Jamie's and Marceline's. I could see the bags under his eyes even in the pink glow illuminating us both. He reached to tie his hair back, as if he were suddenly aware of its messiness.

I scanned the sky, pointing toward the sun. "Mercury should be right there."

"The messenger."

"The psychopomp," I said, turning to him.

I wondered how I could have missed the obvious resemblance as he smiled.

"He—*Holden,* told me that you used to stargaze together," I added.

"Since we were old enough to sneak out onto the roof."

"I think you can learn a lot about someone by their favorite constellation."

Dane cast his gaze over the rooftops, smirking just slightly. "What is your favorite constellation?" he asked, taking the bait.

"Cygnus."

"Why Cygnus?"

"Well, there are many things to admire about swans."

"Like…"

"For one, they mate for life."

"And that's something that's important to you?" he asked. "Mating for life?"

I tucked my cheek into my cupped hand, feeling myself blush. "If I had any interest at all in mating—which I *don't*—then yes."

"I see," he replied, continuing to gaze forward. "You really *can* learn a lot about someone by their favorite constellation. Already I have learned an interesting thing about you."

"Not only that" —I cleared my throat— "but certainly you're familiar with the swan song? They sing to mourn their dead."

"You think that is admirable."

"I think it is brave." I turned to look at him. "It is much easier to run from pain."

"When I think of Cygnus, I think of the swan who seduced Leda," he replied. "Mother of Castor and Pollux."

Castor and Pollux, the celestial twins, one born mortal, the other immortal.

I leaned forward, hugging my knees. "Is that *your* favorite, then? Gemini?"

Dane didn't answer, but he didn't have to. I was plenty familiar with the story of Castor's death, and how Pollux chose to split his immortality with his half-brother so they'd never have to be apart.

After all, it was Holden's constellation.

"He would've been thirty yesterday," Dane said finally.

His rueful tone was one I knew well. The grief of what could have been.

"I don't know what came over me last night," I said. "Sometimes, I just..."

Dane squared his shoulders. "The wounded do wound," he said, walking away.

"How did you know it was me?"

"I didn't until you said something. But your reputation precedes you." He grinned. "A tiny brunette with a tongue like a knife."

Taking a knee next to a recent painting, Dane began to collect stray brushes, dunking them in the jar with the others. I could assume by the richness of the paint colors where most of his money went.

"Did you paint that last night?"

"Not entirely," he replied. "Just touching it up."

I slipped down from the windowsill and made my way to the canvas for a closer look. Layered thickly with oil paints in an impressionistic style was another cathedral, similar to his painting that hung in the Thompsons' hallway.

"Duomo di Siena," he said. "One of the most magical places I've ever set foot in."

"How long did you live in Italy?"

"About two years." He paused. "I didn't know you lived in Paris."

"I moved here for work—we might have passed each other on the street and had no idea."

A breeze brushed past me, rustling a few of the letters on the table. The flat took on a whole new identity in the dawn, and was rather charming when fully illuminated in daylight.

"May I look at the rest?" I asked.

"Be my guest."

I fingered through the canvases that leaned against the wall—some Parisian street scenes, some landscapes, some abstract. "You're very talented," I murmured. "Are you self-taught?"

"Experience is the best teacher."

I held up a small portrait. "Who is she?"

"I don't know," he admitted. "I saw her in a dream."

"You must have dreamt of her quite a bit to remember her face so well."

"On and off through the years," he said, walking over.

I handed the canvas to him. "Do you think she looks like me?"

"A little," he said, staring hard at the painting before handing it back to me. It was obvious he had more thoughts on the subject, but he kept them to himself.

"Do you know where I can find Theo?" I asked, returning the canvas to its resting place.

"I can take you to his flat," he replied, gathering the jars. "If you give me a few minutes to clean these."

I circled the room as he tidied, turning my head to read the book spines stacked on his desk. "*A Spring Harvest* by Geoffrey Bache Smith."

"Do you like poetry?" asked Dane.

"Well enough."

"The author was killed in the war. His collection was published posthumously by a friend."

I picked up the thin paperback, opening to a random page.

ONE I LOVED WITH A PASSIONATE LONGING,
BORN OF WORSHIP AND FIERCE DESPAIR,
DREAMED THAT HEAVEN WERE ONLY HAPPY
IF AT LENGTH I SHOULD FIND HIM THERE.

"It's quite heartbreaking, as you'd imagine," Dane added.

I looked up at him, shutting the book. "Just like my life."

He looked for a moment as if he might laugh.

"I know," I said. "That *does* sound like something Holden would say."

"He always did have a grotesque sense of humor."

"Indeed—like the time he told Marceline's husband that he was the eldest because you'd been *lost to them* in France."

Dane looked me over with a stunned grin, blinking once. "*That* was the joke, then," he murmured.

"I'm sure you can envision the charade," I replied, mirroring his smile. "With all his dramatics."

He nodded to himself, biting his lower lip.

"Are you all right?"

Dane let out a laugh, meeting my gaze. "Nothing quite like finding out you've died."

Chapter Twenty-Three

"Chez Theo," Dane announced.

The flat, overtaken with ivy, had been only a short walk from his own.

"Thank you," I said, turning to him. "For everything."

"Good luck." He held out his hand. "It was nice to meet you, Lou."

"It was nice to meet you too," I said, taking it in mine.

I could almost see it—a tangle of invisible thread stretching from one of his fingers to mine—as if it were the fabric of Holden himself, tying us together.

"Perhaps we will bump into each other again, if fate allows it," I added.

His brow rose in amusement as he pocketed both hands. "Perhaps."

A melancholy settled in my chest as I watched him disappear around the bend, and I wondered how much I could learn about Holden from Dane. If I could somehow come to understand who he had been *before.*

I peered through the window of Theo's duplex, my eye following a trail of garments to the back of the sofa, where I could see his arm dangling. I tapped on the glass, loud enough to wake him.

Theo jolted upright, looking aghast at the sight of me.

"Lou?" Edie mouthed, shooting up from the other end of the sofa.

I shouldn't have been surprised to see her there, but I still ducked with embarassment. A minute or two passed before Theo opened his door.

"What— "

"I'm sorry," I pleaded.

"Lou," said Edie, joining him in the doorway. "What are you doing here?"

"Yes, what *are* you doing here? How do you know where I live?"

"It's kind of a long story."

Theo pinched the bridge of his nose, still looking half-asleep.

"Dane brought me here," I said. "I stayed at his flat last night."

"You what?"

"I said it was a long story…"

"I see that," Theo replied. "You know, you didn't have to get so angry with me last night."

"This sounds personal, so I'm going to leave you two to it, all right?" Edie squeezed past him, her shoes and coat gathered in both hands. "I'll see you back home and you can tell me all about it." She glanced back at Theo, blowing him a kiss. "You know where to find me, Theodore."

Theo's gaze slid past me as he watched Edie make her way down the cobblestones, barefoot.

"Theo, please don't—"

"Come inside," he said, stepping back so I could enter. "From the beginning, please."

"This is going to sound strange," I warned.

"With the way things have been, I very much doubt it," he said, closing the door behind me.

"He found me wandering around outside his apartment. I was lost."

"And you spent the night."

"Not like that," I clarified. "Though it was a kindness on his part that I didn't deserve."

"It's in his nature. Did you talk about Holden?"

"Some."

"And you got on well?"

"I think so."

"Well, I'm glad to hear it." Theo's sigh was one of relief. "I meant to formally introduce you, for the record. I was just a little…distracted."

"I see that." My eyes darted to the sofa. "How did you even *find* him?"

"I tracked him down when I was in Italy and wrote to him. He convinced me to come to Paris for a while since he'd just moved back."

"I'll admit, I've wondered about him…where he was living, what he was doing. I never imagined I might run into him." I smirked. "Then again, I didn't imagine I would be running into you, either."

"As a matter of fact," Theo added suddenly, "I'm glad you're here—there's something I want to give you." Disappearing around the corner, he returned with a familiar black box. "A gift."

"Holden's typewriter?"

For all its importance to him while he was alive, I'd never once questioned where it had ended up.

"I've been lugging this thing across Europe," Theo went on, handing it off to me.

I ran my fingers over the silver latch. "How did you…"

"Bette," he said, reading my mind. "I met up with her once at their old cottage before I left the States."

"She's living there?"

I'd almost forgotten they'd still legally been married when he died.

Theo nodded. "Last time we spoke, she'd been offered a job cleaning the artist's studio next door."

I let out a laugh, fighting teary eyes. "What am I going to do with this, Theo?" I asked, lifting the box with a limp arm.

"Write a goddamn masterpiece, Lou," he replied. "That's what you're going to do with it."

I could see a sadness falling over him, as if something were bubbling that he couldn't quite pinpoint.

"You know," he said, taking a seat on the sofa, "sometimes I still wake up in the middle of the night in a sweat thinking he hasn't done it yet and I still have time to stop him. Fucking *bastard.*"

"He told me that you hit like a girl."

Theo laughed, but when I turned to look at him, I saw that he'd buried his face in his hand.

And I realized he was *weeping*.

Stoic Theo, who'd been my rock the day of the funeral.

"I'm not the one who should be here, living the life he wanted to live," he stuttered. "It's not supposed to be me, and for fuck's sake—just when I think I've gotten to the bottom of this godforsaken well of grief, I realize I've been tricked, and it just keeps coming."

"But if not us, then who?" I asked, kneeling at his side. "Who picks up his torch if it's not us?"

Theo raised his head to look at me.

"Theo..." My voice shook. "Don't you think—that by some strange design—we *are* supposed to be here?"

"Like we were led?"

"I know how it sounds, but sometimes I—I swear he's speaking to me in some sort of language I can't decipher."

"His spirit, you mean."

"I don't know," replied, backtracking. "I don't know what I mean. But I refuse to believe his life was for nothing."

• • •

It was around ten-thirty when I finally got back to my flat, desperate for sleep. But that fantasy died when I turned the corner and saw Edie waiting outside of my door.

I greeted her in a tired stupor, clutching Holden's typewriter to my chest as if it were made of gold.

"Lou," she began, blocking my entry, "you *have* to tell me what happened between you and that man last night, I— what's that?" She motioned to the box.

"It's nothing," I mumbled, nudging past her.

"It doesn't look like nothing," she said, following me into my flat and closing the door behind us.

Laying the black box on my bed, I collapsed next to it.

"Let's have breakfast."

I lifted my chin to see Edie tapping my wall with her long nail.

"You absolutely cannot say no, because I'm buying," she chirped.

Running on about three hours of sleep with far too much on my mind, I found myself sitting in a chic deco style restaurant with Edie chattering next to me.

"You should have the salmon benedict, Lou. It's divine."

"I'm not very hungry," I said, eyeing the peacock feathers frilling the banisters.

"Espresso for her, then, s'il vous plaît." She glanced up at our waiter with a smile. "And tomato juice."

Edie's breakfast arrived looking enticing.

She dabbed her lipstick on a napkin, taking a sip of her coffee. "Tell me, who is Dane and why do you detest him so much?" she asked, pushing the plate in my direction.

She must have heard my stomach growling.

I smiled, picking up my fork. "Dane is Holden's brother."

"And you hate his brother, why?"

"I don't hate him," I replied, cutting into the poached egg.

Edie leaned inward, her eyes full of questions, and I thought this must be what it feels like to be on the other side of myself.

"A lot of complicated family business," I warned.

"Shall we order a second benedict?"

It came more easily than expected—summarizing it all. "I didn't want to marry him at first," I confessed. "I didn't want to marry anyone. I was just a nervous child, which perhaps time could have fixed, if only we'd had more of it."

"I don't suppose you want to hear this right now, but I like to think it'll happen to you again someday. You can have more than one great love story. I would know!"

"Speaking of" —I pointed my folk at her— *"please* be gentle with Theo."

Picking up her napkin, she wiped off her smile.

"Besides, I'll never find another Holden," I said somberly. "I don't know if I'd even want to."

"What about his brother, then?"

It was a joke. I knew it was a joke. But I could feel my cheeks turn *hot*. "Now you're being ridiculous," I said.

"Am I?"

She wasn't. If the gentleman in the brown coat hadn't been Holden's brother, the night might have ended quite differently. I wouldn't lie to myself, but I *would* lie to her.

"I'm not interested," I replied plainly.

"Famous last words."

"Nothing happened! He was just—"

"Shhhhh."

I could tell by the way she tilted her cheek that a nearby conversation had attracted her attention. Edie was a shameless eavesdropper.

"What is it?" I mouthed to her.

She held up a finger.

"A Romani camp just outside the city," she said finally. "I'll be damned." Her eyes lit up. "Lou we've *got* to go."

"You want to have your fortune told?"

"You *don't?"*

"We could go to Montmartre for that."

"Montmartre is full of charlatans! We need a *real* fortune teller."

"You don't even know if that's what they're talking about," I said at last.

Edie flashed me a pearly smile, and before I could stop her, she was walking toward their table.

"*Excusez-moi,* ladies. I couldn't help but overhear..."

I watched from our table as the women paused their meal to speak with her. It took Edie longer than I would've expected to extract the information—probably because she was so fluent in flattery.

"Drabadi Vadoma," she said, swiftly taking her seat. "That's who we need to seek out."

"What does she do?"

Edie grinned, smoothing her hair. "I hope you don't mind, but I shared a bit about our *situations.*"

"You don't mean—"

"What do you think, Lou?" she asked. "Would you like to speak with Holden?"

I watched the shifting scenes of streets and cars fade into rural pastures from the backseat of a taxi. The drive out of the city was quiet, and an opaque fog lingered in the air, both of which only added to the ghostly ambiance of our journey.

Speak with Holden, she'd said.

I thought to myself as Edie buzzed in the backseat next to me: what would Holden want to say to me? And how could I be certain it was him? The thought made my stomach churn.

The driver stopped abruptly, pulling onto a grass-covered road. "It's over that way," he said, motioning to the edge of the woods. "This is as far as I can take you."

"Would you wait for us?" Edie asked, slipping him a few bills. "One hour."

I shuddered, squeezing my arms in my raincoat as we stepped

out. Through the fog, I could see a village of colorful wagons with a glowing campfire at its center. Edie looked over at me but made no move, as if she were second guessing herself.

"This was your idea," I reminded, stepping ahead to lead the way.

I began to feel equally uneasy as we walked through the dewy grass. A young girl with dark hair, about fourteen I guessed, popped out from behind a tree.

"Bonjour," I greeted. "Hello."

"What is your business here?" the girl replied in broken English.

I could tell that she was wary of me, so I didn't approach her. "We're here to see Madame Vadoma."

She held out her hand expectantly, and I looked to Edie, who was quick to pull out the payment.

"I will take you to her," the girl replied, clasping her fingers over the coins. "I am Tzeitel."

"Lou," I replied, bringing my hand to my chest. "And Edie."

Tzeitel lifted the length of her skirt, motioning for us to follow. We cut through the smoky woods to the campsite, which was much bigger than it looked from a distance. The jumble of wagons, in a patchwork of color and varying states of disrepair, had a cacophony of life teeming both within and without, and the inhabitants stared as we walked by.

Holden had told me once that the Parisian attitude toward the Romani people was generally an unwelcoming one, which was all the more reason for them to avoid the city.

"Drabardi's vardo," said Tzeitel.

Edie turned to me. "Do we just walk in?"

Tzeitel climbed the three stairs, disappearing behind the mauve, tasseled curtain. I'd hardly taken in the intricacies of the jewel-toned wagon when she reappeared, pointing at Edie.

"You first," I murmured.

I found a seat on a nearby bench as Edie disappeared behind the curtain. Cinders from the crackling fire floated on the breeze, catching on colorful, patterned blankets that hung on a nearby clothesline. The fog from earlier was dissipating, and I hoped I might take that as a metaphor.

When Edie stumbled down the stairs of the caravan fifteen minutes later, she was as white as a specter. I tore myself from my seat as she approached me.

"I feel like I've just woken from the longest dream," she whispered.

I wanted to ask her what happened, what she'd been told, but Tzeitel was beckoning to me. Edie held my troubled gaze as I pulled away, mouthing to me "good luck."

The inside of the caravan was lit by a single clerestory, which was enough to showcase the craftsmanship of its wooden interior; its built-in drawers and shelves, painted with green and gold. The elderly drabardi waited on a cushioned bench to my right, directly across from a cast-iron stove. Another set of curtains draped over a bed in the back.

Tzeitel ushered me to the bench. "Sit here."

The drabardi peered past me with colorless, cloudy eyes as I sat beside her, in front of a deck of playing cards. When she began to speak, it was in her native Roma tongue.

"Drabardi Vadoma says a little bird told her you would be coming," said Tzeitel.

I glanced up at the young girl, realizing she'd be translating between us.

"You are here to speak with the young man with eyes as blue as the sea," Tzeitel went on, talking over her. "Is that correct?"

Tongue-tied, all I could manage was a whisper. "Yes."

"She says he visits you often."

"Is he haunting me?"

Tzeitel turned to the drabardi, repeating my question in Roma. "She says he is *guiding* you. To follow the thread he has left."

I wiped my hands across the cushion, watching Tzeitel meet the drabardi's gaze with a shake of her head. "Your name…is not Natalia," she said, turning to me. "Correct?"

"It is Louisa."

The drabardi mumbled something, then pointed to the playing cards that sat between us.

Tzeitel nodded, collecting them. "We will not use these for you," she said, opening one of the many drawers. "Draw four cards," she said, handing me a *different* deck.

Feeling their dual gaze, I shuffled the cards as best I could, then took one off the top and flipped it over onto the cushion.

LE MAT

The first card showed a jester, off on an adventure with a little dog at his side. Tzeitel spoke in Roma as I drew three more cards in succession, laying them all in a row. A French description stretched across the bottom of each.

L'AMOUREUX

LA MAISON DIEU

LE BATELEUR

The second card showed an illustration of Cupid, aiming his arrow of love toward three unaware people below. The third card —the *House of God*—was frightening in appearance, with people tumbling from a tower that seemed under attack.

• • •

"They tell a story," Tzeitel began, speaking over the drabardi. "A story of a young soul that comes to a crossroads where she must choose." Tzeitel paused. "Then the choice is made for her."

I pointed to the final card, which looked to me like an alchemist at his station. "And what of this one?"

"The fourth card has not happened yet," Tzeitel relayed. "It is your future."

I studied its image—of a man at his desk, surrounded by tools.

"It means to give form."

The drabardi lowered her voice, speaking in long, drawn out sentences.

"She says to look for him in the wind, the sky, in the people you meet. That you will always find him there."

The right side of my face began to tingle, as if I were being touched—caressed, even—by some invisible force. I wanted to laugh, I wanted to cry. I wanted to reach right back through the ether.

Tzeitel gathered the cards, handing them to me. "She would like to give the cards to you."

I searched the drabardi's eyes, framed with crow's feet. "Thank you," I whispered.

I burst out of the caravan, feeling as though my insides were on fire, and that no amount of air or water would calm the burning.

Edie shot to her feet. "Lou!"

I met her, clutching the deck of cards.

"What happened?"

I laughed, still stunned, hardly able to get the words out. "The universe whispered back to me."

Chapter Twenty-Four

After my visit to the camp, everything seemed to fall flat in comparison. Staying out all hours of the night had lost its appeal, and even my Parisian apartment had taken on a dull and uninspiring flavor. But the world around me—the moving, *breathing* world around me—felt somehow more alive.

I sat on the floor of my flat, with all the cards of my deck laid out in a half-moon in front of me. I'd spent a lot of time studying their imagery, but with no guidebook or instructions, I didn't know how to use them. It was unlike any deck I'd ever seen, at least in comparison to the ones folks traded in the cafés of Montmartre. They had not been the drabardi's usual deck either, I had surmised. Gathering them up again, I shuffled mindlessly as I circled my room.

I didn't know what to do with myself.

I'd been feeling a pull to write, but my half-hearted scribbles on the newest summer fashions had ended up in the waste bin. It was hard to care about trends and tabloids with the thought of Holden's spirit lingering around, probably wondering why I'd yet to take his Royal out of the box.

I missed him. No amount of spiritual revelation would change that.

I walked to the nearest window and looked onto the street below. Couples walked hand-in-hand alongside the hungover bachelors and wealthy businessmen that littered the rue. The sky was bright but cloudy, almost too blinding to look at. My gaze wandered across the street as I absently shuffled, with no intention of drawing a card. But one slipped from my fingers, falling to the floor.

ROY DE COUPE

"King of Cups," I murmured, reaching for it. I'd no sooner risen to my feet when a figure on the other side of the window caught my attention. He walked briskly past the other pedestrians, sporting a worn overcoat and tied-back hair.

Dane?

I hadn't seen him since our chance encounter, though I'd considered inquiring about him to Theo—if I ever saw Theo again. I'd hardly seen him *or* Edie since they'd first met.

I banged on the windowpane and the figure halted, almost as if he'd heard me.

It had to be him.

When I burst onto the crowded rue, I was still trying to shove an arm through my raincoat. I'd left in a hurry, pocketing my deck and flying down the stairwell, hoping I could still catch up. It was busier than it had looked from above, and a few cars honked their disapproval as I skipped across the road. I sprinted down the street, at last catching sight of my objective about to cross the street—

"Dane!"

I swallowed my words when the man turned around, looking at me with a puzzled expression. The eyes were a different color, the smile was all wrong.

I laughed, a bit winded. "Je suis désolé—I thought you were

someone I knew." I directed my attention back to the fork in the road, feeling suddenly grateful the man had been just another phantom.

What the hell would I have said if it were Dane? I hardly knew him.

A market swarmed to my left, carrying the smell of sweet pastries through the warm afternoon breeze. I followed the scent into the crowd, just bored enough to peruse the vendors, who were camped out with their produce and artisanal goods. It was always the flower carts that attracted me most, filled to the brim with lilies, dahlias, roses and peonies, and I gravitated to the first one I saw.

Nodding to the vendor with his newspaper, I fawned over the mid-summer blossoms. It was an especially lush cart.

"I do believe you have walked into my painting…"

I looked up from the tulips to see Dane Thompson standing to my left, wearing a white shirt with an open collar that was covered in paint. "I…" I turned over my shoulder to see his station set up behind me. "I have *quite literally* walked into your painting!"

"We meet again after all," he replied, looking amused. "This is what happens when you taunt the fates."

I laughed, tucking a stray hair behind my ear. "Do you come to Montparnasse often?"

"Often enough. And you?"

"I live around the corner, next to the Lenox Hotel. Do you know it?"

"I do."

"May I see what you're working on?"

Dane motioned me over to the wet painting on his easel, where milky whites, pinks and yellows were painted on in thick swirling patterns.

"It's not finished, but" —he took a few steps back— "stand back a bit, and then look."

I obliged him. "Oh!"

"Do you see the picture better?"

"I do. Would you look at that."

"*Kalopsia,*" he added. "The illusion of things being more beautiful than they actually are up close."

I caught his eye, but he wouldn't hold my gaze.

"Something is off on this side, though," he critiqued, picking up a brush.

Fascinated, I watched his hand make the indigo brushstroke.

"I've missed this," he murmured, dipping the brush.

"What?"

"Having someone stand over my shoulder and watch." He looked up at me with a hint of a smile. "I work well under pressure."

"Then it's my—"

"Non!"

Dane and I turned to the flower cart in front of us, where a woman stood before the irate vendor with her daughter, no older than five. He was yelling and pointing at them, spewing hateful words from beneath his mustache, and saliva all over the blooms.

"Why is he speaking to them that way?" I asked.

"They're German." Dane laid his paintbrush down, rising to his feet. "Guten tag," he called, walking over to them. "Was möchten Sie kaufen?"

The woman pointed to the lilies, speaking too quietly for me to make out her words, not that I could understand them anyway.

"How much for six lilies?" Dane asked, turning to the man behind the cart.

"I don't sell to Germans. How many times do I have to say it?" he replied in broken English.

Dane stepped closer. "I'm American. How much?"

The man glanced between him and the German woman with a look of pure disdain.

"How much?" he asked again.

"For *you,* three francs," said the man.

Dane stared at him for a moment, not moving an inch. He

must've known he was being overcharged. Still, he dug into his pocket and handed over the money, returning to the woman with a bouquet of lilies. He chatted with them for a few minutes before the woman reached into her pocketbook and tried to repay him, which he declined.

"It really is a beautiful language," said Dane, again finding my side.

"That was kind of you."

"She was visiting the grave of the girl's father." He took a knee, beginning to pack up his things. "A French soldier."

"I see." I posted myself against a tree as I watched him carefully place the painting in a pochade box.

"It is a tiresome mentality," he added. "The need to hate someone because they are different."

Already, I could see the ways in which he and Holden were alike.

Dane shot to his feet, wiping the dust from his pants. "Anyway, what are your plans for the rest of the day?"

"Oh," I replied, caught off guard, "I was just going to get something to eat."

"Are you hungry?"

"Just for a croissant or something small—the pastries smell lovely."

He nodded, meeting me with an enthusiastic grin. "In that case, would you like to try the best pain au chocolat you've ever had?"

"Right now?"

"It's a bit of a walk, but" —he shrugged— "if you don't have any plans..."

"I don't." I crossed my arms over my chest. *"The best I've ever had?"*

He stepped into the crowd of market goers, coaxing me to follow. "I swear it."

We abandoned the noisy industriousness of Montparnasse for the quiet stillness of the left bank as the overcast skies of the morning dimmed under another thick layer of clouds. I couldn't help but study him as we walked. Dane was a bit taller than Holden, closer to their father's six-foot-three, but his build was similar. The coat he wore with patchwork on the elbows looked as if it had braved many winters. Bits of dried paint could be found on nearly every part of him, from his hands, to his hair, to his clothing.

"Word on the street is that you're a journalist," he said, making small talk.

"I write for the *Herald Tribune*."

"The *Herald Tribune*." He sounded impressed. "You must be a wordsmith."

"I cover Arts and Culture for the paper," I replied. "But between you and me, I'm most proud of the two pieces I wrote for *Vogue*."

"*Vogue*? I feel underdressed," he joked.

"Your coat is well-loved."

"It used to have holes." He extended his elbow with a laugh. "Holden fixed it for me."

"Did he?"

My smile fell, and by the way Dane turned forward again, he must have noticed.

"I'm sorry, I'm just not used to having anyone to talk about him with," I said as we turned onto rue de l'Odéon. "I went so long without even saying his name."

I could sense Dane felt more or less the same, but he wouldn't say it out loud.

"Here we are," he said, halting in front of a cornflower blue shop front.

I peered into its magnificent front window, gaping at the countless pastries stacked behind the glass. Delicate sponge cakes topped with whipped cream and cherries sat on display, begging to be tasted as we entered the pâtisserie.

A young lady behind the counter turned to us with a warm smile. *"Dane,"* she gushed.

"Comment ça va, Camille?"

"I'm well. I—what a delight!" Wiping her hands on her apron, she walked around to greet him properly. "And how are you?" she asked in a low, tender tone, finding his arm with her hand.

It was immediately clear to me that the two of them had a history, but what kind of history, I couldn't say.

"I'm all right," Dane assured. "How is Lady?"

She giggled, beaming up at him. "She's the fattest cat you ever saw!"

This brought a smile to Dane's face.

"And who's this?" she asked, turning to me.

All smiles and dirty-blonde curls, Camille's beauty was intimidating, and I couldn't help but feel very plain next to her. She was sunshine incarnate.

"This is Lou," Dane replied. "My friend."

His *friend*. It felt almost strange to hear Holden taken out of the equation entirely.

Camille looked between us. "Welcome, Lou," she said, taking my hand.

I almost felt a familiarity in her brilliant hazel eyes, as if a mysterious thread connected us too.

"What would the two of you like?" she asked, turning to Dane.

He brushed his hair from his face, stepping toward the glass. "I promised Lou the best pain au chocolat she's ever had."

"Bon, deux pains au chocolat." Camille ducked behind the counter, collecting our pastries with tissue paper. "On me," she said, handing him the bag.

Dane only grinned, once again confirming their closeness. "Merci beaucoup, Camille."

"It was lovely to meet you, Lou."

"And you," I said, trailing Dane out.

By the time we stepped back outside, the wind had picked up. We took a seat on a nearby bench, surrounded by a few pigeons scrounging outside of the pâtisserie.

"As promised," said Dane, offering me the bag.

I pulled out the flaky croissant, sinking my teeth into it. A look of amusement washed over Dane as I nodded my satisfaction.

"She is the best in the city," he said.

"Who is she?" I asked, bringing my hand to my mouth to catch the crumbs.

"She…" He found the sky above us with a nervous smile, as if he were pondering the best way to answer. "Camille knew Holden."

I swallowed hard, lowering my croissant. "I didn't realize he'd had liaisons in Paris."

Dane met my eye. "Many."

I could have assumed so from what little he had told me, but being confronted with it was another thing entirely.

"She's very beautiful," I added, biting awkwardly into the croissant.

"Believe me—you got the best version of him."

"I had thought it was *you* who had courted her," I admitted.

Folding his arms over his chest, he leaned back on the bench. I studied Dane's profile—the hint of a smirk—as though he couldn't help but acknowledge the irony. Now I understood.

"She chose him," I said, realizing.

"It was hardly a choice." He shifted in his seat. "Holden was…much better at that sort of thing than I am. He talked to her first."

I stared into the hollow caves of my croissant. "And when he left?" I asked.

"We kept in touch until I moved to Italy, and she got married."

My eyes followed his fingers as he picked the paint off of his knuckles. "She has a fondness for you. I could see it."

"But it was him she wanted." His eyes glimmered when he turned to me. "No one wants to be somebody's second choice."

I took another bite of my croissant. "There's still so much I don't know about him," I mumbled through my chewing.

"Perhaps there are some things you'd rather not know," said Dane.

"No," I replied truthfully. "I want to know everything."

Dane grew quiet, crossing his leg over his knee.

"Of his liaisons," I began, "does the name Natalia ring a bell?"

His brow furrowed, but he shook his head. "No one named Natalia. Why do you ask?"

I cleared my throat, settling in. "Edie and I visited a Romani camp, and the name came up when she read cards for me."

"In regard to Holden?"

"It wasn't entirely clear, but yes, I think so."

Dane tore off a piece of his croissant, dropping it to the pigeons below. "Tell me, what did you think of the camp?"

My lips parted to speak, but nothing came out. For the first time since I'd left my flat, I thought of Holden's spirit, and I wondered if he might be around us. "It was eye-opening," I said, glossing over the details. I pulled the deck of cards from my pocket. "She gave me these."

"Tarocco di Marsiglia."

"You're familiar with it?" I asked, handing them off.

"It is a Tarot de Marseille." Dane flipped through the worn, colorful cards. "A peculiar deck to be found at a Romani camp."

"How do you know all of this?"

"I've met a few Travelers in my day," he replied.

"The deck did seem out of place there," I admitted. "She originally had another in her hand."

"Lenormand," he said, handing them back. "Most likely."

"Do you know how they work?"

He shook his head. "That is where my knowledge ends."

"I wish I could read them."

"I'd wager that you can. The folklore says the most special decks are given as gifts, and this one seems to have found *you* rather than you finding *it*."

I flipped over the top card. "This one is following me," I joked. "I drew it in the caravan." I looked over to Dane, who seemed absorbed in thought. "He looks to be some sort of alchemist or magician."

"You know, Holden used to say this thing about writers being magicians—I forget the exact phrasing." He shrugged, tapping the card with his finger. "Maybe the card is supposed to symbolize you."

"Or him," I added.

"Or him."

A pair of pigeons cooed at my feet as I took in the surrounding shops, noticing the blocky exterior of a storefront across the way. "Shakespeare and Company," I said.

"You've never been?" Dane replied, reading my mind.

"Blasphemy, I know."

"Let's go," he declared, picking up his pochade box. "Maybe we can find a guidebook for your deck."

"Do you think?"

"You wouldn't believe the things that end up there. The things people leave." He shot me a coy grin. "I know the owner."

I stood up beside him. *"Oh,"* I replied, brushing the crumbs from my dress. "Another one of Holden's *liaisons?"*

He laughed over his shoulder. "No—not this time."

The sky was darkening as we crossed the street to the buzzing, literary mecca. The inside of the shop felt more like a boarding house than an establishment, with folks trading books and sorting their mail on the counter. A gentleman lay across one of the many cushioned benches, one leg propped with his typewriter on his lap. Surrounded by stacks of books teetering on every nearby surface, the petite, sophisticated woman who smiled at Dane looked completely in her element.

"Sylvia," said Dane. "This is my friend, Lou. She's a journalist with the *Herald Tribune."*

That garnered the attention of a few of the men floating about the room.

Her short waved bob swung above her shoulders as she reached to shake. "A few of our friends have written for the

Herald," Sylvia replied. "Welcome, welcome! Don't mind the mess—I can't seem to get rid of these loiterers."

"Sylvia," teased one of the stragglers, "have I told you how becoming your hair looks today?"

The way she rolled her eyes confirmed that she was kindred with them.

"Make yourself at home," she added. "*As you can see,* everyone else does."

Leaving Dane to converse, I strolled through the narrow doorway into the back, where another gentleman typed away at a desk with a copy of Joyce's *Ulysses* at his side. The titles were numerous in every direction, with each shelf stocked to capacity. It was the kind of place you could walk through a hundred times and still not see everything.

"What do you think?" Dane asked, popping around the corner.

"I could get lost in here."

"I have. Many times."

"I remember when you used to send Holden books in the mail," I said as we began to wander. "Did you come here often with him?"

"This is the newer location," Dane replied. "But Sylvia opened it in the fall of 1919, when Holden first came to stay with me."

I laughed, perusing the multitude of spines. "He's told me about the flat you shared above the Bal Musette."

"If you can call it a flat, yes." Dane shivered as if he'd felt a sudden chill. "It was close quarters."

"This might come as a strange question," I said suddenly, "but what was he like *before?*"

"Before what?" He eyed me intently, in a way that made me wonder if his response was a trick question.

"I don't know—the war, I guess?"

"Ah." There was relief in his voice. "He was…studious, highly creative. He loved animals."

"He sounds much the same, then." I walked over to a shelf in the corner, noting the leather bound volume of *Greek Mythology* inscribed with gold cursive. "But he always used to talk of *before.*"

Dane turned his back to me. "See anything you fancy?"

"A good many things, but I never buy on the first visit."

A low rumble filled the dense room, shaking the chandelier above our heads. From the doorway, I could see the thunderheads on the horizon. Men hanging around the shop's window gathered their things, joining everyone else inside.

"I should head home," I said.

"I'll walk you back to the crossroads."

"You don't have to."

"I want to."

Another crack of thunder.

Dane guided me to the door, looking back over his shoulder to wave at Sylvia.

"Stay dry!" she called.

A few raindrops had left their mark on the stoop of the shop.

"Do you think we'll make it?" I asked.

Dane held his palm to the fast-approaching storm clouds above. "We've got plenty of time," he said.

We did *not* have plenty of time. A block and a half away, the sky opened up. We hurried down the sidewalk, ducking under a shop awning as fellow street goers disappeared into shops and cabs.

Dane slid down the wall, taking a seat as the thunder echoed through the streets. "I stand corrected," he murmured.

"Is your painting all right?"

He picked up the pochade box, wiping the remaining water off with his hand. "All's well that end's well."

I turned to him, mirroring his grin. "One of my favorites of Shakespeare."

"There's a line from that play that I've always loved." His eyes glazed over as he looked outward. *"The web of our life is of a mingled yarn."*

My voice was a mere whisper. "I adore that."

Dane watched the downpour with heavy eyes and a worn expression. I could tell he was thinking about him.

"The night after Holden died, there was a huge storm just like this one," I added.

"How is the family getting on?"

"I haven't spoken with any of them since I left," I confessed. "You could write and ask?"

"I have. I've just never sent the letters."

I thought about the unfinished letters piled on his desk.

"It's not for lack of caring, despite what people may think," he said, rubbing the paint marks off his wet hand.

I felt a sudden ache, realizing the cutting effect my words must've had on him when we first met. "We didn't know where you were or if you'd received the telegram," I said.

"I did." He began to wring his hands, in the same anxious fashion that I did. "I was painting someone's ceiling when a friend I was living with brought me the telegram."

"The ceiling commission," I whispered. "I remember him telling me about it."

"I couldn't bring myself to write back. I know it seems cold. I just don't know how else to be and I don't know what to say."

The rain slowed as I sighed and looked over at him. "Words are fickle things, aren't they?"

"They are."

An unspoken understanding settled between us as we sat there together, damp from the rain and humidity. After some time, the sun was drawing steam from the puddles in the road, which we took as our cue to move on. Neither of us said much as we resumed our walk to the crossroads, joining the rest of the city as they too began to emerge from their hiding spots.

"Thank you," I said finally. "For the company and the croissant."

"I have one last thing to offer you…" Dane reached into the lining of his coat, pulling out a pocket-sized booklet.

"You found one! When?"

"I asked Sylvia when you went off on your own," he replied, handing it to me. "She had one right behind the desk."

I fanned its stained, worn pages. "*Rider Waite Tarot,*" I read. "1909."

"It's for a different deck, but the meanings should be the same."

"Thank you, Dane."

Thanks didn't seem to suffice. And with the Lenox in view, I felt the impulse to share.

"Life has felt so dull lately," I admitted. "But *you*—I feel like I've stumbled upon this missing puzzle piece of his life. Holden always talked so highly of you."

Dane nodded to himself, as if he were pondering how to feel about it all.

"I—I loved him very much," I blurted out. "I hope you know that."

"That makes two of us," he said, turning to me.

"Do you want to come up and dry off?" I asked.

I sensed a slight discomfort from him as we crossed the deserted street to my apartment.

"I should probably go," he said.

"Of course. I have some things I need to do anyway," I lied.

"Au revoir, Lou."

It took everything in me not to call after him as he walked away. Then, as if he were considering the same thing, I watched him slow to a halt and turn back.

"Perhaps we can try running into each other on purpose sometime?" he asked.

Chapter Twenty-Five

"And then—" I could hardly catch my breath I was laughing so hard. "*Then,* Holden went over to her and said what Dane had told him to."

Edie giggled as she folded a blouse, adding it to the pile of clothes on her floor. "And what was he told to say?"

I doubled over in a cackle. "*Tu es moche.*"

"Oh, that is *cruel!*"

"It still worked out in his favor if you can believe it," I added. "That was Holden's charm."

Edie dropped her lashes to her lap, reaching for another blouse.

"Why are you looking at me that way?"

"It's a joy to see you so happy, that's all."

"You don't think I was happy before?"

"Not like this…"

I reached for a dress. "Edie, don't—"

"You've been spending *a lot* of time with him," she added. "I've hardly seen you all summer!"

"That's because you've been with Theo," I reminded, motioning to the mess of clothing that surrounded us.

Edie had all but moved in with him, slowly giving away or

getting rid of her belongings, which meant a wardrobe update for me.

"That's not the only reason and you know it," she teased.

Dane and I had spent many wine-soaked evenings on the patio of one café after another, recounting our stories of Holden and drawing tarot cards. He'd told me all about the trouble Holden had gotten into when they lived together—how he'd begged Dane to teach him French so he could flirt better with the French women, and how he'd frequented the bars of Montparnasse, smoking opium and making unlikely friends. In return, I'd shared stories of home—of living above the shop, where he'd lived as a child, and working beneath. I told him about Jamie and Marceline and what they were like, since it had been so long since he'd seen them.

"It's been such a comfort to have someone to connect with over his death," I said finally, turning to Edie. "Grief creates ties between people. And Dane—he's…a lovely person."

"I'd be curious to know what he thinks," she jeered. "Perhaps I'll ask him when we meet up at the Dôme."

"*Please,* don't," I cautioned.

Edie shoved the pile of blouses off of her lap. "Speaking of the Dôme, this should suffice for today—we need to get ready!"

I watched from my place on the floor as she began to rummage through the dresses on the bed. "I thought you were wearing your crimson gown with the fringe?"

"No." She laughed as if I should know better. "I'm looking for something for *you* to wear."

"I was just going to wear this…"

Edie pouted at my black and tan set. "Oh, wait," she said, reaching into her closet, "I have just the thing!"

She quickly tore the paper bag off of the hanger, revealing a sheer, sage green cocktail gown. The flapper dress was sleeveless with a low collar lined with gold, and threaded hummingbirds on the bottom.

I held the dress up to my reflection in the mirror.

"It brings out your eyes," she said, resting her chin on my shoulder. "You can have it. It suits you much better."

I threw the dress over my slender frame. I'd never worn something so revealing.

"Shall I draw a card for the night?" I asked, dabbing my lips with a maroon lipstick.

"You're getting quite good at those," she said, kneeling next to the vanity as I pulled out my deck. "Ask if Dane will like your dress."

"Don't tease."

A card slipped out of the deck as I began to shuffle. Edie and I exchanged a glance, then looked down.

"La Maison Dieu." I grimaced at the illustration of a tower being struck by lightning. "The Tower."

"What does it mean?"

"Unexpected upheaval."

Having begun my own study of the tarot, I'd come to associate it with Holden's death.

"It just fell out," Edie assured, likely noting the way my face paled. "It probably doesn't count."

I nodded to her, returning the cards to my purse.

If it weren't for my gnawing anxiety, I might have taken more interest in the plethora of stares we attracted as we walked in the twilight toward the noisy café. I was filled with a thought that frightened me beyond belief. That history might repeat itself somehow, that the same thing could happen again if I—

"Good evening, gentleman!" Edie ran up ahead to Theo, planting a kiss on his cheek.

"Now I feel *very* underdressed," Dane murmured to me as I found his side.

"I was helping Edie declutter her closet."

Arms around Theo's neck, she turned to Dane. "She cleans up well, doesn't she?"

I could feel myself blushing.

"Why don't we go to La Rotonde instead," I said suddenly. "The Dôme looks packed."

There was one table left under the neon lights with a full panoramic view of the crossroads. Edie sat down and immediately lit a cigarette, resting her legs over Theo's knee. He ordered a bottle of champagne for us, then another. By the third bottle, Edie had started a conversation with a rowdy table of expats to our right.

"You're quiet tonight," said Dane. "And...I've come to know you enough to say that is unusual."

I grinned guiltily.

"Are you all right?"

"I am," I lied, reaching for Edie's cigarettes across the wobbly bistro table. "I just, um—I've been thinking a lot about you and me."

Dane's brows peaked just enough for me to notice.

"Just what wonderful friends we've become," I added. "I cherish it so much. Having another person to talk to."

"Oh—so do I," he answered quickly.

Too quickly.

Was he disappointed?

"Do you think you're going to stay in Paris for good?" I asked, feeling myself turn red again.

"I can't say," he said, swirling the bubbly in his glass. "What about you? Are you ready to move on yet?"

I was feeling it.

I'd felt this feeling before...

This warmth.

"At some point I'll have to go home, won't I?" My hands were fidgeting so badly I couldn't strike a match. "Do you ever think about going back?"

"I don't think there's much for me to go back to anymore."

Shocked by his answer, I looked at him, perplexed. "Not even to visit?"

"I think it's a bit late for that," he murmured.

"...not like this lovely lady!"

A lit match descended as if from the heavens, lighting the end of my cigarette. I closed my eyes and inhaled, feeling an arm wrap around the back of my chair.

"Has anyone ever told you that you could be in the pictures?"

I reopened my eyes to see one of the expats from the neighboring table extending a hand to me.

"I'm Alex," he said.

"Lou," I said, taking his hand hesitantly.

"This is my brother Freddie and his lady." He motioned to another man who'd joined our table, and the seductive redhead who accompanied him.

"Listen," said the brother, stroking his mustache, "after we're finished up here, we were going to head down to Le Select. Do you want to join us?"

Ever the social butterfly, Edie turned her attention to our new friends with an enthusiastic laugh. "Le Select. We'd love to come, wouldn't we, Theo?"

"Whatever you want."

"Le Select..."

I turned to Dane, who spoke as if he knew it well. "What's it like? I've never been."

"It's a bit rough around the edges," Alex interjected. "But it's a lot of fun."

Upon entering the loud, crowded bar that smelled heavily of whiskey, it was clear that Edie and I were overdressed. Alex kept bumping into me, but whether it was an irritating flirtation or just clumsy drunkenness, I couldn't say. The seven of us made our way toward the back, commandeering a large round table and ordering several bottles of Chablis. Edie listened with frightened eyes, clinging to Theo as Alex and Freddie began to tell war stories, both becoming more belligerent with each sip. I would've rather spent the evening walking the Seine with Dane, who now sat adjacent to me, looking just as bored and agitated.

He must have felt me staring, because he met my eye from across the table. "What?" he mouthed to me.

I only smiled and shook my head.

"Do you really think it's true?" Edie took a hefty sip from her glass. "That it was the war to end all wars?"

Alex let out a belting laugh.

"It's magical thinking," said Dane, chiming in. "For as long there is man there will be war."

Freddie turned to him. "You don't think we showed them well enough?"

"I don't believe the world has seen the full impact of what happened here." Dane folded his arms over his chest. "People are mistaken if they think this won't be a stain on human history. Children will be holding their fathers' grudges for years to come."

"What about you, then?" Alex asked. "Did you serve in the AEF?"

"My brother did. I was in Italy with the Red Cross."

"I didn't know that," I interjected.

Dane shrugged at me shyly. "It just never came up."

"Well thank God for you Red Cross boys. Especially for the Brits, poor lowly bastards needed all the help they could get," said Alex, gulping his glass of wine.

"What was your brother's name?"

Dane looked to Freddie. "Holden Thompson. He was a captain —108th infantry regiment, 27th division."

"No shit!" Alex slapped the table. "You're brother to the Reckoner?"

The Reckoner.

The wave of recognition that washed over Dane told me that he'd connected the dots to Holden's story too.

"I was with the 106th in Ypres," Alex added. "Your brother led a huge counter assault with my regiment! He had this shotgun, see—just charging a trench, blowing them to bits. I'd never seen anything like it."

Dane was unnerved. Uncomfortable. Caught off guard—I could tell.

"It's a small world," said Theo, breaking the silence.

"What happened to the old Reckoner, anyway?"

Dane tapped on the table, dropping his gaze. "He hung himself last year."

"That's disappointing," said Alex. "I expected more."

"What the hell does that mean?"

Alex met my gaze under the beads of sweat forming on his forehead. "Things were heinous. That's the way it was. You don't see me indulging in cowardice—"

"You don't know when to stop talking, *do you?*"

The table went deathly silent.

Alex only smirked. "It seems, ladies and gents, I have hit a sore spot," he said, clutching his chest. "I didn't realize his widow was present. I assume that's you?"

I held my head high, unashamed. "Yes."

A smug smile took hold of him. "He made a mistake leaving such a pretty little thing behind," he said, tracing my neckline with his gaze. "Are you lonely?"

"Pig," I spat.

"I would be more than willing to take his place in your bed."

And then it happened.

The Tower.

Dane cracked the empty wine bottle over his head, sending shards of green glass flying.

Freddie shoved him violently against the wall as Alex hit the floor. "Do you want to join your brother!?" he shouted, squeezing his neck.

"Maybe I do," Dane replied, struggling to breathe.

Theo lunged across the rickety table, jumping to his defense. Grabbing Freddie by the collar, he yanked him off just in time for Alex to spring to his feet like a wild poppy. In a screaming rage, Edie grabbed another wine bottle and launched it at him. Freddie's redhead took cover as its glass rained down over her—and over Dane, who coughed on the floor.

"That's it!" yelled the bartender. "Get the fuck out of my bar!"

"Excuse you!" Edie shouted back. "How dare you speak to a lady that way?"

I grabbed her. *"Edie—"*

Another smash quieted the room.

When I turned back around, Dane had Alex pinned to the wall with a broken piece of glass to his neck.

Alex relaxed in his grip. "I took you for a pacifist."

"Do not *fucking* talk to her like that," Dane breathed.

Alex laughed as the glass point pressed into his neck. "Oh, this is rich...does she know?" His gaze slid past Dane to me. "Does she know how you feel?"

I could see the way Dane's shoulders tensed up. I could feel the burning in his chest as if it were my own.

Alex's smile was full of blood. "I guess she does now," he taunted.

"Are you deaf!?"

Dane released Alex and dropped the glass, revealing bloody imprints on his palm.

"I said get the fuck out of my bar!" the barman yelled again, grabbing Dane by the arm and shoving him toward the door. "That means all of you!"

Dane was already hustling down the street by the time I stumbled out the doors of Le Select with Edie and Theo.

"Dane, wait!"

"I don't want to talk about it," he called back, crossing the road in a hurry.

"Your hand—" I picked up my pace, following at his heels. "Is your hand hurt?"

Dane turned around to face me as we stepped up onto the sidewalk. "I don't want to talk about it," he said again, stumbling over his words. "When he said that to you I...I completely lost control in there."

"It's my fault—I'm the one that antagonized him."

"Holden wasn't some sort of merciless killer, nor was he feeble-minded—his life was *stolen* from him, he never should have been here." He brushed the hair from his forehead, leaving a small streak of blood. "He didn't die with honor on some foreign field. He just died." He turned to look at me. "And I couldn't save him from that."

I wanted to speak, to comfort his agony, but the words were impossible to find. "Is it true?" I asked. "What he said in there?"

Dane shook his head and cast his gaze across the street, more as a refusal to answer than a no. "I'm not Holden," he said, turning back to me. "I never will be."

"I—"

He held his hand up in protest when I tried to walk with him. "Don't follow me, Lou."

A breeze whipped around my face as I watched him leave. I knew that his grievances were about more than Holden's death, or him and me. It was the mangled intersections of our lives, and the feelings of loyalty and guilt that knotted our stomachs.

"Is he all right?"

I turned to Edie, who'd found my side, along with Theo.

"Cocksucker had it coming," Theo mumbled, pulling out a cigarette. "He deserved everything he got as far as I'm concerned."

Edie tugged on my arm.

"I need a car," I said.

"Didn't he say…"

"He did." My eyes darted between them as I stepped toward the curb, holding up my hand. "But grief does strange things to a person."

I wouldn't make the same mistake a second time—of letting someone go who was clearly in distress.

Not with The Tower nearby.

Dane's apartment was dark when the cab dropped me off. A fog had started to fall along the riverbank, blanketing the city lights in an otherworldly glow. Taking a seat outside of his door, I plucked a few pieces of grass and began to shred them anxiously. It was an all too familiar wait.

Dane *wasn't* Holden, but my heart braced for impact all the same, as though I were back in the shop, looking down at his initials in the appointment book.

Don't follow me, Lou.

I closed my eyes, breathing deep.

"We've got to stop meeting like this." Dane's silhouette walked into view beneath the streetlamp as I reopened my eyes. "I told you not—"

I could tell by his rigid stature that he didn't know how to react as I leaped to my feet, squeezing him to me with all my might. Slowly, he wrapped his uninjured arm around me.

"I was scared," I whispered.

He pulled back to examine me. "Scared?"

Looking into his mossy-colored eyes, I didn't know how to say it, or if I even should. "I was afraid you…"

He pulled me in close, with all the tenderness that Holden had shown the bluebird with broken wings. "Life is too short already," he murmured. "I have no desire to end it prematurely."

I didn't loosen my grip on him.

"Do you want to come in?"

I looked up at him, timidly. "May I?"

He grinned, cocking an eyebrow. "That was much easier than last time."

I hadn't been back to his flat since the night we'd met, and following him through the door filled me with a fond nostalgia.

Dane lit a lantern, then dipped into the kitchen to clean his hand. "I'm going to be paying for this one for a while," he called back.

"Why do you say that?"

He emerged with his left hand wrapped in gauze, holding a bottle of wine and two glasses.

"Your painting hand!"

"How's Theo?" he asked, uncorking the bottle.

"A little beat up, but I wouldn't worry. Edie will take good care of him. How are *you?"*

Dane smiled with a slight wince as he poured me a glass. "I feel like I got the shit kicked out of me," he admitted, handing it to me.

A laugh slipped out. "I thought you excelled for someone who claims to be nonviolent."

"You could say I've been caught in Holden's crossfire once or twice," he said, taking a seat on the sofa. "I don't want you to think that's something I normally do."

"Defend a woman?"

He grinned from ear to ear, but looked away.

"Thank you," I added, sitting next to him. "By the way."

"It was my pleasure." He took a sip from his glass. "Truly."

"Why didn't you ever tell me about the Red Cross?"

Dane shrugged. "It never felt worth bringing up."

"You're far too humble."

There was a slipperiness to the flow of our words—as if either of us could, at any moment, say something that might veer us into dangerous territory. And then of course there was the *other thing.*

What Alex had said at the bar.

"I think I should try to sleep off this self-loathing," said Dane finally, downing the rest of his wine.

One glass was good.

One glass was *wise.*

I stood up rather abruptly. "All right, well…"

"It's late," he added. "You're welcome to stay if you like."

My gaze found the bedroom door. "I'll stay, then."

"Uh, do you—"

"No," I interrupted.

"I don't mind the sofa."

"But you're hurt." I tucked my hair behind my ear. "You need it more."

"We could just…"

"Share the bed," I finished.

It was very well where I might've ended up the first night we met, had I not discovered his identity. Instead, I'd spent an entire summer getting to know the gentleman in the brown coat—never once acknowledging the initial, undeniable spark between us. Was it the spark of sincere attraction? Or the spark of Holden drawing us together?

I didn't know.

Dane kept to his side of the bed—in fact, he seemed to lie as far away from me as possible. His breathing was shallow, much like mine as I stared into the darkness. And then, I felt him flip onto his back.

"I don't…"

I turned over to face him.

"I don't expect anything from you," he said. "I respect what you had with Holden. You made his life better."

I smirked in the dark, tucking my hand under my cheek. "He told me once that of all the things in his life he was proud of, his relationship with you was the first."

A few minutes passed before Dane spoke again, and when he did, I could hear that he was on the verge of choking up.

"I would give anything to have him back."

"Like Pollux did for Castor?" I whispered.

"Like Pollux did for Castor."

I reached for his hand in the dark, taking it into mine. "Do you ever…" I swallowed hard with a throat full of fire as he inched closer to me, bringing our faces mere inches apart. "Do you ever think that if you let yourself feel, then" —I blinked, allowing a tear to trickle down the side of my nose— "what you love will be taken away from you?"

Propping himself on his elbow, Dane leveraged himself over me. I could feel his stare in the dark. Soft and hesitant. And then I felt his lips brush across the wet streak of my cheek. His thumb trailed the kiss, wiping away the last of my tears as his mouth found mine. His hair was soft and wavy in my hands—his kisses, wonderfully deliberate.

"Yes," he whispered, withdrawing just enough so he could pull me in closer. "I do."

I turned onto my side, and feeling his sigh on the back of my neck, I closed my eyes.

I returned to my flat in a conflicted state of mind the next morning, blind to any and all the commotion happening in my hall as I hustled toward my door.

We'd fallen asleep that way—with entwined limbs and pulsing heartbeats. And I'd woken up counting the freckles under his eyes, watching as his eyelids fluttered with dreams. Dane had stirred only slightly when I left—when I'd whispered only that I had to go.

Had it been our connection through Holden, or was it something else?

Could there *be* a "him and me" without Holden?

"Yes!"

"Well then, unlock the box!"

I slowed my step, stopping to observe the husband and wife three doors down from me. Two large trunks partially blocked my path. The couple seemed to be bickering, and yet, their conversation had somehow aligned perfectly with my inner dialogue.

"Oh—sorry for the mess," the woman said suddenly, reaching to maneuver the trunk that obstructed me. "My aunt just died and we're in the process of going through her estate."

"It's all right," I replied softly, walking around them. "My condolences."

Holden's portrait, caught in the lining of my vanity mirror, was the first thing my gaze fell on when I opened my door. But as I closed myself inside, it was something else that seemed to watch me.

Holden's Royal, sitting on my desk.

"Unlock the box," I whispered, unclipping the latch.

It was as pristine as I remembered it, with its intricate gold lettering. I pulled it carefully out of the box, setting it on the table. "I wonder if you still work," I mumbled, peering down into the typewriter. I blew sharply, sending bits of dust flying.

Then I saw it—

The ribbon.

Dismantling it, I unwound the roll delicately, holding it up to the window so I could read it.

Bette,

I know the last conversation we had wasn't the most pleasant and I'd like to apologize for that. I hope you don't feel that our time together was in vain. I do not. We learned a lot from each other, you and I. For all of our grievances, you are still important to me and I hope that you are well, always.

Love,

Holden

The last message he'd ever written. I wondered if Bette had ever received it. If it had ended up in the burn pile, or if it had gotten lost when he died. I laid the unraveled ribbon carefully on the desk and loaded a new one into the Royal as if I'd used it a hundred times before. And I began to type.

"Hello up there! Lou?"

Abandoning my half-typed letter, I opened my balcony door to see Edie waving frantically below.

"Down here!"

"What is it?" I called down.

"It's Dane! Do you know where he is?"

Unable to resist the gossip, street goers stopped to listen.

"Hold on," I said, leaning over the rail. "I'm coming down."

Only a few hours had passed since I'd left him asleep, and I couldn't imagine what Edie could possibly want with him so early—

"Lou!" she hurried over, meeting me just outside the door to our building. "Theo went to check on him this morning to make sure he was all right after last night. And—and he's not there! Everything is gone!"

"Gone?"

"He left this." She pulled a folded note from her purse, handing it to me.

GONE TO FIND CASTOR

"Who is Castor?"

"A myth," I murmured.

"Did he say he was leaving?"

"No." I was still as stone. "He didn't."

Edie looked me over as she bit her nail, looking unsure of what to say.

"Well," I breathed, handing the note back to her, "everything is really gone?"

"All of the important things. Typewriter, clothes, some painting supplies. Why would he just vanish without a trace?"

I knew why.

And I'd forgotten that like Holden, he *too* had a reputation. That trying to hold onto Dane was like trying to hold onto water.

THE MAGICIAN

manifestation – agency – creation

December 1922 — March 1923

Chapter Twenty-Six

I shot up in bed, clutching my satin sheets.

It was the same dream I'd been having for months. The same field of yellow flowers, growing in tall stalks. Each time, I'd be standing on a hill looking down on Dane. I'd call his name, but he wouldn't hear me. Then I'd charge down the hill full force, only to collide into *Holden,* who would dissolve beneath me into numerous butterflies.

A blustery December had fallen over Paris, blowing away my memories of summer and memories of him. No one had heard from Dane since the end of August, and I'd all but given up hope of seeing him again. Though, without so much as a single letter, I wasn't sure if I even *wanted* to see him again. He had torn open my stitches—the stitches he'd helped to sew—ripping away the inkling of faith that maybe things *did* happen for a reason. That good things could grow from bad circumstances, just as bad things could grow from good circumstances. That, at the very least, there was an order to the things that happened to us.

Sliding out of bed, I trudged to my desk. Even the morning light beaming through my balcony door felt cold. Picking up my tarot deck, I inhaled and closed my eyes.

"What is the meaning of my dream?"

• • •

L'AMOUREUX

"The Lovers."

I'd grown used to the card, but had yet to understand what it might mean in my own life.

Who were the lovers?

Who was *my* lover?

Was it Holden, or was it Dane?

Castor or was it Pollux?

I flipped the card over.

Maybe it was neither.

Maybe it was a pain au chocolat.

I peered through the window of the pâtisserie, watching as Camille tidied the counter for opening. Aside from the chocolate croissant, I felt like something *else* had brought me to her doorstep. Something I couldn't explain.

When I walked through the door, she greeted me with the same sweet smile. "Bonjour!"

The distance from the door to the counter felt like miles.

"I stopped in with Dane over the summer," I said.

Her smile fell as I approached, despite her best efforts to retain it. "Yes—Lou. Hello again."

A pendant sparkled on her hat—a jeweled bluebird brooch.

"I know that you knew Holden." I wrung my hands with a nervous grin. "Rather intimately."

Camille pursed her lips. "Dane told you?"

I nodded, tucking my hair behind my ear.

"I remembered your name from Holden's letters. Dane would tell me how he was from time to time." Camille grazed her fingers over the register. "I was so sad to hear about what happened to him," she added quietly.

It was a *real* sadness that emanated from her, unlike that of

May and Bethany at the wake. This Camille—this woman I hardly knew—she had loved him. I could feel it.

"What was he like when you knew him?" I asked.

She brought her hand to her mouth, concealing a faint laugh. "He was charming, interesting…they both were, really."

"Dane?"

Camille nodded, relaxing her face. "I was always so taken with their bond."

"I regret that I never got the chance to know them together."

"They are so alike, and yet, so different," she said. "Like two sides of the same coin."

I looked to the window. "Do you mind if I ask if Holden was your great love?"

Her voice softened. "One of them."

"You believe we can have more than one?" I asked, turning back to her.

The ring in her irises glowed golden. "I do," she replied with a smile.

I crossed my arms, overcome with a sudden desire to hug her.

"The funniest thing…I actually dreamt of Holden last night." Her grin grew wide. "He walked in here asking for a chocolate croissant."

I could have sworn I stopped breathing, and my gaping look was enough to break any remaining barrier between us.

Camille started to laugh as she reached for a piece of tissue. "It must have been for you," she said, grabbing one.

"It is the best in the city," I admitted. "Dane wasn't exaggerating."

"Here you are, then." She slid the wrapped pastry across the counter to me. "From Holden."

I met her eyes. "Thank you, Camille. For loving him."

"He was a good man," she said, reaching for her apron. "As is Dane."

I walked out of the pâtisserie feeling lighter. I tore the corner of my croissant, stuffing it into my mouth. It was early, and most of the shops in the neighborhood still looked dark. *Except* Shakespeare and Company.

Whether they rose early or just never closed, the door was propped open. This time, Sylvia was surrounded by her loiterers—all with an eagerness about them—talking over each other to make themselves heard. Empty glasses and mugs scattered every surface. I scurried past the intimidating crowd to the back room, where the lone gentlemen sat at his desk.

Greek Mythology was still there, seemingly waiting for me. I dusted off the cover and opened to the first page, spotting a name in the top left corner.

Natalia Perlman

An electric jolt pulsed through my veins, and I wondered if maybe *this* was what the drabardi had seen.

The men mumbled hellos and tipped their hats, breaking away from the desk so that I could pay for my book.

"You have an interest in mythology," said Sylvia as I handed it to her. "Who would be your favorite goddess?"

I thought for a moment. "Perhaps Hecate, the torchbearer. She lights the way for others into the underworld and I think that's very admirable."

"*Hecate,*" she repeated. "The torchbearer."

I emptied my coat pockets on the counter as she wrapped the book, trying to find my change.

"What's that you've got there?" A man with a mustache pointed to my miniature notebook. "The next great American novel?"

I turned to look at him, but my mind went blank.

Don't you know the best characters are always real people?

A vision of Holden at the Goolrick's counter appeared in my

memory. It slid forward, to the petals in his hair, the bluebird in the maple tree, and the brother that would have given his own immortality to bring him back. Then I paused, suddenly recalling something Tzeitel had said in the drabardi's caravan—

It means "to give form."

"I've seen that look before..."

"Thank you, Sylvia," I said, grabbing the book in a haste.

"Follow that thread!" the man called after me.

My coat hit the floor as I rushed to Holden's Royal, standing at attention at my desk. The cab ride home had been a fever dream, filled with visions and dialogue of another place and time. I reached for a clean sheet of paper, took a seat, and then...

I turned over my shoulder, remembering Holden's portrait in my vanity mirror. "This is how I bring you back," I whispered.

Chapter Twenty-Seven

"Lou, are you in there, love?"

I could hear Edie tapping her nails on the other side of my door from my place on the floor.

"You've been cooped up in here for *days* now! You must open up"

I opened the door, cautiously closing my silk robe over my nightgown. Edie and Theo stood in my hall, covered in melting snow flurries.

"My God, Lou."

Edie walked right past me, into my mess of an apartment. Typed pages lined the floor and tarot cards scattered my vanity and bed. A candle with Holden's picture and The Magician sat on my windowsill.

"Uh…" Theo stepped inside with wide eyes that followed the room. "What is all of this?"

"I'm giving him form."

Edie and Theo exchanged a confused glance.

"Take a look," I pressed, handing Theo a paper.

His eyes skimmed it. "A story about Holden?" he asked, lowering it.

"It's a novel," I corrected. "About all of us."

Edie gaped. *"A novel?"*

Theo studied the page with increased curiosity, then motioned to the Royal behind me. "I told you that you'd get more use out of it."

"This is remarkable!" Edie gushed. "Can we take you out to celebrate? Distract you for a bit?"

"I have a lot of work to do."

That first night, I'd written well into the early morning hours, propelled by instinct and adrenaline. Something had opened inside of me in the bookstore, and I couldn't stop until I'd poured everything onto the page.

"Well," Edie went on, "if you change your mind, you can find us at the Dôme."

Theo inched toward the door. "Are you certain we can't convince you?"

"Go on, you two," I scolded playfully, showing them out. "Another night."

"Good luck on your masterpiece!" Theo called back.

Locking myself back in, I laughed to myself, reclaiming my seat at the desk. I watched from the warmth of my porch as snowflakes accumulated on the balcony railing. Edie and Theo insisted I wasn't a third wheel, but that didn't make me feel any less like one. I was glad to have a project to keep me company on cold winter nights.

Knuckles cracked against my door a second time.

"Edie," I murmured, shooting to my feet.

They just wouldn't take no for an answer tonight.

"Back so soon?" I joked, opening the door.

My expression fell flat when I saw Dane in the hallway, covered in snow. His cheeks were red from the cold. My gaze dropped to the bags at his side.

I trembled with months of pent up rage. "Why are you here? Why did you come back?"

"You know why I came back."

"Because you've thought of nothing but me?" I scoffed.

"Someone who thinks of me would have written—or at least said goodbye." I crossed my arms tightly over my chest, hiding behind the open door. "You can't just vanish and reappear at your own convenience and expect me to be glad to see you. I am not so delicate that I fell apart in your absence."

"I would never think you delicate."

Dane set his bags down at his side, taking a knee. I watched as he unlatched one of his suitcases, pulling out a sketchbook. He cleared his throat, handing it to me.

"What is this?"

He motioned for me to open it, so I did. A portrait of my face covered the first page, and the second. The third was a full body sketch of me on his windowsill. More and more charcoal drawings, all of me.

"You can only draw a person so many times," he added.

"You *have* thought of me."

"And you?"

My gaze snapped up at him, standing before me with snow melting in his hair. "I have thought of little else," I whispered.

Dane reached for my face with his icy hands, bringing his lips to mine. And I dissolved into him—wholly, fully—with every ounce of my stitched heart. I pulled away, trying to warm his cheeks with my hands as the melted snow dripped onto my face.

"Is this wrong?" I asked, gasping for a breath. "Is it wrong for me to love you?"

He kissed me again, lifting me off of my feet. Knocking past my open door, I struggled to take off his wet coat as we stumbled over my papers. The slip of his hands up my robe sent a wave of chills through my body, aching with desire, with need. My back hit the bed. Our noses brushed and I opened my mouth, impatiently awaiting the next time our lips would touch.

"Say it," I breathed.

He paused as he held himself over me, eyes roaming the peaked silk of my nightgown. Then his fingers found my temples, catching in my hair. "I have loved none but you," he said softly.

. . .

I watched the snow fall with my cheek against his tanned chest. Dane kissed the top of my head, running his fingers gently through my hair.

"Is it detestable that a part of me will always love him, too?" I asked. "I'm not sure I can help it."

"I wouldn't ask you to stop," he whispered back. "If you didn't love him, you wouldn't be here."

Perhaps The Lovers was meant to represent them both. Like Castor and Pollux, Holden and Dane were a package deal. In loving and losing the first brother, I would come to meet the other.

"I refuse to believe there is some divine reason we lose the people we love," Dane added, "but if such a thing existed, I feel like you and I would be part of it."

I hugged him to me.

"Besides, I think we have his blessing."

Lifting my head, I turned to look at him. "Where have you been all this time?"

"I'll show you," he said, slipping out from under me.

I watched from the warmth of the covers as Dane dressed. He reached for his coat on the floor, pulling a small blue book from the pocket.

"I pressed this for you while I was gone," he said, opening to the center. "It's yellow mullein from the Somme—I thought you might want something extra to remember him by."

I would go back to France just to pick one for you.

"The Somme…"

Dane sat on the bed next to me. "It feels sometimes like I've lost my other half. I just wanted to try and understand where it went."

"Did you find him?" I asked, sitting upright. "Castor?"

"It will sound bizarre." He laid the dried, translucent flower across my palm. "I'm still questioning if I imagined it…"

"What?"

"Butterflies," he replied. "Dozens of gold butterflies in migration. I saw them fly right over me one morning."

My heart skipped a beat. "I saw them," I whispered. "The butterflies, the field—I saw it all in a dream. You were there, and Holden too." I stood up, wrapping my robe around me. "I've experienced them too. The signs…they led me to start writing this story." I walked to the window sill, grabbing The Magician. "You were right. I *am* The Magician, but so is he."

Dane looked around the room, as if noticing the mess for the first time. "The divine frenzy has you in its grip," he said, picking up one of my papers.

"Read it," I said.

He took a seat on the edge of the bed as I tidied my flat.

"You describe my father's shop just how I remember it," he remarked. "Even the apartment."

"When did you last visit?"

"Something like eight years ago." Dane read on, remaining silent other than a small whimper of a laugh. "You will immortalize him through your writing."

"Like Pollux did for Castor," I said. "I'm not only writing it for me—it's for you too. For all of us."

"Lou," he said, meeting my gaze from across the room. "Did you mean it when you said there's nothing you wouldn't want to know?"

I nodded with a furrowed brow. I could see that he was deep in a thought that distressed him as he again reached for his coat, this time pulling out a letter.

"Here."

I walked over to his shaking hand.

To Dane From Holden
May 27, 1921

I apologize that this isn't thoroughly thought out, and if my words seem jumbled. I'm writing to you to share some news that may upset you, so will you please have a seat? And Dane, promise that you'll read this to the end. It's the most important letter I'll ever send you.

I'm thankful for our time together and I consider myself lucky to have been your brother, which is why I needed you to hear this from me before you hear it from anyone else. I've decided that it's time for me to move on—please don't fret, don't panic as you read this. I'm already gone.

My life has been a decent one, despite the injury I've both endured and inflicted, and for that, I'm grateful. I am grateful to have loved and been loved. I will carry this with me to the glass castle in the sky. I do hope to be looking down on you some clear, winter night.

We'll see each other again, Dane, someplace better. I am certain. I can see only sunshine from here. Isn't it a damned funny thought, to be nothing at all?

In the summer and in the winter,

Holden

I didn't speak for a long time.

"I got the telegram first," Dane murmured. "The letter came about a week afterwards."

I read the words over again with a detached numbness. "Dane..."

"I know what you're thinking." He let out a shaky sigh. "That I should've told them—that at the very least he wasn't in pain and I've robbed them of knowing that."

"No," I whispered, carefully refolding its worn creases.

I wondered how many nights alone he'd spent with this letter. How many times he'd read it.

"You were an ocean apart."

Dane collapsed in my arms when I reached to embrace him.

"And who's fault is that?" he mumbled dismally.

"Not yours."

He shifted himself on my lap until he was looking up at me. Tears rolled from the corners of his eyes, but his face was still. I thought of the childhood bedroom I'd slept in after Holden died, and tried to imagine the years they'd shared together, and all the ways Dane thought he'd failed him.

"We are just the children in the middle," I whispered, stroking his sandy locks.

Chapter Twenty-Eight

"What did you say you were doing?"

Theo turned to me as we walked down my stairwell. "I told her I was with Dane."

"Theo!" I scolded. "I told her *I* was with Dane!"

"What?" He chuckled. "Can we not both be with Dane?"

I rolled my eyes as we rounded the lobby, feeling the chill of outside seep through the open front door. "Theo, remind me to check my mail when we're finished, will you? It's been a few days."

"I'll try my best to remember to remind you."

We stepped onto the lively street, inundated with men in wool coats and women in fur hats. I admired the window displays as we walked, bedecked in their season's best. It was a few days out from Christmas and Theo had yet to find Edie a gift. Edie was generous with her money, especially to Theo, who would have drained his savings a long time ago if they hadn't linked up. For that reason, he wanted to find her something special—something *thoughtful*. And something she didn't already own.

"Tell me, how is the story coming?"

"It's not," I admitted. "The divine frenzy has dried up."

Before Theo had come knocking, I'd been staring blankly at an empty page for over an hour. Writing about 1920—all parties and protests—had come easily. But 1921 was a year I'd tried so hard to forget that it seemed I had succeeded.

"Ah—the infamous writer's block. Did you ask your witch cards?"

I turned to Theo flatly. "Yes," I murmured. "I did consult my witch cards."

"What did they say?"

I shrugged. "Nothing I didn't already know."

"Well, what is it that has you stuck?"

"I'm not even sure how to articulate it—it's just missing *something*. It needs more of his voice, somehow." I turned to him suddenly. "Do you remember anything meaningful about his funeral? Or the wake?"

His smile fell as he tried to think. "To be completely honest, I try not to think about it much."

"Here," I said, motioning to a perfume store.

Theo opened the door and we walked inside; my senses were immediately overpowered with the cloying scents of rose, amber and musk. Three women worked at the counter, sampling perfumes and wrapping Christmas gifts. Looking overwhelmed by the multitude of choices, Theo glanced to me for guidance.

"She loves vanilla," I said.

"I *do* remember how hot it was the day of the funeral," he went on. "But I wouldn't say that was meaningful."

We browsed the multitude of glass perfume bottles, walking circles around the store.

"Is it such a bad thing to not remember?" Theo asked, turning to me.

"Normally, I'd say no."

"Well…"

"What?"

He eyed me with a hesitant grin. "Have you thought about just going back?"

"Back home?"

"Back to the past."

I watched as Theo sniffed a perfume bottle with a grimace. The last time he'd mentioned going home, I'd almost laughed in his face. But this time…

"It's just been so long," I said, finding his side at the counter. "I don't know anyone anymore."

"We can't run forever. None of us can. I know I have to go back home eventually, if only to visit."

A young girl walked up to us, looking exhausted from the holiday foot traffic. "Can I help you?"

"This one, please," I said, handing her a small, oval bottle.

"Is it vanilla?" Theo whispered to me.

"No—it's one of mine that she's always borrowing."

"Even better." He grinned, turning back to the tired eyes of the girl.

"Will this be all for you?"

Theo nodded, paying reluctantly after hearing the price.

"I couldn't imagine seeing Marceline again," I said, following him out the door. "Or any of them, really."

"Maybe their pain has subsided some."

I pocketed my hands in my coat, looking over at him. "Has *yours?*"

"It is a bit more tolerable now. Most of the time. Don't you think so?"

It *was* more tolerable, but so much of that had to do with Dane. I wondered how he might feel about going back to the States for an extended stay to see his family, and Holden's grave. I could even introduce him to *my* family. I'd be willing to brave them with him by my side, and maybe I could do the same for him.

"I don't know, Theo," I said at last. "I've built a life here."

"It's not my job to convince you, Lou," he reminded kindly. "Whether you want to go back and face it—it's your choice."

I looked ahead through the crowd. All it would take was a sign—some *otherworldly* guidance—to convince me that Theo was right. But there were no bluebirds or butterflies to be seen, no perfectly timed comment of a bystander.

"Do you and Dane have any Christmas plans?" asked Theo.

"We agreed not to give each other gifts, but he's taking me to Notre Dame to see the decorations. I've still yet to visit."

"Me too," Theo admitted. "We're sorry excuses for Parisians."

I looked up at my familiar balcony from the street, thinking of my blank paper still waiting for me in the Royal.

"Thank you for the help," he added.

"And for yours as well," I replied, heading toward the door. "You've given me something to think about."

"Merry Christmas, Lou." He pointed to me. *"And check your mail."*

I laughed, waving back to him. "Merry Christmas, Theo. To you and Edie both."

Making a beeline for the postage box, I pulled out my tiny gold key. There were three envelopes that I skimmed in a hurry, at last landing on one stamped clearly with a Fredericksburg address.

My sign.

To Lou From Bette
November 24, 1922

I received your letter a few months ago. I'm sorry it's taken me so long to write back. I'm not sure entirely what to say about what you sent me, except that it was my first time reading that message. Thank you for sending it. If you ever find yourself in town, don't hesitate to look me up.

Bette

Chapter Twenty-Nine

According to Dane, the best time to see Notre Dame was close to sundown; when it was dark enough to see the lights, but early enough to avoid the crowd for midnight mass. We packed a picnic basket and took it to the Champ de Mars, deciding to relax on the lawn for a while beforehand. It was the emptiest I'd ever seen it, too cold even for the pigeons.

I lay in Dane's lap, warmed enough by the champagne we'd brought along in the basket. "What was Holden's favorite church in Paris?" I asked, looking up at him.

"His *favorite* church?"

"The one he would frequent from time to time."

"Saint-Étienne-du-Mont," he replied. "We lived right down the street from it."

I looked up at him and smiled, hugging onto his arm that wrapped around me. "Why that one?"

"I remember him carrying a pendant of Saint Stephen around —it had belonged to one of his friends who died. I think he might have left it there, but I'm not sure."

"Interesting coincidence that you lived so close to it."

"Meaning seemed to follow him, whether he realized it or not."

"The whispers of the universe," I added, sitting upright.

Dane reached into the basket, spreading jam across a piece of baguette before offering it to me.

"Thank you," I murmured, taking a bite. "What do you do when you feel blocked artistically?"

He bit his lip and thought for a moment, proceeding carefully with his words. "I stop looking for inspiration."

I laughed.

"I find that when you let it go, it comes back."

"What about changing your environment?"

"I've done that too," he replied, spreading jam across another piece of bread. "Many times, as you know."

"I've been thinking…"

Dane looked at me with curious attention. "Oh?"

"Tonight," I said, suddenly losing my nerve. "I've been looking forward to it all week."

He kissed my cheek. "Me too."

I leaned back onto his shoulder, taking a deep breath in as I followed the height of the tower to the sky.

"I know we agreed that we weren't going to exchange gifts—"

Surprised, I turned to him.

"But there's still something I wanted to give you."

"We agreed!"

"It's small and it cost me nothing," he assured. "Close your eyes and open your hand."

"You shouldn't have."

Something light brushed across my palm.

"Thread?" I asked, holding up the thin red string. "Certainly there is a story to this."

"It's a Chinese legend that a red thread of fate runs between two people that are always destined to find each other, regardless of time or circumstances." He showed me the other half tied to his wrist. "It can be tangled and stretched but it can't be broken."

I held out my hand, watching as he tied it in a delicate bow around my wrist. "It is perfect," I whispered.

Dane's painting in the Thompson's hallway, as stunning as it was, hardly did the real cathedral justice. The city came alive with lights as we walked toward the medieval church. The entryway was a marvel on its own, with statues of unrecognizable faces guarding both sides of the timeless wooden doors, reaching heavenward in their height.

We joined the line of eager tourists, all there to catch a glimpse of the Christmas festivity.

"Do you ever miss being with your family for Christmas?" I asked.

"I've become so accustomed to being alone," he replied. "To be honest I always felt a bit out of place there."

"You did?"

He nodded, slipping his hand in mine.

"I'm sure they would love to see you, though."

Dane pulled me along into the luminous sanctuary, glowing with gilded candelabras. The echoes of footsteps on tile filled my ears.

"I don't know about that," he murmured. "I'm afraid I would just be a reminder."

I knew Mr. Thompson well enough to know that wasn't true.

"Perhaps you are possessed by your own story," I added, noting the wood carvings and festive foliage that adorned them. "In the *Rider Waite* book, the eight of swords shows a depiction of a woman surrounded by swords, blindfolded. It is much the same idea—she is a prisoner to her own narrative."

Dane swung around to face me, halting beneath the multicolored Romanesque glass that overlooked the sanctuary. "Lou…I'm not going back."

My lips parted as he snaked his hand around my waist.

"There's no reason to," he added, pulling me in.

"You don't really believe that, do you?"

He raised my chin, answering with an ardent kiss. "We have everything we need here," he said, nuzzling my temple.

"You know I have to go back at some point, if even just to visit," I replied, looking up at him.

"I'll wait for you here."

"And if the stay is extended?"

Dane's brow furrowed under the colors of the stained glass.

"I don't think I'll be able to finish this story until I go back and face this. You could visit his grave..." My fingers trailed the lining of his coat. "Will you not come with me?"

"You know I can't," he said, averting his gaze.

"Why not?"

"You *know* why not. How could I show my face after all these years with no explanation, and with that letter?"

"I suppose staying here and punishing yourself forever is a better option, then," I said, releasing myself from his hold.

I walked over to the altar, waiting for Dane to speak, but he said nothing.

"No one blames you for what happened," I added. "It's your passivity that hurts."

It was an incredible irony, that what was destined to bring us together would just as soon tear us apart.

"It seems you've already made your choice," he said finally, finding my side.

"I have," I said. "I'm choosing myself."

Dane's tone was rather flat. "Then who am I to stop you?"

I *wanted* him to stop me—at least to try to.

Anything but nothing.

"It's your story to rewrite," he added. "Not mine."

Chapter Thirty

"What about this one?" Edie held up a dress.

"I don't think I'm going to be going out much, Edie."

She didn't understand how quaint and quiet Fredericksburg was. I'd planned for a six-month stay, but even that was up for negotiation. Edie had promised to look after my flat in the meantime.

"What if you run out of clothes?"

"I have an entire closet at my parents' house," I replied, throwing a couple of blouses into my suitcase.

"From *when?*" She looked at me, aghast. "Lou, those will be horribly out of style!"

"I don't need to be in style," I argued.

"Will you be hiding out?"

"You could say that," I replied.

I'd told no one stateside about my voyage back home, mostly because it would only take Dane telling me to stay for me to change my mind.

"What about this?"

I turned my attention back to Edie, who was holding my hard-cover of *Greek Mythology*.

"Careful." I reached for it. "It has pressed flowers inside."

Taking the book into my hands, I ran my fingers over its gold script. "Edie, do you think I'm making a terrible mistake?"

She looked at me as if I'd just said something blasphemous. "What kind of mistake?"

"That I'm leaving behind my only real chance at happiness." I sighed, looking down at the red thread tied around my wrist. "I can't ask him to wait for me."

"It must be for a reason you feel compelled to go."

I nodded. "A reason I can't explain, yes."

"Then trust that," she said softly.

Dropping my gaze to the book, I opened to the pressed mullein in the center. Beneath it, an illustration of Hecate. The triple goddess. The *torchbearer*.

It was my story to rewrite, so I would.

"You were right." Dane let out a soft laugh. "We certainly couldn't have said a proper goodbye at the train station."

I grinned, dragging my fingers through his waves across my chest. The orange glow of sunset shined through the window of his flat, warming our bare skin as we lay on his sofa.

My breath had formed clouds in the frigid cold as I'd stood outside of his flat, rehearsing the words I wanted to say to him. But it had all been in vain, because as soon as he'd opened his door, there were no words spoken at all. We hadn't even made it to the bedroom.

His fingers brushed against my shoulder. "You've always been an ocean away, but now I've had the pleasure of knowing you," he murmured.

Reaching for his face, I turned him to me. "I'm coming back."

He smiled weakly, but his eyes were hardened, as if he'd already accepted that I might not.

"When is your train tomorrow?" he asked, lifting himself off of me.

"Three o'clock."

Dressing himself, he handed me my skirt.

"You'll be there to see me off, won't you?"

"Of course."

Dane walked to the window, pulling his sweater over his shoulders, still freckled from his summer travels. I could sense his perturbations—that this was the last time, that he'd never see me again. That this was the edge of the final goodbye.

Rising to my feet, I buttoned my blouse.

"Come here," he said, turning to me.

I inhaled and closed my eyes, trying to sear the details into my mind. The softness of his sweater on my cheek and the little bits of dried paint on his hand. All the little pieces of him that I would miss.

Dane leaned over, grabbing a bundle of letters from the top of his desk. "You'll need these."

"Holden's letters?" I looked up at him, shocked. "I can't take these from you."

"The Magician needs her tools." He placed them in my hand, closing my fingers over them. "It's all but the last. I know you'll keep them safe."

"Thank you," I whispered.

"Take this too," he added, handing me his copy of *A Spring Harvest*. "Inspiration for the road."

The day of my departure was mild and sunny, despite the January air. Between last minute packing and the myriad feelings I had over leaving, I hadn't slept well. Head against my pillow, I'd ruminated on every possible outcome of my trip, and every reason Dane wouldn't be waiting for me when I returned.

I tugged on the red thread around my wrist as I waited on the platform with my luggage.

"Now," Edie began, "let us know when you get to Liverpool—"

"And again, when I get to New York," I added. "I will."

The whistle of the steam engine echoed through the station, and I looked up to the ticking clock hand above our heads. Folks were beginning to say their farewells, and Dane was nowhere to be seen.

"I'm sorry, love," Edie cooed sympathetically. "Maybe it was too hard for him."

"He said he would be here."

Edie and Theo exchanged a glance that spoke volumes.

They didn't believe he'd show.

"Theo?" I asked, trying to formulate my thoughts. "If you…"

"Don't worry," he said, cutting me off. "I'll tell him you said goodbye."

I looked around once more as the whistle blew and passengers began to board.

"Tell everyone hello for me," Theo added. "And don't forget to write."

The three of us huddled in a final embrace before I picked up my bags and began my walk up the stairs. There was still time for Dane to make it, to show up at the last second. I halted on the middle step, waiting. Hoping. But I turned around only to be reminded of his absence.

The train was comfortable, albeit crowded, and it took me no time to find my assigned box, which I shared with a mother and her son.

"Bonsoir," I said.

The young woman nodded to me. She was a lovely creature, with copper curls as red as fire. Setting my luggage down, I looked out the window, spotting Edie and Theo in the crowd. Then, I felt a tug on my skirt.

"Oh" —I looked down— "bonsoir."

Two aqua-blue eyes looked up at me. Something was so striking about them—about the little boy himself—that I couldn't help but stare back.

His mother called to him in a language that sounded like Dutch. The toddler returned to his mother, who seemed to be telling him not to touch strangers. But in her string of musical words, I swore I thought I heard *Holden.*

Perhaps another spirit glamour.

The little boy reached up, catching his mother's necklace in his little fingers as she brought him onto her lap. She eyed me apologetically, but I just smiled.

Edie blew me a tearful kiss among the ocean of waving hands on the platform. Another young woman, a bright and bubbly Brit, joined us in our box as the train whistled.

"Hello," she asked, taking a seat next to me. "Are either of you English?"

The redhead and I exchanged a look.

"I'm American," I replied.

"Oh, where are you headed?"

I tore myself from the window with a bittersweet smile and misty eyes. "Home."

Chapter Thirty-One

I watched sleepily from the car window, fiddling with the red thread around my wrist, as rural fields replaced cityscapes.

Having grown so accustomed to the easy-going tempo of Europe, the fast-paced city had taken me by surprise. Nothing could have prepared me for what it would feel like to step back onto American soil. What it would feel like to walk into Grand Central Station and see the homage to Castor and Pollux plastered across the ceiling.

I'd walked into the terminal two years ago wanting only to leave it all behind. But a new part of me had grown from what was buried with Holden; like a sprig of yellow mullein taking root on a blood-soaked battlefield.

I glanced down at *A Spring Harvest,* which sat on my lap. Despite traveling for almost a week, I'd still yet to open it.

Half of me felt foolish. The other half couldn't help but look for him in every lone traveler with sandy hair.

Begrudgingly, I began to thumb through, when I noticed something caught between its pages. I held my breath as I pulled a folded paper from the crease and opened it, holding it against the late afternoon sun.

• • •

DEAR LOU,

I IMAGINE BY THE TIME YOU FIND THIS LETTER YOU'LL BE FAR AWAY FROM ME, IN SOME OTHER PLACE ENTIRELY. YOU SAY THAT YOU WILL BE BACK—BUT I HONESTLY CAN'T IMAGINE I'D DESERVE YOU AFTER ALL OF THIS. YOU'RE A MUCH BRAVER PERSON THAN I. I AM LUCKY TO HAVE BEEN LOVED BY YOU, AND I KNOW HOLDEN WOULD FEEL THE SAME. BE HIS WORDS WHEN HE CAN'T SPEAK.

YOURS,

DANE

The early evening air smelled of burning wood when I stepped off the train, no longer the rebellious youth that I'd once been. I looked down Caroline Street from the station bridge, glimpsing the familiar Goolrick's Pharmacy sign.

I was home.

The Rappahannock River looked murky brown from the back seat of the cab, framed only by the tangled branches of hibernating trees. I could see the stark white brick of Chatham manor showing through in all its restored glory, and I wondered if Holden's spirit ever walked the gardens there with Walt Whitman.

I thanked the driver and stepped onto the dirt road, sliding my suitcases across the backseat. The sun was beginning to hide behind the trees, giving the familiar cottage an orange winter glow. Clementine appeared around the corner to bark at the stranger in her yard.

"Hey old girl!"

It only took her a minute to recognize me, and she charged full force in my direction.

"Clementine!" Bette called from the porch. "What are you—"

The look on her face when she saw me was one of absolute horror.

"Hello!" I called to her.

Bette walked down the stairs, squinting at me suspiciously as the dog bombarded me with wet kisses.

"Remember me?" I asked, looking up at her.

"Lou Morgan, what the hell are you doing here?"

I shot to my feet, brushing off my dress. "You told me to look you up if I were ever in town."

"I have to admit" —her gaze circled my suitcases— "I didn't think you would actually show up."

"Can I stay with you for a while? A few weeks at most."

"A few *weeks?* I'm sorry, I'm…" Her eyes fell on the typewriter box that I held at my side. "You want to stay here—with *me?*"

I nodded. "I would greatly appreciate it."

Bette turned away, seating her chin in her palm. "You're not here to try and take the house?" she asked, whipping back to me.

I laughed. "No."

"Then, sure. I guess you can stay. Though I don't know why you'd want to."

While the cottage looked the same on the outside, the interior had changed dramatically, with an eclectic mix of nouveau style furnishings. Emerald deco fans wallpapered the room. All of Holden's things—all traces of him—had vanished.

"When did you move back?" I asked, setting my suitcases by the door.

"About six months after." Bette lit a cigarette and sat at the table, motioning for me to do the same.

"No more Roy?"

"I turned the bastard in for bootlegging. He shouldn't have hidden his stash in my house." She exhaled. *"His* house," she murmured.

I scanned the room. "It looks like your house," I replied.

That *almost* made her smile.

"You still haven't told me why you showed up here unannounced."

"I'm writing a novel."

"About him." Bette flicked her ash into a crystal tray. "And what does that have to do with me?"

"I was hoping you might know where I could find some of his writing."

I could tell she was wary of me by the way the nails of her free hand dug into her arm.

"We all end up as parts of people's stories," she said, taking a shallow breath. "Am I the villain in yours?"

"There are no villains in mine."

I watched as Bette abandoned her seat and made her way to the hall, where she disappeared around the corner. She returned with a stack of papers.

"Stay as long as you want," she said, plopping them on the table in front of me. "This is everything he didn't burn."

Chapter Thirty-Two

"Tell me," Bette began, as we both sat at her table with a glass of Roy's illegal whiskey, "why didn't you stay with Marceline or any of them?"

I raised my eyebrows, taking a sip from the glass. "Politics."

"I suppose it's not the worst thing in the world to have some company."

I smirked, reaching for my pack of cigarettes on the table.

"Even though you're not my first choice," she added.

"I always knew you didn't like me."

"It was because he liked you so much." She dropped her eyes to her glass, which she tapped with her fingernail. "The way he looked at you was the way he used to look at me…like he was captivated."

My cheeks turned warm.

"Oh, *don't.*"

"What?" I squeaked.

"I didn't marry him blind," she added. "I knew who he was."

Who he was. I wondered which version of him she'd known.

"He let me stay here when I didn't have anywhere else to go."

Bette reached for a cigarette, and I leaned forward to light it.

"You can imagine what happened next," she added, blowing

smoke. "I knew he would be just as quick to fall out of love as he was to fall into it."

I met her gray eyes, looking especially large and glossy. "Then why did you say yes?"

Bette shrugged, and her voice softened. "He was special."

"He had a bewitching effect on people."

"He was so passionate...so sad." Bette thought to herself. "It was as though someone had just broken his heart open."

A vision of Camille baking croissants in her pâtisserie came to mind. "I think maybe someone had," I replied.

"He proposed to me in the middle of the night, while we were having a drunken swim in the Rappahannock." She exhaled a cloud of smoke. "It doesn't feel right that I should inherit his house."

"No." I shook my head. "Things are as they should be—how he would have wanted them."

We both fell silent, and for the first time, I thought about what had happened there.

"It was in the bedroom. That's where I found him," she said, quick to read my thoughts. "I don't go in there."

I looked toward the hall.

"I'm afraid it's the only spare room I have."

I turned to her. "Will you show me?"

The bedroom in which Holden had died was disarmingly ordinary, smelling of stale paper, as though it hadn't been aired out since Bette had sealed it shut. Books sat on every table and every chair, bookmarked with postcards, begging to be dusted. Holden's clothes lay piled high on a trunk in the corner next to his old desk.

"I didn't know what to do with all of his things," Bette added.

I lifted my suitcases, laying them across the small bed. "It will suit me just fine."

Bette looked uneasy as she stood at the entrance of the room.

"Thank you," I added.

"Listen." She took a sip from her glass, squaring her shoulders. "I'd love to drink and smoke all night, but I need to get going."

"Are you still cleaning the artist's studio?" I asked. "Theo told me he offered you a job when I met up with him in Paris."

"You can come up and see the studio, if you want. He wouldn't mind," she said.

"All right."

Bette nodded. "I'll get the whiskey."

The climb to the iron gates was a steep one, and I couldn't help but admire the white Georgian home, perched atop the twilit grounds. Bette closed the gate behind us, making her way toward a sandstone building to the right of the house.

"He's usually finished working by sunset," she said, pulling out her key.

The studio was a marvel to behold with its vaulted ceiling and enormous north window. Dozens of paintings covered the walls, lit by the last remnants of daylight.

Dane would have been awestruck.

"Whiskey?"

I looked at Bette, hesitant.

"I do it all the time," she added, tying an apron around her waist. Passing the whiskey jar to me, Bette reached for the string of a small lantern, chasing away the shadows of the fast-approaching sunset.

I examined the paintings, many of them nameless portraits, looking European in nature.

"Melchers is his name, the artist," Bette replied. "That one is called *In Holland."*

I studied the brush strokes of the windmill. "I would like to visit Holland."

"I would like to visit Europe," she replied. "The way Holden talked about it...we were supposed to go and visit his brother there, but obviously we never made it."

"Dane lives in Paris now." I sipped from the jar. "We met by coincidence."

That got Bette's attention.

"Word on the street is he's a hard man to locate."

"For once, the gossip is right."

"What was he like?" she asked, starting to wipe down surfaces. "I always wanted to meet him."

"He was charming, but not in the way that Holden was charming. He had a quiet wit to him. A wisdom. He was so…" I laughed under my breath, picking at the thread around my wrist.

Bette looked up at me as she carefully dried the paintbrushes, one at a time. "*My, my,*" she teased. "You have lived an interesting life, Lou Morgan."

I took another sip of warm whiskey, feeling the burn slip down my throat.

"What happened?"

I tapped my fingers against the jar. "I haven't quite figured that out yet," I replied.

The stars were clouded by a thick overcast when we left the studio. My eyes struggled to adjust to the darkness outside as I followed Bette to the gate.

"Bette—"

She sighed. "Please, don't."

"I'm sorry," I said, passing the jar to her. "For coming between you and Holden. I never meant to."

"I was just as guilty," she admitted. "I met Roy, and he promised me all these things…I think Holden and I knew things between us had run its course, even though he felt the need to stick around."

The song of an owl pierced the dark woods as we walked side-by-side.

"By the end, I was happy for him," she went on. "That he found what he was looking for."

"I don't think he ever found what he was looking for," I replied, folding my arms over my chest.

My thoughts drifted to the bedroom I would be sleeping in, and if there might be any trace of his spirit still in it.

"I'm sorry about the comment in the bar," she said, taking a sip. "About his coat. I figured you hated me as much as the rest."

"I don't think anyone ever hated you, Bette. It's all just crossed threads."

"The irony of it all," she added, almost playfully. "Holden always told me that he thought we'd get along."

Chapter Thirty-Three

The brown glass of Holden's prescription whiskey bottle sparkled on my windowsill. One by one, I slipped a bluebell down its short neck, arranging them as needed. I'd found a patch growing near the wood line, where Holden had once told me he'd buried the bluebird, and remembering his fondness for them, I'd returned with a few handfuls.

Satisfied, I stood back to admire the bright purple flowers, and how they complimented the worn colors of my Marseille deck next to them.

Sprucing up the room had been an undertaking—a few days of dusting, sorting and rearranging—but by the end of the week, it was looking perfectly inhabitable. I'd returned the Royal to its place on Holden's desk, next to *Greek Mythology, A Spring Harvest,* and a few of his books that I'd helped myself to. His writings sat to the right of my typewriter, next to a melted candle that I used to light the pages of my own draft at night.

He hadn't left much, just a few short stories and untitled prose. The letters, however, were bountiful.

"Look at this one," Bette called.

I returned to the emerald sitting room, where she and I had scattered Holden's letters across the floor to try and sort them by date. There were hundreds of them—spanning from his Princeton era, to his time in France, to his days living with Bette.

Like Dane had said, *all but the last.*

I took a seat next to Bette on the floor, taking the letter into my hands.

"March 1917," I murmured, reading the date.

"Who is Frank?"

"I think" —I reached behind me, aimlessly feeling around for a letter I'd read earlier— "Frank was one of his professors? Holden mentioned him a lot in his early letters."

Bette rose to her feet, lighting a cigarette as I read.

To Dane from Holden
March 14, 1917

You will not be happy to hear this, but I went to New York over the weekend and enlisted with the AEF. The only person unhappier with my decision than you is Bonnie. Who can blame her, really. When we started dating, I was set on becoming an English professor. She never signed up to be with a soldier.

But that's the other thing, Dane. I've gotten myself into a mess with her sister, and we are careless with it. So much so that I know I'm bound to get caught—yet, nothing deters me. I don't know when I became so careless about everything.

Please don't ask about Frank—I don't see much of him these days between my drills and extracurriculars. I can hardly find the time to read my own writing, much less his. The drills really are quite rigorous.

Anyway, I do hope you will not disown me after reading this. I told Scott and Theo that you very well may.

Holden

"I still can't believe he didn't leave a letter," Bette said, pacing the room.

I froze.

"Quite unlike him not to leave a letter."

"Indeed," I agreed, half-heartedly.

"It's the *least* he could have done," she added.

I could only imagine what Bette had seen that day, and how it had changed her.

"Well." She sighed, extinguishing her cigarette. "Are you joining me this evening?"

I folded the letter, laying it on a nearby pile. "I have something I need to do."

"You should take a break," she scolded. "It would do you good."

"No—this is personal."

Bette eyed me knowingly under those thick, dark lashes as she grabbed her coat. "Something personal," she said. "Clementine will keep you company, then."

I glanced at the dog, who was sprawled out half-asleep across the wood floors.

"I'll be back tonight," Bette added, finding the door.

I looked down at my wrist, and the red thread around it.

It had only been two weeks, but I'd yet to receive any mail. I tried to tell myself that Dane was notoriously bad at correspondence, but it did little to curb my anxieties; in particular, the worry that in my absence, he would find the notion of *us* to be morally questionable, and seize his chance to slip away quietly.

The deep glow of a February sunset cascaded through the bedroom window as I walked in, clearing the top of Holden's desk, stacked with last night's progress. Each night since I'd arrived, I sat before the Royal and bled. All that I thought, all that I felt—I unraveled it before my priest like a typewriter ribbon. Much like Holden, I *too* had found safety within the walls of my fictional castle.

Writing Dane a letter would be another task entirely.

Loading a new sheaf of paper, I took my seat.

Dear Dane,

~~I am writing you from Holden's desk at the cottage.~~ I have arrived safely in the States and I'm staying at the cottage. Bette and I are getting on well, and I've gotten lots of work done. Thank you for your note. I must admit I was surprised to find it. Tell me, have you thought of me at all?

Ripping the paper out of the Royal, I balled it up, tossing it over my shoulder. I loaded a new one.

Dear Dane,

I was hoping I might hear from you by now. I think of you often, even here. Bette and I have been reading Holden's letters, cataloging them for you. The writing is going well. ~~Writing your character has been my favorite part.~~

I sighed, crumpling that one as well.

Dear Dane,

Please write. If there is anything I can't take from you, it's silence.

Hearing Clementine's nails scrape across the floor, I glanced over my shoulder to see her standing in the hall with her ears perked. Dropping a hand to my side was usually enough to call her over, but this time, she didn't move.

"Here girl," I said, abandoning my chair. But Clementine only stepped back, disappearing around the corner. Kicking the nearest ball of paper, I collapsed onto my bed.

The hole in the ceiling stared back at me like an eye, a constant reminder that I was sleeping in the exact place where he'd died. Admittedly, the thought comforted me. That I might slip across the same threshold he'd crossed in my dreams, and find him there. Even now, my eyelids were heavy. Strained from reading in low light…

"Lou."

When I opened my eyes, I saw Holden leaning in the door frame—arms crossed, smirking at me. The under-eye bags I'd remembered were gone, replaced by an almost iridescent shimmer. I blinked hard, shifting onto my side to look at him. His body looked solid, yet as translucent as glass.

We stared at each other for what felt like hours in the in-between. I had so many questions—the bluebirds, the novel, about Dane and the letter, but as I spoke, only one came out.

"Are you all right where you are?"

A soft nod with an even softer smile—the sight of which filled my chest with a peaceful, easy feeling.

"Having a pleasant nap?"

My eyes shot open, and this time, it was Bette standing in the doorway.

"I take it…" Her gaze fell to the crumpled papers on the floor. "You were unsuccessful?"

I turned back to the ceiling. "Do you ever have so much to say that nothing comes out?"

"Every day."

I didn't expect her to walk into the room and lie down next to me on the bed. For as long as I'd been there, she'd never once stepped inside. I heard the strike of a match, followed by the smell of tobacco.

"Do you want to know what happened that day?"

I turned my head toward her on the pillow. "Do you want to tell me?"

Bette stared upward, tears freezing in her eyes. "I stopped by in the hopes of picking up some of my things," she began. "I remember having this feeling of dread, standing outside the front door. He didn't answer when I called."

She passed me the cigarette, marked with her lipstick, and I took a drag.

"The neighbors let me use their telephone and the first person I could think to call was Theo."

"He didn't mean for you to find him," I said, handing it back.

"Someone had to find him, didn't they?" She pursed her lips. "Did he really hate everyone so much?"

"Bette—there was one letter Dane didn't give me." I shifted on the bed to face her. "One he purposefully left out."

Bette did the same, allowing the ash from her cigarette to fall onto the bed. "A goodbye letter?"

"He's had it this whole time—he's been torturing himself with it, trying to bear the cross alone because he's too afraid to show anyone."

"What did it say?" she asked, voice trembling.

"That he was grateful. And that..." A faint smile found my lips. "He hopes to be looking down on us, some clear winter night."

Chapter Thirty-Four

"They're eager to meet you," said Bette. "Mr. Melchers has been to Paris."

"It looks as if he's been all over," I replied, climbing the hill behind her.

My nose tickled from the pollen in the air. By mid-March, things were beginning to bloom, and new life was returning to the landscape. Bette didn't seem to mind that I'd been there longer than I'd originally planned.

"Are you ever going to tell your family you're home?" she asked, reaching for the iron gate.

"At some point."

"As someone who doesn't have parents, I'm not sure I understand your aversion."

"Aversion is too strong of a word." I squinted past the budding rose bushes to Mrs. Melchers, who was defending her tablecloth from the morning breeze. "I just know they'll find a way to patronize me," I admitted. "And…"

Bette glanced over her shoulder expectantly. "And?"

"And I *may* have written to them about Dane." I buried my face in my hands. "I made it sound quite serious between us because I thought it was."

"Did they know about Holden?"

"He was married..."

"You *do* care what they think." The surprise in Bette's tone was almost humorous.

"I was going to tell them eventually, it all just happened so fast. And then I met Dane and I..."

"You thought he would come back with you."

"I got ahead of myself." I paused. "Speaking of Dane..."

Bette tried to smile, as though she already knew what I would say.

"I know you would tell me if I got a letter, but..."

She shook her head. "I'm sorry."

"Good morning!" Mrs. Melchers called. "I hope you don't mind that we'll be outside, I just thought it would be a shame to miss this beautiful morning."

I turned my attention to the iron garden table and its lace tablecloth, weighted down by four blue patterned china plates and a carafe of orange juice.

"My friend Lou I've been telling you about," said Bette. "Lou, this is Mrs. Melchers."

"Hello!"

"It's a pleasure to meet you," I replied.

"I hope you like quiche."

I recognized her at once from Mr. Melchers's portraits in the studio. She was, I suspected, around the same age as my mother, with a soft complexion and a dimple on her chin.

"Would one of you be a dear and fetch Gari from the studio?"

Bette turned to me. "You should see it in the daylight."

"I'd be happy to," I said.

I made my way to the sandstone building, past the square-cut boxwoods and tulip bulbs ready to burst.

"Mr. Melchers?" I called, opening the door.

Light streamed through the massive north window of the quiet studio. It was immediately clear to me that he was elsewhere, but I called out again for good measure.

"Mr. Melchers…?"

Rich colors exploded all around me, brought to life by the morning sunshine. It had been a few weeks since I'd come up with Bette, and I took notice of a new addition in the corner as I walked to the center of the room. I tried to imagine Dane thirty years from now, with gray hair, painting in a studio of his own. The thought brought a smile to my face.

I made my way over to the easel in the corner, and the new painting that sat on it, covered by a cloth. Curiously, I pulled it to the floor, revealing a half-finished bluebird sitting in a tree.

"Do you like bluebirds?"

Startled, I turned around. "I have an odd connection with them," I admitted, meeting the eye of the older gentleman. "I'm sorry I uncovered it—I'm Lou, Bette's friend."

"Pleased to meet you, Lou." He smiled beneath his peppered white mustache, sliding his gaze past me. "Someone told me once, long ago, that bluebirds carried messages between lost lovers."

I tugged the thread on my wrist. "Did they?"

He walked over to examine his work. "I found this one sitting in a pear tree at the end of Caroline Street."

The pear tree.

I'd been looking for a reason—a sign, perhaps—to cross the bridge into town.

"Anyway, shall we have breakfast?" he asked, motioning toward the door. "We're very interested in hearing about your novel."

I took one last look at the painting of the bluebird as I followed him out, remembering what the drabardi had told me that foggy morning in Paris.

Look for him in the wind, the sky, in the people you meet.

"Where to?" Bette asked.

I held the edge of my seat as we wound around the turns; my hair whipping around wildly under my hat.

"The cemetery," I replied.

Bette turned to me with a grimace. *"The cemetery?"*

"Do you want to join me?"

"No thanks," she replied. "I make drastic efforts to avoid the cemetery. The whole street, actually."

I looked to the blooming pear tree as we zoomed past the shop. "You don't ever visit his grave?"

"I don't need to," she replied. "Or want to."

Bette parked in front of the iron gates of Saint Mary's cemetery, not bothering to cut the engine.

"It looks like rain," she said.

I turned to her, opening my door. "I'll take a taxi back."

She nodded, fiddling with her hands in her lap. "Lou—"

"Yes?"

"Tell him hello for me, will you?"

I reached over, squeezing her hand. "I will."

The cemetery smelled of cut grass and pollinating flowers, unlike the sweltering smell of the river that terrible day. I walked toward the locust tree, skimming the headstones, until I finally came across a modest one that read *Holden James Thompson, June 17, 1894 - May 27, 1921*.

I couldn't help but feel significantly aged as I stood there, surrounded by all of the new neighbors Holden had acquired in the past few years. Despite the evened lawn, the grass around his gravestone had not been properly cut, and clover grew wildly at my feet.

And then I saw it.

"For luck?" I leaned down, plucking the four-leaf clover. "Quite predictable for an Irishman, Holden," I teased.

I felt a couple raindrops hit my hat as I turned it between my fingers, making a note to press it next to the Great Mullein.

Bidding Holden farewell, I continued my pilgrimage down Princess Anne Street as it began to drizzle. I walked past the Princess Anne Hotel and wondered about Molly, wishing I'd kept in touch. Down on the corner of George and Caroline, folks took shelter from the rain under the awning of Goolrick's Pharmacy. I passed the café where Holden and I had had breakfast, and the nearby postage box.

Soon enough I'd have something else to mail to New York.

I'd saved my most poignant visit for last, and was thoroughly soaked by the time I reached 1111 Caroline. It had been repainted a dark naval blue, but otherwise, it hadn't changed much. A small sign read *James Thompson Jr., MD* beneath *Thompsons' Tailoring*.

It was no mistake that I was visiting on a Monday when the shop was closed. I'd planned it that way.

Stepping up onto the stoop, I peered through the window on the side of the door. The warm floors were still bright cherry, though they were dimmed by the overcast skies. The memories in its foyer were ones I'd never forget—from dropping my Corona down the stairs, to Holden carrying me to my flat with a twisted ankle, to receiving that dreadful phone call—they were burned into my memory for the rest of eternity.

Yet, standing in the rain outside my former home, surrounded by memories of my former sweetheart, I longed for *him*.

I stepped down from the stoop, only to be met with a mirage of my past. There, on the curb stood an unmistakable face, shutting the door to his car.

"Jamie!" I called. "Jamie Thompson!"

When his gaze found me on the street, a screaming recognition washed over him.

"*Lou?* Is that really you?" He sprinted over to me. "What are you doing here? You're soaking wet!"

Only two years had passed but he was no longer the young man he had been when we'd seen each other last. He'd grown a mustache, and seemed so much more like Holden, somehow.

"I was just taking a peek through the window," I admitted. "I didn't think anyone would be here."

"Well—come in," he urged, ushering me to the door. "Come in and out of the rain."

Jamie unlocked the door and I followed him into the foyer, mirroring the first time we met. We'd only been kids then.

"Congratulations on your practice," I said with a shiver. "Aren't you closed?"

"I was just stopping by to pick something up."

"*Jamie,* is that a wedding band?"

He laughed, holding up his finger. "Last August."

"The nurse from school?"

"I asked her name after all. It was Carolyn."

"Oh, Jamie!" I couldn't stop smiling. "I am so happy for you."

"And what about you?" he asked. "I don't imagine you crossed an ocean to peek through our windows."

"Why wouldn't I?" I laughed. *"She's got good bones."*

"Yes." Jamie grinned. "But the heart feels a little wicked here."

I stepped into the doorway of the dimly lit shop, hit by nostalgic smells of linens and leather. "To tell you the truth, I am working on a novel inspired by my time here with Holden."

"In that case" —he glanced toward the stairwell— "would you like to see the upstairs again? Spare a little time for an old friend?"

"I'd like that very much."

I thought I might be flooded with feelings upon entering my old flat, but Jamie had made the space his own. The foyer was finely furnished, and degrees hung above the mantle as if it had always been an office.

"I'll make us some coffee," he said, disappearing around the corner.

I took a seat on the settee—a new one, not the one in which I'd nursed Holden's black eye. Not the one Theo had slept on the week after his death.

Jamie set a tray of coffee, sugar and cream on the small coffee table. "How are you, Lou?" he asked, taking a seat.

"I'm well," I said, struggling to find the right words after so long. "How is everyone?"

"Well, Marceline and Arvin had their first baby about a year ago—if you hadn't heard. A little girl."

"Oh—I hadn't heard."

"The last couple years have been tremendously hard on my mother," he continued. "And my father…well, in a lot of ways he's the same as he's always been, but he's aged as well. They've been in touch with my brother lately so they're happy about that."

"Dane?"

The red thread peeked from beneath the sleeve of my coat as I reached for one of the mugs.

Jamie chuckled. *"I know,* it's a shock. It's been years since he's written."

I grinned down at my lap, dropping a sugar cube into my coffee. "I can't tell you how happy I am to hear that," I said, watching it dissolve.

It was the truth. I *was* happy.

But I was also sad. I'd written Dane two weeks ago and had yet to hear a thing. I tried to smother my sadness as Jamie and I talked. Even after years apart, it was like we'd never stopped.

"Where are you staying, Lou?" he asked at last. "I need to get going, but I can give you a lift."

"I'm staying with Bette across the river."

Jamie knitted his brow. "At the cottage?"

I nodded.

"I forget sometimes she still lives there," he admitted. "Is she…well?"

"Quite. I mean, as well as she can be."

Sliding his empty cup onto the tray, he rose to his feet. "Things really have come full circle, haven't they?"

Rays of sunlight burned through the rain clouds as we drove across the Falmouth bridge, making the trees look even more verdant than usual. I picked at the thread on my wrist, wondering if it might be time to retire it.

Dane had written, but not to me.

Maybe he wouldn't.

"You know," Jamie murmured, "I was mad at him for so long.

Then one day I realized that even my anger couldn't bring him back."

"You weren't the only one with conflicting feelings," I replied.

He paused for what felt like a long time, and I waited for him to speak as we turned onto River Road. "I miss him something terrible."

"So do I." looked over at him with a weak smile. "But I don't think he's gone. I think you just have to know where to look for him."

"Do you think you'll come into town again to visit?"

"The draft of my book is almost finished," I replied. "So at the very least I'll be in town again next Monday when I mail it off. I have an editor friend in New York."

"Maybe I could tell my parents and Marcie that you're here and we can all have dinner one night."

"I'm not sure if Marceline would want to see me," I confessed. "We didn't part on good terms."

"I'll at least tell my parents you're back—if that's all right with you?"

"Of course, Jamie. I'd love to see them."

Bette was lounging on the sofa reading one of Holden's letters when I walked into the cottage, still damp from earlier.

"Who dropped you off?" She asked, lifting back the curtain.

"Jamie."

She lowered the letter. "No."

"Yes."

"Jamie Thompson," she said, refolding it.

"He has his own medical practice now above the shop. And he's married!"

Bette looked me over as I slinked off my coat. "Is it still raining?"

"Not currently, but I'm not sure it's finished."

"I'll take an umbrella," she murmured.

"I'll be in my room," I added. "I have two chapters to go and I'll be finished."

"Oh—" Bette reached for an envelope on the end table next to her. "You got a letter today."

She must've seen how my heart caught in my throat as I leapt for it.

"From Edie and Theo."

"Oh." I forced a smile. "Jamie said that Dane has written to the family."

Bette grabbed her pack of cigarettes next to her, pulling one out and offering it to me. "You sent your letter?"

"A few weeks ago." I watched as she struck a match, lighting the end of her own cigarette, which she then used to ignite mine. "I thought he was just bad at correspondence."

She blew a ring of smoke. "How will you end it, then?" she asked, handing me the lit cigarette.

"What do you mean?"

"This story of yours. Your characters."

I shrugged, folding my arms over my chest as a stream of smoke wafted up from my fingers. "I suppose I'll give them a happy ending. It's what we all want, isn't it?"

"That would be a kindness," she said, taking a drag. "Since closure isn't so straightforward in real life."

I brought the cigarette to my lips limply.

Closure isn't so straightforward in real life.

"I've got to go," Bette added, jumping to her feet. Throwing her raincoat on in a haste, she swiped the umbrella from the corner behind the door.

"See you tonight."

Stopping only to give Clementine a scratch behind the ear, I made my way to the bedroom and stretched myself across the bed. I couldn't remember the last time I'd cried. The last time I'd *allowed* myself to cry.

But as my cheek hit the quilt of the bed, the tears began to flow. A pitter patter of rain began on the other side of my open window.

A cool breeze rushed past the curtains, blowing a tarot card off of my windowsill. I peeked over the edge of the bed, shivering from the moist chill that had taken the room.

The Lovers lay on my floor, face up.

Chapter Thirty-Five

Maybe the card is supposed to symbolize you.

I reflected on Dane's words from the day outside the pâtisserie as I stood before the postage box.

Perhaps I'd always been The Magician, or perhaps Holden's *divine frenzy* had found a new host.

Perhaps I would always carry that part of him within me. That precious, eternal flame that I'd glimpsed behind his eyes. I would stoke it against the wind, guarding it away for safekeeping until the pen called again.

I smiled to myself, clutching my packaged novel.

"May you dance across the imaginations of others for years to come," I whispered, dropping it into the postage box. It hit the bottom with a reassuring thud.

Scanning the bustling street, I studied the folks of my hometown, unsure where I fit in among them. I wondered how many of them had felt what I'd felt, and if they, too, could feel the warmth of the sunshine on their skin better than before.

I wondered if they, too, could hear the whispers of the universe and all of its ecstasies.

Pocketing my hands in my new high-waisted trousers, I began

my walk back down the street when something stopped me dead in my tracks.

Stepping out of a black Chrysler, the familiar strawberry blonde froze as she stood on the curb, dressed to impress in a brown tweed blazer and tan skirt, with hair cut short, laying under her fitted hat.

Marceline.

Forever seemed to pass before I dared to cross the no-mans land and walk toward her.

"Jamie told us that you were in town," she said, stepping forward to meet me.

I grinned. "Of course, he did."

"Well, how are you?"

"I'm well—and you?"

"Quite busy, actually," she replied.

"Jamie told me about the baby."

Marceline smiled like a smitten mother. "Our Celia June."

Habitually, I reached for the worn red thread on my wrist. "Dane's mother's name?"

"And Holden's birth month," she added. "For my father."

"Congratulations to you and Arvin—to all of you."

"And to you as well on your novel. That is a birth of its own."

"Thank you. I just dropped it in the post box." I paused, squinting more closely at the tweed pattern of her blazer. "Is that…"

"Holden's blazer?" She laughed. "It is. I made it into something I could wear. It's amazing you noticed, I actually found it upstairs one day—"

"On the bed," I finished. "Right where I left it."

Marceline seized me in a tight embrace. "Welcome home," she whispered. "I'm sorry for what I said to you all those years ago."

"*I'm* the one who should be sorry," I replied. "You were right —I wasn't part of the family."

She released me with teary eyes. "You'll always be part of the family."

A soft breeze blew between us, carrying the smell of the river.

Marceline sniffled. "They say that time heals all wounds..."

"But the void is bittersweet," I added.

She turned behind to Arvin, waiting in the car with the baby.

"Is that a bluebird on your purse?" I asked, catching a closer look at the embroidery on her pocketbook.

She looked down at her side, smiling sweetly. "It is. I have been seeing them so often lately..."

I turned my attention back to the car. "Do you and Arvin want to have coffee and catch up?"

"Ah." Marceline glanced down at her watch. "I don't think we can today—but maybe we can all have dinner soon? I'm sure Molly would love to see you too."

"I look forward to it."

"You surely have some celebrating to do, anyway." Her smile seemed both ambiguous and all-knowing. "We'll catch up soon." Marceline was halfway to her car when she halted and turned around. "Oh—one more thing. Tell Bette I asked after her, will you?"

I was at peace, but still feeling aimless when I began my walk to Saint Mary's gates. I *would* have celebrated if I'd had someone to celebrate with, but since I didn't, a walk in the cemetery would suffice. An older gentleman standing over a fresh grave caught my attention as I walked by, and I couldn't help but stop.

"Morning to you," he said, holding his hat over his heart.

"And to you. I'm sorry for your loss."

"Does it ever get easier?"

Remembering the words of Mr. Thompson that day in the foyer, I shook my head. "Not easier. Just...different."

The grass around Holden's gravestone had finally been cut.

"Well done with Marceline," I began, approaching his carved name. "I saw the bluebird on her pocket—"

I swallowed my words, noticing something glinting in the sun atop the slate stone. A platinum ring, topped with a six-pointed star of sapphires and diamonds. The ends of a red string blew in the breeze beneath it, secured by a delicately tied bow.

I heard someone approach from behind, but didn't dare move.

"It belonged to my mother."

"Dane." His name was a shallow inhale as I turned around. "You…" A tear fell as I lifted my sleeve, revealing the other half of the untangled, unbroken red thread around my wrist.

Standing with his hands in his pockets, he inhaled excitedly, only wiping the smile from his face so he could speak. "Words are fickle things, aren't they?"

To the Thompson Family from Dane
April 6, 1923

I know it's been far too long since I've written, and I hope you will accept this apology. Please know it is sincere. I know there isn't much I can say to make up for my absence. The honest truth is that I couldn't face any of you because I hadn't faced myself. There's more to the story than you know, and I've kept it from you, selfishly.

I spent the past summer visiting the battlefields where Holden fought in France, most notably the Somme. One morning while it was still dark, I walked out to the edge of the wasteland to watch the sunrise and saw something truly remarkable. Out in the field, I saw the wildflowers that he'd so often mentioned to me. He told me stories of the men and how they picked posies of Great Mullein for their dead friends, which grew wildly between the bodies—and he always said that all the yellow posies reminded him that love could grow anywhere, even in the midst of decay. Now I see he was right.

I know you'll be surprised to hear this, but I've met someone special. She urged me that we are free to change our own narrative at any time—you might recognize her, actually. If the invitation is still open, I'd like to come and stay on for a while, to see if I might make it up to you.

Dane

Acknowledgments

All the Yellow Posies was first born in April 2021 as a standalone novel. It began as a pile of journals—documentation of my personal journey with grief. I decided to revisit the manuscript in February of 2024 and do a full re-write. It is now the first book in the *Threaded Entanglement* series.

To my own found family: this story would not exist without your impact and contributions—every last one of you. You know who you are.

To Gloria and my grief writing group: I couldn't possibly convey how much you've taught me about the healing nature of writing. And the multitude of people who have approached me with their own stories of suicide loss—thank you for sharing such profoundly personal stories. I can only hope I have represented you well in this narrative.

To Megan, my developmental editor: even from the beta stage, you helped me mold my vision and the emotional depth of these characters, and I'm still convinced that you're the only person that could have done this job. Thanks for taking a chance on me.

To Joey, my partner: oh, what a life it is to be married to a writer—and to me, no less! Thank you for meeting my all-consuming creativity with compassion and support, even when it requires my absence.

To Kathryne and Laura, my best friends: thank you for letting me talk in circles about my characters. I would have never survived this rigorous rewrite without your support, influence and favors!

To Sarah Bachman, my cover artist: thank you for helping me breathe new life into this book with your magic paintbrush.

And lastly, to my readers who read the original version, and to everyone who was touched by this story: you have my undying appreciation. Thank you for investing your hearts in Lou. In doing so, you have invested your hearts in me.

About the Author

Elaine DeBohun is a historical fiction and fantasy author, astrologer and Fredericksburg native. *All the Yellow Posies* is her first novel and is book one in the *Threaded Entanglement* series.

facebook.com/elainedebohun

instagram.com/threaded.entanglement.series

Made in the USA
Middletown, DE
29 September 2024

61229459R00176